WHERE THE WICKED TREAD

WHERE THE WICKED TREAD

JOHN A. CONNELL

NAILHEAD PUBLISHING

COPYRIGHT

WHERE THE WICKED TREAD

A NailHead Publishing book

ISBN 978-1-950409-18-1 (hardcover)

ISBN 978-1-950409-17-4 (paperback)

ISBN 978-1-950409-16-7 (ebook)

www.johnaconnell.com

Austria 1947

Two British Royal Military policemen had me by both arms, dragging me down a drab prison corridor. After lying most of the night on a cement floor in a frozen jail cell, my leg muscles refused to work very well. The chains around my ankles didn't help. They were either in a hurry or enjoying a moment of sadism. I had to admit some responsibility because of a comment I made about being treated better by the Nazis in several prisoner-of-war camps I'd spent time in during the war. They hadn't taken too kindly to that remark.

I'd been a guest of the Royal MPs at their prison in Graz, Austria, for four days, living off cold soup and stale bread. They'd roused me every night and interrogated me, though I didn't have much to tell. I was sure the interrogations were mostly to deprive me of sleep. The scant food, sleep deprivation, and rough treatment were all punishment for my beating a Brit army major so badly that he was now in the hospital.

What they didn't know was that I'd been through cruel and unusual punishment before, by far more sadistic men.

I figured my friendly tormentors were taking me for another hours-long interrogation, but we turned down another corridor that was unfamiliar to me. They dragged me past two doors before propelling me into a windowless room with two chairs and a square table. One of them put his foot out and tripped me. The only thing that kept my face from slamming into the tiled floor was my chest hitting the table. Marginally better, but it still hurt like hell.

"Cute move," I said. "They teach you that in dungeon school?"

They lifted me off the floor and shoved me into one of the chairs.

"Fellas, is this any way to treat a fellow cop?"

The one with a brushy mustache pinned my hands to the table, while the other attached my handcuffs to a ring in the center of the table. After flashing me satisfied smiles, they both walked out of the room and shut the door.

Maybe someone with more authority was about to pay me a visit or someone who had a real panache for inflicting pain. Or they were about to hand me over to the Austrian police, who wanted me for murder from my time in Vienna. None of the options offered a good outcome. The only thing I could do was take advantage of the relative comfort of the wooden chair and the warm room. I settled in and immediately started to fall asleep.

Someone pushed the door open until it hit the wall with a bang. I opened my eyes but kept my gaze fixed on the opposite wall.

"This is getting to be a bad habit," the man said.

I recognized the voice and looked around in surprise. "Mike? What the hell?"

Mike Forester assaulted the chair opposite me before dropping into it. He let out a long sigh and leaned back. "What is it with you and getting into trouble? Is this some kind of self-flagellation? Or do you get a kick out of spending time in jails?"

"What are you doing here? This is the British zone," I said, referring to the British area of the occupation of Austria.

"They called me because they found that CIC travel pass. The one I issued you so you could get *out* of Austria."

"I was working on doing that."

"Not hard enough, apparently."

"I ran out of money and was looking for work."

"I could have gotten you out of Austria and to the States a couple of months ago. And now look at you. What is it with you that you refuse to go home?"

"Did you come here to play parent, or do you have something for me?"

Mike Forester was an intelligence agent in the CIC, the U.S. Army's Counter Intelligence Corps. We'd known each other since the beginning of the war—him in the CIC and me in the army's G-2 intelligence agency. After D-Day, we lost track of each other until meeting up again in Munich, then getting into trouble together in Vienna. He was a good and loyal friend, as well as one of the few people I let get away with giving me a verbal slapping when I screwed up.

Forester righted his chair, and his expression turned serious. "I'm here for two reasons. The first is Laura called me, because she couldn't get in touch with you."

That revelation hit me like a punch to the heart. I went rigid in my chair. "Is she all right?"

"She's fine. She called me about a week ago. But knowing her, anything could have happened between then and now."

Laura was the love of my life. Ever since we first became an item in Munich, we'd had an on-again, off-again relationship. The last time we hooked up was in Vienna, and we'd gotten pretty serious. At least I thought that until she left Vienna while I was awaiting my fate in an army stockade. I understood her need to visit her deceased husband's parents in England, but it felt final somehow, and I wondered if I'd ever hear from her again.

Forester said, "She called me from Hamburg, saying she was about to board a ship destined for Naples. She wants you to meet her there."

"A ship? Why not by train? And why Naples?"

"She wouldn't or couldn't share that info with me. The only other thing she did say was she'd be arriving in about three weeks. So that gives you a couple of weeks to get down there."

"Two weeks? I'm sure the Brits plan to keep me longer than that. Mike, you've got to get me out of here."

"I'm pulling some strings, but there aren't any guarantees. I don't have much sway over the Brits, and plus, you put one of their majors in the hospital."

"He was beating and raping a woman."

"You managed to attack a guy who has royal connections, and he claims it was consensual, that you attacked him for no good reason. Plus, the woman wouldn't refute his statement."

"Come on, Mike. If the military cops had done their job …

That guy knew exactly where to strike her without leaving bruises."

Forester said nothing, as if his silence was enough of an answer—it didn't matter since the man was a major with connections in high places.

A thought came to me. "You could have told me all this without leaving the comfort of Vienna. You really came here for the second reason."

Forester glanced at the door as if making sure no one was listening. "About a month ago, a couple of agents caught up with a Gestapo lieutenant hiding out in a cabin in the mountains above Salzburg. He'd been on our arrest list since the end of the war for torture and murder, mostly in Poland and Czechoslovakia."

The mention of Gestapo and Czechoslovakia together made my stomach churn.

Forester continued. "I wanted him tried and hanged, but my superiors said that because he'd been in German intelligence on the Eastern Front before moving over to the Gestapo, and because of his connections in East Germany and Poland, they determined he'd be a valuable asset to use for counterintelligence against the Soviets."

"Why are you telling me this?" I asked. Though I had my suspicions, I found it hard to believe them.

"The man I'm talking about is SS Obersturmführer Theodor Ziegler."

The mention of that name made every muscle in my body tense as if being hit in the stomach. On pure instinct and adrenaline, I shot up from my chair, only to be restrained by the handcuffs attached to the table. A hot sort of bile rose from my guts and burned my throat. "Where is he?"

"Sit down and I'll tell you."

It took me a moment to get control of my muscles and sit, but only on the edge of the seat.

"I wanted this man bad," Forester said. "Not only for his trail of torture and murder but because of what he did to you. Unfortunately, before I could do anything about it, headquarters released him with the understanding he'd work for the CIC."

"And he disappeared."

Forester nodded. "Three days ago." He started to explain the circumstances and extend his apologies, but I wasn't listening. All I could concentrate on were the events of that horrible day. I'd escaped from a POW death march just months before the end of the war. Starved and frozen, I lay down in a snowy forest to die. Then a little Jewish girl named Hana appeared out of nowhere, looking to me for help. My need to save her brought me back from the dead. Only I failed her when the Gestapo showed up at the farmhouse where we'd taken shelter. Obersturmführer Ziegler shot Hana in front of me, then murdered the Czech family for harboring us. He took delight in the murders and my anguish. I never forgot Hana's face as she stood before me one minute, then lay broken and bloody in the snow the next. Those images haunted my dreams on most nights. I never forgot the lieutenant's sadism, and I swore to take him out of this world if we ever crossed paths.

Forester snapped his fingers in front of my face to bring me back to the present. "I didn't come here just to watch you fall apart. I need for you to concentrate." He paused, waiting for me to acknowledge my full attention.

When I nodded, he said, "I'm not as enraged as you, but

letting this man go really got under my skin. The more I heard about this guy, the more I wanted to break something. But my hands are tied. No one in the CIC is authorized to go after him. He's small potatoes as far as headquarters in concerned."

"No need to say any more," I said. "You get me out of here, and I'll go after him. And I won't stop until I find him."

Forester nodded. "I thought you would." He leaned forward and lowered his voice. "The problem is getting you out of here. I think I've got a solution, but there's a risk for both of us."

"Say no more."

Forester got up from the table and exited the room. I could hardly sit still, but I didn't have to wait long before he came back in accompanied by a Royal Military Police captain and the two Brit MPs who had dragged me out of my cell.

The captain glared at me, then tilted his head in my direction, prompting the two guards to step over and unlock my handcuffs and leg chains. They lifted me by my arms and escorted me out the door, with Forester and the captain in the lead. In an outer office, Forester and I both signed papers. An MP sergeant handed Forester my backpack, including my M1911 pistol, and we were out the door.

My friend said nothing as we walked briskly to a car. We got in, and he drove up to the guards at the security gate. I held my breath until they waved us through, and we got out onto the road. Forester hit the accelerator hard and raced down the streets like we were in a getaway car.

"This is the second time you've gotten me out of a jam," I said as I used the dashboard to brace myself. "I'm not sure I'll ever be able to repay you."

"You're not out of a jam yet. I got you out of there on false pretenses."

"I figured that's why you're in a hurry."

"I drummed up fake extradition orders. They think I'm taking you to the stockade in Vienna for murder. As soon as they realize the ruse, the Brits will be coming after both of us."

"You want me to go after that Gestapo bastard pretty badly to jeopardize your career."

"They might make the next couple of weeks of my life a little rough, but they won't be able to touch me. After you helped bust up a crime ring and expose a double agent, I was promoted to the top of command in Vienna. So you could say I owed you. This makes us even. But it's not going to be smooth sailing for you."

"Get me past the British zone checkpoint and near Vienna, and I can take care of the rest."

"Your quarry is in the opposite direction. West and south. Meaning, you're going to have to go through the British zone on your own."

"I'll make it. Do you know where Ziegler is now?"

Forester shook his head. "He was last spotted in Innsbruck and heading south. That was two days ago."

"South? Italy?"

"Almost certain. We believe he's joined up with a group of fellow Nazi war criminals hoping to get through the Brenner Pass, a known ratline and one of the Nazis' favorite escape routes."

"A group? They travel in packs?"

"Sometimes. It can be safer that way. And they can pool their money for bribes and find havens through multiple contacts in South Tyrol. That area was part of Austria until the end of World War One, and the vast majority of the people there feel it should still be a part of Austria."

"The group has to get past the British zone checkpoints."

"Some of them hire local guides to get over the mountains and bypass the checkpoints, but some still manage to get through the Brit border guards. How they do that is still unknown. My guess is someone or some entity is feeding them official travel passes or refugee status papers under false names. Watch your step down there; you're going to find more foes than friends. And with all the post-war chaos in Italy, the Italian authorities tend to look the other way."

A few miles north of the Graz city limits, Forester pulled off the highway and parked near a rock quarry. He removed an envelope from his coat pocket and handed it to me.

"This is the best I could do for you," he said.

I opened it. The first thing I pulled out was a 4x6 black-and-white photograph of Ziegler. Looking at his face sent a chill through me. It was an official portrait, with him dressed in his SS uniform. I had memorized his looks long ago, and I figured Forester had provided the photo for me to use in questioning people about his whereabouts. His head looked like it'd been put in a vise, leaving the sides of his skull in proportion but squishing his face into his cranium. The jawline was pronounced but lacked a chin. His deep-set eyes were almost obscured by bulging cheekbones. I put the photo facedown on the dashboard and checked out the rest of the envelope's contents: two hundred Austrian schillings in paper and coins,fifty U.S. dollars; and a U.S.-issued travel pass for a Gregor Witt. Witt was the alias I used when I first got to Vienna.

"The forged *Soldbuch* you had under that name is in there too," Forester said.

The *Soldbuch* was the identity book every German soldier received during the war, and this one claimed I was Gregor Witt, supposedly a soldier released from a prisoner-of-war camp in Italy six months after the war.

"I thought I'd lost this," I said. "How did you get it?"

"I have my methods. It might get you past the Austrian authorities, but not the British."

"I still have that CIC travel pass you gave me."

"That expired two months ago."

"I'll figure something out." I put the contents back in the envelope and held it up. "Thanks for this and getting me out of the bind."

"There's one thing I want you to do for me. I'd like you to report back any fleeing Nazis you come across. There are still fifty or more high-profile Nazis we haven't caught yet, or they were released in the confusion. The CIC has some agents in that area. Some for prosecution, some for intelligence gathering. Anyone you can identify, you pass that info on to me, and I'll alert the agents down there."

"Will do," I said and started to get out of the car.

Forester took my arm to stop me. "Be careful out there. I don't want to think I put my ass on the line only for you to get killed. And give Laura my best."

I nodded and got out of the car. I retrieved my backpack from the trunk, and Forester drove away.

I looked around: the rock quarry was to my left, the snow-covered fields to my right, and one road between them. I had to cover about 250 miles to get to Brenner and the beginning of the pass through the Italian Alps. It was freezing and snowing. I didn't have a car, only a fistful of money, one forged pass under an alias, and an expired CIC pass. That and the contents of my backpack. Wanted by the Austrian police and the British authorities.

All in all, a daunting task ahead of me.

But I had a mission: If I could find the Gestapo commander, I might be able to put to rest one of my worst nightmares by sending him to hell. I just had to do it in the two weeks before getting to Naples and finding out what was so urgent with Laura.

2

Someone was following me. The best I could determine, there were two of them dogging my every move. I had no idea who they were, but one thing I did know was that they weren't professionals. Maybe they didn't care that I'd detected them after leaving a butcher shop ten minutes ago. Maybe it was an intimidation tactic to scare me off from asking so many questions about Ziegler.

I was in the Austrian town of Matrei am Brenner, about ten miles from the Italian border. After hot-wiring a car outside of Graz, I went straight to Innsbruck and hit a number of bars, restaurants, and hotels in the city center and showed the photo of Ziegler around to the proprietors and clients. The range of reactions went from cold shoulders to outright hostility. I left that city before I attracted too much attention, and headed south toward the Brenner Pass.

There was only one highway from Innsbruck to the Brenner Pass. It followed the Sill river valley that cut its way through low mountains. I'd hit the half dozen towns and hamlets along the way, striking out at each location. But I must have hit a nerve at one of my stops in this current town, enough of one, at least, to have picked up my two companions.

Matrei am Brenner had one main street that went for about eight blocks or so and paralleled the highway and railroad tracks. I figured the railroad must have had some strategic importance for the Allies during the war, because bombs had damaged a number of buildings. Those left intact were like most buildings in the small Austrian towns, charming three- and four-story structures decorated with flower boxes and eighteenth-century-style ornamental tracery around the windows.

It was after six p.m., and the few streetlamps were lit. Reconstruction on the damaged buildings had stopped for the day, and most of the stores were closing.

I slowed my pace near a bay window protruding from a ground-floor shop so that I could see the two men reflected in an angled window. They slowed when I did, giving me ample time to observe them. They both wore long black coats. One looked to be in his twenties and the other early forties. The younger guy's hands were free of weapons, but the older one, who also had the build of a heavyweight boxer, carried a pistol at his side. They weren't curious about me; they had no intention of asking me a few friendly questions. I was prey, and the only reason they'd avoided confrontation up to now was because of the people still milling about.

I planned to turn the tables on them and ruin their evening.

Just past the train station, I turned right on a street not much wider than an alley and headed for a sharp curve about a hundred yards ahead. I'd taken this darkened alleyway on purpose, as I knew they'd make their move on me once I took the curve and I was out of sight from the main road. I wiggled my fingers into the brass knuckles I had in my right pocket as I approached the curve.

I should have guessed that in these small towns were hotbeds of die-hard Nazis and Nazi sympathizers.

I took the curve and tucked into the doorway of a wood-shop closed up for the night. There were no streetlamps and only a handful of other buildings on my side of the road, with an open field on the opposite. When I heard footsteps hoofing it up the street, I made sure I had a firm grasp of the sap in my left.

The two men stopped just short of the doorway, probably surprised that the street ahead was empty. This made it trickier, and I had a flash of regret that I'd left my pistol in my backpack. I charged out of the doorway and went for the bigger man. The man's eyes widened in alarm, and he started to bring up his pistol. I struck his wrist with the sap and heard bones in his wrist snap. He cried out. The gun clattered to the asphalt.

I slammed the brass knuckles into the bigger man's jaw. Stunned, his knees buckled, and he hit the asphalt. The younger guy had frozen in place, but when he saw his partner go down, he cried out in fear or rage and charged me.

He led with his shoulder, like a linebacker trying to take down the runner. That was a mistake. I simply swung my body away, grabbed him, and used his momentum to hurl him into the wall of the woodshop.

He crashed into it and recoiled, though he managed to stay on his feet. He turned to attack once again, but I scooped up his companion's pistol and aimed it at him.

"Stop right there," I said in German.

He did.

"Get on your stomach with your hands behind your head."

With a defiant glare, he lay next to his partner just as the big man came out of his daze and started to rise. I gave the big guy one more good hit with the sap to the back of his head, and he stopped moving.

I turned my attention to the younger one. "I know why you were following me."

"We weren't following you," the young man shouted.

"Keep your voice down, or I'll give you the same treatment I gave to your friend. Now, you'll tell me what I want to know, and I won't throw your corpses in the river."

The young man said nothing.

"I'll take that as a yes." I knelt down and put the barrel of the gun against his head. I had no intention of shooting him, but he didn't know that. I fished Ziegler's photo out of my overcoat pocket and laid it on the ground next to his face. I got a cigarette lighter out of my other pocket, lit the wick, and put it close to the photo.

"Where is he?"

"I've never seen that man before."

I pushed the barrel harder against his temple. "You know him, all right. Asking around about him is what made you come after me. So don't waste my time denying it." I leaned in next to his ear. "'Cause lying makes me crazy. And when I get crazy, my trigger finger takes on a life of its own. People wind up with holes in their heads. Stay silent or lie to me again, and I'll do that to you and your partner." I shoved the gun so hard that it forced his head against the ground and flattened his cheek. "Where is Ziegler?"

He grimaced from the pain. Tears of fear and frustration filled his eyes. "He's not here. He hired a guide to take him to Italy."

"When did he leave?"

"Yesterday."

"Why did he hire a guide?"

"To avoid the checkpoints and go over the mountains."

"Is he traveling with anyone else?"

"I don't know. I heard he was going to meet up with others somewhere in the pass."

I let off the pressure on his temple and grabbed the collar of his overcoat. "Get up."

I jerked him to his feet and pointed to the field. "Start running and don't stop. I can hit a moving target with this at a hundred yards."

The older man groaned as he came awake. He tried to get up on all fours, but he collapsed and stopped moving.

"What about him?" the young man said and nodded at his companion.

"I'd worry about what I'll do to you if you don't start running. Now!"

Like a starting gun, my shout caused the young man to burst into a frenzied sprint like a runner in a 100-yard dash. I waited until he disappeared into the murky darkness, and took off for my car.

I REACHED a clearing on a mountain slope about two hundred yards from the British checkpoint at the Austrian/Italian border. That was after parking my stolen Opel in the parking lot of a burned-out one-story building and climbing up the mountainside to search for a view of the road below. I got the binoculars out of my backpack and trained them on the guardhouses and series of gates controlling the border crossing. There seemed to be more uniforms than usual for a checkpoint, even one at the border of two countries. At least fifty British Royal MPs manned the Austrian side, with a platoon of Italian police on the opposite side of the triple barrier.

Every car waiting to cross was stopped, and the occupants were told to get out. A handful of inspectors would then go over the vehicles with a fine-toothed comb and double-check the occupants' papers. Something was up, and bigger than a dragnet for a small fish like me. They'd grab me up for sure, but they were definitely after bigger fish. Regardless, crossing over into Italy through the heightened security would be impossible.

I stuffed my binoculars into the backpack and looked up at the snow-encrusted mountains looming above me. I was going to have to slog my way over the mountains for miles. I'd done it before via another pass to enter Austria on my way to Vienna, but the memories of that brutal journey were still fresh in my mind. And that had been in October. Now I would try to do it during the worst time of the year, when the snows were deep, and the days were short.

I tossed the keys to the car into a clump of trees, hoisted my backpack, and started climbing.

3

Not for the first time in the last two days I told myself that I had no business being in the Italian Alps in February, on foot no less. I was roughly paralleling the Brenner Pass, which was a narrow valley at over four thousand feet of elevation and hemmed in by high mountains. I stayed about thirty yards west of the road that ran through it, and twenty yards above it.

It was around seven p.m., and the sun had set a couple of hours ago. The snow had finally stopped, leaving a foot or so on top of the previous day's layer. The Swiss pine and spruce branches were laden with snow, and clumps dropped every now and then. My feet were frozen. The frostbite scars on my feet were howling at me to find warmth.

I'd just passed a village, but it was shut up tight, reminding me of the many abandoned villages I'd passed through during the war. The map I'd picked up in Matrei am Brenner indicated there was a small city about two hours to the south—two hours if I didn't freeze to death beforehand. As long as I kept my eye on the road and adhered to the contours of the valley, I wouldn't get lost.

I rounded a bend and came to an area of more rocks than trees. Beyond the edge of my hood, I could see the inky-black silhouettes of the mountaintops against the gray dome of clouds radiated by an obscured full moon. In the distance, the mountains muscled in on the valley, squeezing it from either side, then the pass doglegged to the left. Steep slopes came up quickly on either side, and I was forced onto the road.

Not two minutes later, I came upon a stone bridge. It spanned a gorge cut by a narrow river running perpendicular to the road. In the dimness, I heard more than saw the water rushing as it forced its way through the gorge. Then, just as I stepped onto the bridge, a truck's engine roared up the road behind me. I scurried for the tree line in case it was an Italian police patrol.

I got a couple of yards into the trees when the truck barreled past me. It was a five-ton British Army troop carrier. Its canvas covering flapped in the wind.

What was a British troop transport doing here? At the end of the war, the U.S. had taken on the administration of Italy, but they were gradually relinquishing control to the Italians. And while I'd seen a few American military vehicles on the road further north, this was the first Brit.

The truck suddenly stopped halfway across the bridge. Curious, I shifted my position to get a clearer view. The rear canvas flaps parted, and without a word, two men in British Army uniforms climbed out of the back. They reached inside and forced another man to get out. That man was bound at the wrists, blindfolded, and in civilian clothes. The two must have snatched him from an indoor location, as he was without a coat or any winter gear.

The two men led the blindfolded one to the edge of the bridge. The captive didn't struggle, though he shivered violently. Frigid temperatures and terror had that effect on a man. Nothing was said. They just stood there for a brief moment. Their captive seemed to have no idea of his whereabouts. Maybe they were letting him pee.

One of the men whipped out a pistol and shot the blindfolded man in the head. Surprise and shock caused every nerve to spark, as if the bullet was meant for me. The guy's legs buckled in death. The two Brits caught him before he fell, lifted him, and flipped him over the railing.

A thick branch rotting just under my right foot broke with a snap. I'd been leaning out to get a clear view, and it was as if the ground beneath me had given way. I tumbled down the hill and landed on my backpack onto the road. I looked up toward the bridge. The two soldiers swung around and looked in my direction. In the dim light I caught a glimpse of their faces, and I figured they had seen mine.

A split second of hesitation was followed by both of them pulling out their pistols. I'd put my M1911 pistol in my backpack, leaving me no choice but to scramble to my feet and dive for the trees. I clambered up the hill but quickly came up to a rock face that rose sharply. I grabbed onto tree branches and roots, anything to help me climb, but I couldn't climb faster than the men could run on the road.

I heard two pistols being cocked behind me.

"I advise you to raise your hands and come down," one of the men said in British-accented German.

I stopped my struggle and looked back. The two men

stood on the tarmac with their pistols aimed in my direction. I figured if they'd wanted me dead, they would have shot me by now. With no other options available, I complied.

I raised my hands and began to climb down. The bulky backpack made it a tricky descent, and about ten feet from the level of the road, I slipped and slid down the rest of the way on my back. I came to a stop at their feet with my hands still up and inches from the muzzles of their pistols. Both men were in their late twenties, early thirties. One had a handsome face blemished only by a long scar from his ear to the base of his chin. The other wore glasses over big cow eyes, though even under his heavy coat, I could see he had the musculature of a swimmer.

"*Wie heißen Sie*" the one with glasses asked.

"I'm an American," I said in English. "Mason Collins."

A flash of confusion and skepticism flashed across their faces.

The one with the scar said, "A bloke daft enough to be on foot in the mountains, at night, in the winter? Who speaks German? Not likely."

He spoke British English, but there was a tinge of another accent underneath that.

I shrugged. "You want the short or the long explanation?"

"I want to hear why we don't shoot you and toss you over the bridge to join our friend."

"Look, I don't know who you are, so I'm not likely to report you—"

"I say we kill him and be done with it," the handsome one said to his partner.

"We're not here to kill people just because they're stupid

enough to blunder onto the scene," the one with the glasses said.

"I have no interest in getting between you guys and your work," I said. I decided to avoid any talk of my mission or showing them Ziegler's photograph, as I wasn't entirely sure what team they played on. "I'm just hoofing it south to meet up with my sweetheart in Naples. I got into an altercation with a Brit officer in Austria, and I had to ditch my car. That's it. End of story. So I'd appreciate if you'd keep to your plan and spare this idiot, who happened to be in the wrong place at the wrong time."

"He sure sounds like a Yank," the one with the glasses said. "You got some identity papers?"

While keeping my hands high, I pointed to my overcoat. "Inside coat pocket."

The one with the scar reached into my coat and pulled out my leather pouch. He searched inside and found my papers. I just hoped he'd grab the right one, as I had two forged identities, one claiming I was a German ex-soldier with a transit pass. I held my breath while the two men examined the paper by the glow of a cigarette lighter.

Both of them then looked at me simultaneously. My heart bumped into high gear. The one with the glasses put the paper back into the pouch and dropped it onto my chest.

"That travel pass is expired," the scarred one said. "We're not MPs, so we don't care." He leaned into me. "I just wonder what a CIC intelligence chap is doing in the middle of nowhere. Have you been spying on us?"

"Come on, think about that. That would imply that I knew exactly where you'd be and masterfully timed it so I could— on foot—be here just before you stopped on that bridge."

The one with the glasses tapped on his companion's arm. "If we're not going to off him, then let's get out of here."

The one with the scar took a moment longer to stare at me before he straightened. "If we hear you tried to report this, we will find you. Do you understand?"

"You go your way, and I'll go mine. We'll both be happy."

"Stay there until we're gone," the one with the glasses said.

"Then could you make it snappy? The snow has soaked through to my ass."

The two men backed away while keeping their eyes and guns on me until they disappeared from my view. I raised my torso enough to watch them jump into the truck's cargo area, and the truck raced away.

I clambered down the incline to the road, brushed the snow off my coat, and slid off my backpack. I'd thought the prudent thing was to keep my Colt .45 in the backpack in case I was surprised by the cops, but now an unease and a sense of vulnerability crept through me. My fingers found the holster with the pistol nestled inside. I drew it out, checked the magazine, blew my warm breath on the cartridges, reinserted the magazine, and strapped on the holster. I waited another moment to make sure they hadn't changed their minds. The road remained empty. The only sounds were the wind in the trees and the rushing water in the gorge.

After one more glance at both ends of the road, I headed for the bridge. I began crossing it at a quick pace since I was vulnerable on the bridge. Ice had formed on the decking, and the wind whipped through the gorge. I hesitated a moment where the two men had executed their victim and looked down. The clouds had parted enough to expose a full moon that sat on the crest of the highest mountain and illuminated the river. The water roiled forty feet below and hurried chunks of ice along as it rushed to an unknown destination. The only signs of the incident were a few drops of blood on the cement barrier and the boot prints in the snow.

After a couple seconds, I started on my way again. Once I got off the bridge and into the relative safety of the tree line, I turned my thoughts to what I'd just witnessed. Two British Army guys just murdered a helpless man in cold blood. Were they corrupt soldiers involved in a smuggling operation? That seemed the most likely scenario, and they had killed a rival. And what did they mean by not killing innocent bystanders?

From my time in the U.S. Army's criminal investigation division, I was aware of the Brenner Pass being the preferred route for smugglers from the ports in Italy north to the ravenous black markets for contraband and drugs in Germany and Austria. I'd taken an even greater interest in the smuggling routes when Laura had put herself in danger by chasing a news story about the smuggling in this very pass.

As it would turn out, slogging through the ice and snow would be the least of my worries.

4

I t was a relief to come out of the wilderness and into the town of Sterzing. It also went by the Italian name of Vipiteno, but despite being in Italy, for all intents and purposes it was Austrian, from the architecture to the street signs to the names of the inns and restaurants.

I passed under the arch of the medieval clock tower and tromped down the narrow street that was probably once the medieval heart of the town. It was after ten p.m. according to the tower clock, and things were shut tight.

I was so dog-tired that the only way I could go on was to stare at my feet and will them to keep moving. As I walked down the ice-glazed cobblestoned street, however, I couldn't shake the idea that I was being watched. The town was small, with maybe four thousand inhabitants, so a stranger walking out of the forest in the middle of winter probably merited attention. But this seemed different.

I decided to try a small inn wedged between a ski shop and a bakery, but the moment I stepped into the inn's lobby, it crossed my mind to do an about-face and walk out again.

Being an ex-cop and former army intelligence officer, I could read a room better than most, and this one read hostile. A bunch of grim faces had turned my way, a mix of suspicion and apprehension on their faces. I felt like a cowboy in one of those westerns, who'd just ridden into town and entered a saloon full of desperados.

But it was snowing outside, and I was chilled to the bone, not to mention bone tired and hungry enough to chew on one. Plus, this place was the first establishment I came upon and found open where I could get some chow, throw back a couple of drinks, and hit the rack without having to venture out into the cold again until I was damned good and ready.

As I stomped the snow off my boots, the odors of sausages and butter cooking made my stomach fold in upon itself. I took a couple more steps into the room, expecting the owner or an employee to come up and guide me to a table. But the middle-aged guy remained behind the bar, and a woman of similar age was taking orders from three men at another table —at least she had been until I appeared. Now they were all frozen in place, looking my way.

I slipped off my backpack and let it land with a thud on the wooden floor. I pointed to an empty table. The woman hesitated a moment before giving me a nod. Apparently, that was the signal that all could come back to life, and a murmur of voices resumed. I crossed over to the table against the wall, pulled off my wool gloves and thick sheepskin coat, and sat with my back to the wall and a clear view of everything around me.

I didn't expect to be served right away—or at all—so I used the time to survey the room. The inn's lobby consisted of a single space. The dining area with twenty tables took up half of it. A long bar ran along the opposing wall and was book-ended by a check-in desk near the entrance and access to the kitchen at the other end. The floors, walls, and ceiling were of pine paneling that had darkened with age.

Typical of Austrian establishments, stuffed deer and boar heads hung on the walls, along with vintage black-and-white photos of skiers and locals, some grinning, some with grim expressions similar to those of the current occupants. The place was being warmed by two wood-burning stoves, though they added nothing to the dim lighting. A few wall sconces and two lamps on the bar provided the only illumination.

The woman taking orders returned to the kitchen without a glance my way. That made the grinding in my stomach even worse. Out of the corner of my eye, I saw someone step up to my table. I looked up to see a small man with his hat in his hands. He wore spectacles and sported a bushy mustache as gray as the steel wool he had for hair. He looked at me with nervous eyes. His face was so clenched it looked like he was holding his breath.

After he offered nothing in the way of conversation, I asked in German, "Can I help you?"

His face unwound and formed a crooked smile. He sat down eagerly and said, "The snow is falling quite heavily."

I had no idea what to make of that statement. I might have discounted him as simpleminded, but he looked at me so expectantly, that I got the impression he was waiting for the right response. He seemed to think I was his contact. But for what?

"Sir, I think you have the wrong guy," I said.

His face contracted again. He opened his mouth to say something but opted to rise from the table and give me a quick bow before retreating to a table in the corner of the room. There, his hands fought among themselves as he stared at the entrance.

The woman taking orders must have been watching from some concealed place, because as soon as the small man got seated, she exited the kitchen and goose-stepped up to my table. She held up her pad and pencil. "We only have *Wurzelfleisch* and potatoes."

It flashed through my mind to wonder why she'd bothered to bring a pad and pencil with her. "I'll take it. And a *Weissbier*."

She noted my choice, eyeballed me from the top edge of the pad, then did an about-face and headed for the kitchen.

The dish had an unappetizing name, but I'd enjoyed the pork pot roast several times as I'd wandered through Styria, the southeast region of Austria. My reveries were interrupted when two men in threadbare suits stood from their table and approached me. The tall one took the lead. He held his lanky frame ramrod straight, with his head high as if he owned the room. His stocky partner, with his shaved head, thick neck, and homicidal glare, was the one I'd have to watch carefully. He had the air of an attack dog, an enforcer, the tall one's ambulatory muscle.

Everyone else in the place avoided eye contact with the two and pretended to go about their business, though many of them stole glances my way, and the murmur of conversation dropped to a whisper.

It was hard to tell if the reactions around the room were from respect, fear, or simple curiosity, but the hairs on the back of my neck stood up is if reacting to some malicious ether; some would say that was a primal reaction to danger but, for me, it was an early warning system developed from years of getting myself into bad situations.

The two suited men came up to my table and sat without invitation. They said nothing. I returned the favor, and we commenced a staring contest. Maybe this was their way of intimidating me, but I refused to take the bait. I'd spent too much time interrogating murderers as a homicide detective, then captured Nazi soldiers, to break a sweat with these two. Plus, my hunger had made me meaner than a rabid dog.

They exchanged a look, as if unsure what to do next. The tall one started blinking and tapping his index finger. "Who are you?" he asked in German.

By their actions, they hadn't been frontline soldiers or hardened criminals. They could still be dangerous, but I took their threat level down a notch. Plus, I was intrigued. To push their buttons a little further, I said, "Herr Niemand," introducing myself as Mr. Nobody.

The tall one blinked again, but the thick one bristled and said, "You obviously arrived on foot. We want to know why and what you're doing here."

"That must be very frustrating for you."

The thick one stiffened and positioned himself to make a lunge, but his companion put his hand on his arm to stop him. The waitress almost tiptoed up to my table, deposited my beer, and scurried back to the kitchen.

"We've forgotten our manners, Anton," the tall one said to his companion. He turned to me. "My name is Friedrich Kappler, and this is Anton Rudel." He looked at me expectantly.

I took a long swig of my beer instead.

Rudel spoke in pretty clean *Hochdeutsch*, but while his

accent was close to perfect, I still detected another accent—
Slavic was my best guess. However, Kappler spoke with an
accent I could only surmise was somewhere in the northeast
of Germany. Definitely German-born. Not that it mattered,
but they were definitely not natives of South Tyrol or even
Austria.

I wiped the beer foam from my mouth. "Gregor Witt."
That was the alias I'd used in Austria that was now printed on
the travel pass I purchased on the black market, claiming I
was an Austrian businessman.

"There, you see, Anton?" Kappler said to his partner.
"Civility is always better." To me he said, "Now, let us go back
to our original queries. Why are you here? You're certainly
not from South Tyrol."

"By your accents, neither are you," I said.

Kappler's face twisted in impatience. "What are you doing
here?"

"I could ask you the same thing."

"Avoiding our questions only makes us suspect you more."

"That's not my problem," I said and leaned forward. "But I
do have a problem with people trying to stick their noses in
my business. I could also wonder what two Germans are
doing in Italy when Germans are restricted from cross-border
travel. But I won't, because that's not my business."

It looked like Rudel was using every ounce of his
willpower to not attack me. I made a note to remember to
watch my back when I left this establishment.

Kappler sneered and pointed his index finger at me. "It's
everyone's business in this town when a murderer or
murderers have killed five men around here in the last ten
days. Do you know something about that?"

I thought of the two Brits shooting their captive just a few hours ago ... "No."

"Perhaps you do. Perhaps you don't. In any case, I'll give you a word of warning: It's not safe to travel on foot in this area. There are some individuals who would take a stranger as a threat, and others who take advantage of such a traveler. The murders in this area have ..." He appeared to search for the right word. "... put certain people here very much on edge."

"I'll keep that in mind," I said in a neutral voice and leaned back with a smile. I wanted to get rid of them because I noticed the woman exit the kitchen holding my plate of food. She stopped just outside the door, apparently waiting for my two interlopers to leave.

Kappler cleared his throat to get my attention. "Now you understand why we're so suspicious of strangers wandering into our town. Especially ones who speak German with a peculiar Bavarian accent. I can't put my finger on it, but I suspect that while your German is very good, it is not your native language. I would take my warning very seriously."

Any patience I had for these two clowns had vanished. "I bet you two miss the days when the Gestapo, perhaps men like yourselves, could harass and intimidate anyone they pleased."

Rudel launched from his chair, shoving the table aside. I was ready for him and jumped to my feet. He took a swing at me. I leaned back enough that he missed my nose, then I followed up with a quick left-right combination to his jaw and stomach. Breathless, Rudel bent at the waist and staggered backward.

I waited for Kappler to come at me, but he opted for grabbing his companion's shoulders and pulling him to a safe distance. Rudel would have none of it and charged me like a bull seeing red. I shifted to my left, grabbed his coat, and slammed him into the wall. Rudel's head ricocheted from the impact, and he dropped to his knees.

Kappler held his hands out to me in a sign that he had no interest in attacking me. He went over to his stunned friend and helped the man stagger away.

Once I was sure they wouldn't come back for more, I rearranged the table and sat, ignoring the cold stares. What I couldn't ignore was the woman with my food glaring at me, then making a turn and going back into the kitchen. And my beer lay in a puddle on the floor. To top it off, the guy behind the bar—presumably the owner—thrust his finger toward the door and yelled for me to get out.

Not wanting anyone to go for the police, I pulled on my coat and gloves, hoisted my pack onto my back, and walked out into the cold darkness.

5

As I walked down the main street, I remained vigilant for threats in front and behind. There was a good chance those two from the inn might try to enlist some friends to bushwhack me. I slipped down an alley, dug into my backpack, and fished out the holster with my .45 nestled inside. I checked the magazine and the chamber, then strapped on the holster under my coat and got ready for the long night ahead of me.

Before stepping back out onto the main street, I stopped at the corner and glanced down both sides of the street. All seemed quiet. I moved out. After a couple of blocks the main street curved to the right, and I followed it. Not four streets farther, I could see the southern end of the town, and beyond that the moonlit valley and mountains.

I heard footsteps behind me. In a quick move, I drew my pistol, spun on my heels, and aimed at the man's head. It was the small man from the inn. He stood in the middle of the street, frozen in place, his hat once again in his hands. His eyes were wide from fear at the sight of the gun.

"Please, sir, I mean you no harm," the man said in German.

"You nearly got your head blown off. Don't you know not to sneak up on people?"

"I had no choice. I shouldn't be out here. I'm being watched." He gestured to a dark side street. "Could we go over there?"

I took a second to consider whether this was to get me into a spot for an ambush, but I just couldn't figure it with this guy. Plus, I was intrigued.

Knowing that my tendency to be intrigued had gotten me into trouble in the past, I studied the man's face, his pleading eyes, to gauge how deep into the muck he might be leading me. Snow had begun to collect on his bald head and cling to the few hairs left on top.

"Put your hat back on."

He did so and appeared grateful for my concern. I held out my hand for him to go first. He hurried across to the side street and tucked himself into a dark doorway about ten feet down. I checked my surroundings, holstered my pistol, and caught up to him a moment later.

"I'm sorry I startled you," the man said. "I hoped you would come this way after talking to those two men. So I hid in an archway."

Now that I had the man cornered, I dug into my overcoat pocket to fish out Ziegler's photograph. It was gone. The man flinched when I frantically checked my other pockets. Nothing. It must have fallen out one of the several times I'd stumbled on the mountain slopes.

Irritated with myself for losing the photo and letting the man get the jump on me, I took it out on him by jabbing him in the chest. "Next time, step out in front of someone, not behind. You'll live longer."

He just nodded.

"Start talking," I said. "I'm cold and hungry, so you've got five minutes."

"My name is Leo Schwend, and I need your help with an urgent matter."

"I've got my own problems. Go to the police."

His face widened in dread. "The police? I ... I just can't."

"Is that who's watching you?"

He shook his head. "People like those two men you encountered at the inn."

I was losing my patience. The man's answers only created more questions. "Feel free to elaborate, Leo. Your five minutes are ticking down fast."

Schwend leaned in and lowered his voice. "I prefer not to say here. Believe me, it's very serious. I don't know where else to turn."

Two people passed by on the main street. I pushed Schwend deeper into the doorway and squeezed in next to him.

Once the people were out of sight, their conversation inaudible, I said, "In the inn, you came up to me and spoke a phrase like a password. Who were you waiting for? Someone else who might help?"

"I gave a considerable amount of money to a contact here. He was supposed to hire some armed guides to come to my aid. But that was over a week ago. I can only assume the local man took my money with no intention of helping me."

"And what were these armed guides supposed to do for you?"

"I can't leave this town without someone following me. If I tried, I'd lead them to the cabin."

"Leo, you're not making any sense. Who's watching, and what cabin?"

"My sister-in-law and her son are hiding at the cabin. The armed guides I wanted to hire would escort us all to the south and safety. That's what I desperately need for you to do. I saw how you subdued those men. My sister-in-law is in great danger, and we need someone like you. I can pay you." Schwend pulled out a small leather bag from his pocket, undid the string binding the top, and lifted out a gold coin. He held it up for me to see. "There's a thousand Swiss francs worth of gold in the bag. It's all I have left. You do this for me, and it's all yours."

I pushed his hand down and instinctively looked both ways. "Leo, you can't flash money around like that. No wonder those guys are after you."

"They don't want me or my money. They want my sister-in-law. And no telling what they might do to the young boy." He shoved the bag at me. "Take this, please, and go to the cabin. Save them."

I took his wrist and pushed it and the bag against his chest. "I won't take your money. And I'm not going on some sketchy mission to a cabin. I'm sorry, but every time I get involved, it means trouble. The only reason I'm traipsing through the freezing cold like a chump is because I have to get to Naples."

I stepped away and headed for the main street.

"Please," Schwend said and ran in front of me to cut me off. "Just go there and see for yourself. It's not more than ninety minutes from here on foot." His face lit up as if another thought came to him. "And she has food," he said with a smile like a pimp enticing a john. "It's warm, and there's an extra bed. Just stay for the night. And she's quite pretty." He withdrew a piece of paper from inside his coat and shoved it into my upper coat pocket.

I reached for the paper, but my hand stopped halfway there. Schwend's eyes had widened with fear as he stared at something over my shoulder. I turned to see what frightened him. Three men stood a block down the narrow street. Schwend cried out in panic and ran for the main street.

The three men trotted up the street toward us with pistols at their sides.

I drew mine and aimed. "Stop right there."

The three men dived for cover. I took long steps backward, toward Schwend, while keeping my eyes and gun trained on the three men. At that same moment, a car rushed up to the intersection with the main street and skidded to a halt.

Schwend cried out again. I turned my attention to him. Two other men had gotten out of the car—Kappler and Rudel, the two men from the inn. Rudel grabbed Schwend and shoved him toward the open back door of the car. Kappler stood just outside the driver's door.

I charged for Rudel. Shots rang out from behind. I ignored the bullets whizzing by my head and slammed into Rudel. I struck the back of his head with my pistol grip, and he tumbled to the ground.

I grabbed Schwend's coat and dragged him toward the front of the car while aiming my pistol at Kappler's chest. "Get out of there. Now!"

Kappler backed away with his hands in the air. I figured the only reason the three men behind me had stopped shooting was to avoid hitting their own men, but as soon as Kappler retreated, the men opened fire again.

Rounds flew past me or struck the car. I hurried us both around the car to use it as a shield. I fired three times over the roof of the car, then shoved Schwend into the front seat. "Get over."

The men charged forward as they fired. I shot twice. One of the men screamed and tumbled to the ground. The other two jumped into doorways for cover.

I tossed my backpack in the back, jumped into the driver's seat, and hit the accelerator just as the men fired more rounds. The car's tires spun on the snow and ice. The car fishtailed, then found traction. We hurtled out of town.

"Who are those guys?" I yelled at Schwend.

All I got from him in return was a gurgle. I looked at my companion. Blood trickled down one side of his mouth, and red bubbles had formed on his lips.

While trying to navigate the slippery road, I did my best to pull back his coat to see his wound. Blood soaked his shirt. I stopped the car and put on the emergency brake. After one glance back to see if we were being pursued, I turned to Schwend. A bullet had hit him in the side of the neck and left a nasty exit wound on the left side of his chest. Blood surged with each pulse of his heart. His eyes had glazed over, and his mouth gaped wide. A second later he was gone.

I growled and slammed the steering wheel. A thousand volts of pain radiated through my arm and into my chest. It was only then that I noticed the hot, wet liquid flowing down my side.

I pulled back my coat and saw a bullet had entered my

ribcage. Blood was seeping from the hole and soaking my sweater. My head spun, and my chest turned cold.

I had to get somewhere safe and find a doctor. But where? I couldn't go back to town, and there was only a quarter of a tank of gas. Not enough to get to Bozen or Meran—the only possible places where I had a chance of finding a doctor or hospital.

Then I thought of Schwend's request. The cabin. It couldn't be far if it was only ninety minutes on foot. I scanned the road. The car's headlights illuminated the heavy snow that had begun to fall. To find one cabin in the darkness and in time … A thought came to me, and I pulled out the paper Schwend had shoved into my pocket.

On it was a rough outline of the town with a darker line following a meandering one labeled the Eisack river. The dark line changed names a couple of times, presumably street names, then it veered to the left and turned into a switchback to the west of town. I figured that represented a road that climbed up a mountain side, which finally led to an X and the word *Kabine*, or cabin. I could follow it well enough, but the big problem was I would have to head north and go back through the center of town.

I hadn't a second to lose. I released the hand brake, made a U-turn, and hit the accelerator. Like the death coach in Irish folklore, I hurtled into town with Schwend, my dead-man cargo. In seconds I hit the outskirts of the town and prayed I wouldn't encounter a roadblock or run into the shooters. Up ahead, a small crowd had gathered near the intersection or stood outside their front doors, all obviously attracted by the gunfire. Two local constables were sniffing around the side street.

As I got close, all heads turned to the sound of the car's engine. Slowing down was not an option. I honked my horn. People scattered. The policemen pointed and shouted. But I kept going, zooming past them. In the rearview mirror I could see the cops running up the street, probably to their car.

I passed under the medieval tower only wide enough for one vehicle and seconds later found the street that the crude map indicated where I had to turn left. I did so. A couple of quick turns west then north, and I came to the road that twisted up the mountainside.

It came up so fast in the darkness that I almost missed it and had to hit the brakes. The Mercedes slid on the icy road. Schwend's limp body was thrown against the dashboard, then it banged against the door as I made the left turn.

A coldness spread across my chest. My head swam. My vision constricted to the area directly ahead, which was made worse by the narrow beams of the headlights. The windshield wipers groaned as they swept snow off the windshield. Schwend swayed left or right with each turn, sometimes falling on me and forcing me to shove his lifeless body the other way. The whole thing became a surreal nightmare as I strained to stay on the road and not crash down the steep incline.

I hit fog. Or was it my vision? The veil of mist was sparse and insubstantial at first, but then it became a white, roiling curtain as I got higher. I slowed the car to a crawl and leaned forward, straining to see the turns in the road. Going slow probably saved me, because I nearly passed out a couple of times.

I slammed on the brakes again. The road had come to an abrupt end. Had I made a wrong turn? Part of my mind prepared for me to die on that frozen mountaintop. The thought of joining Herr Schwend got my adrenaline pumping through me. I shook off the enveloping blackness, doused the headlights, opened the car door, and peered into the night. In the moonlight I could see that the principal road had ended, but there was a narrow road barely visible in the snow-covered field to the left. It went straight up the slope and disappeared into a pine forest.

Maybe, just maybe. I turned the headlights back on and steered onto the primitive road. The car's tires had a tough time finding traction, the backend fishtailed. The cold had spread from my chest to my arms and legs despite having the heater on full blast. I was down to cursing at the car, begging the car, praying for a miracle.

6

It was like being submerged and slowly rising to the surface. My brain first registered a diffused light, then a muffled sound, like the soft hum of a car engine. A shock wave of alarm crashed into my brain. The car! I was still in the car!

I opened my eyes, and in the dim light, I saw wood beams of a ceiling. The sound became clearer and turned out to be a child's voice simulating a car's roaring engine. My thoughts twisted in confusion and struggled to make sense of it all. I tried to lift myself, but none of my muscles responded. Instead, my entire chest exploded in a fiery pain. I gasped and stiffened in hopes the agony would subside.

A moment later, it did subside, and I became aware that the sound had stopped. I looked down, careful not to move anything but my eyes. Another incongruity. A small boy knelt near my waist. He was looking at me while holding a metal toy car parked on my thigh.

I forced my dry lips to separate. "Where am I?" I asked in raspy English.

The boy jumped to his feet and ran out of my field of view. A door slammed a moment later.

I gathered that I was still alive—assuming heaven didn't consist of a boy using my thigh as a roadway, or the molten pain in my chest, or a throbbing headache, or a mouth as dry as the Mojave. Maybe hell—a more likely fate in my case.

I drummed up the courage to turn my head to take in my surroundings. I lay on a cot in some sort of large, open room. The floor and walls were all of pine paneling. On the far side was a kitchen. To my right and the other side of a door, rustic furniture had been arranged around a wood-burning stove.

The last thing I remembered was being on the verge of passing out while driving in the fog with a corpse as my companion.

Did I make it to the cabin? That didn't seem possible.

Some demon started pounding spikes deeper into both temples, so I righted my head and stared at the ceiling. The door opened, letting in a blast of cold air and the light of day. A woman appeared, standing over me. She furrowed her brow in concern as she looked down on me.

The woman turned her head to someone I couldn't see. "Kurt, *bring mir bitte ein Glas Wasser*," she said, and I heard the boy's footsteps as he ran across the wooden floor. The boy, Kurt, came back a moment later, handed a glass of water to his mother. She bent down, gently lifted my head, and helped me take a few sips.

The water cleared away some of the sludge in my mouth and throat, allowing me to speak. "Where am I?" I asked in German.

"Ah, good, you speak German. My son said you spoke in another language. You are in a cabin. My son and I are staying here. But you must know that, since you're the one who drove up here."

"I did? I don't remember."

"Well, you didn't make it all the way. You stopped a hundred meters from the cabin. Kurt and I saw your headlights, and I found you unconscious." Her eyes narrowed in suspicion or anger. "With my brother-in-law dead in the passenger's seat," she said with a slight quiver in her voice. "Did you kill him?"

I shook my head. "We were attacked in town."

She said nothing to refute my claim, meaning she was well aware of the danger. My throat threatened to lock up again, and I gestured for the water glass. The woman lifted my head and helped me drink. While doing so, her lips were clamped shut, and they trembled as if she were holding back tears. She looked to be in her mid-thirties. She wore a faded, checkered headscarf over brunette hair hastily bundled. Despite signs of an inadequate diet, she had lovely features. Most of her face was soft and rounded, except for her diminutive nose that came to a point. Her cheeks were red from the cold and contrasted her steel-blue eyes that were now moist with tears.

After I had a few sips of water, she placed the glass on a bedside table. "My name is Erika Altmann."

"Gregor Witt."

One eyebrow rose at her skepticism. "You speak with a Bavarian accent, but you're English. Aren't you?"

She'd saved my life, so I decided to be honest with her. "American."

She stiffened upon hearing that. "What were you doing with my brother-in-law? And what are you doing here? Are you a spy or secret police?"

"No, I'm just a traveler trying to get to Naples. Your brother-in-law came to me for help. He wanted to hire me to take you south. At least five guys in town didn't want that to happen—" A wave of pain surged through me, taking my breath away.

"You should rest," she said. "You've lost a lot of blood. Fortunately for you, the bullet must have ricocheted off something solid and fragmented before hitting you. The fragment struck one of your ribs, nicked your liver, then lodged against your chest cavity. Most of your bleeding was because of the laceration of the liver. That's what the doctor said, anyway."

My instinct was to sit up with surprise at hearing that, but I resisted the urge. "A doctor? You shouldn't have done that. He might talk and tell someone where you are."

"I have some friends in the vicinity. I trust the doctor will keep this to himself."

I noticed a slight inflection in the way she said "friends," like they weren't the kind of people you invite over for dinner. Or trust them any further than you could throw them.

"How long have I been out?"

"Three days. But no more questions. I have some chicken broth. I want you to have some of that and get some rest."

In truth, I had a lot of questions, starting with why Schwend risked his life and his remaining money to hire an armed guide to get them to safety. What were this woman and her son doing holed up in a remote location? Why were five men willing to kill in order to stop Schwend and find Frau Altmann? But at the moment, I just hoped I wouldn't pass out face-first into the soup.

∼

THE SHARP CRACK of a gunshot woke me up. I opened my eyes and was relieved to see the cabin's ceiling. All was quiet. No screaming. No more gunfire. Several of my recurrent dreams involved gunshots or explosions, though which dream had wakened me this time was a blank.

I felt the presence of someone and turned my head to the left. Kurt was sitting in a wooden chair and staring at me.

"Good morning to you, Kurt," I said in German.

Obviously, he didn't get the sarcasm, as he remained silent and continued to stare. I'd gotten to know Kurt a little over the past five days. A nice kid, but he didn't say much. At least not as much as other five-year-olds I'd known. He didn't bounce around and never raised his voice. He would sit quietly and read the same children's book over and over again, or watch the snow fall from his perch at the window.

"What'cha been doing?" I asked.

"Watching you."

"Yeah, I get that. How about doing something useful and help me up?"

Kurt got out of his chair and stood by the bed so I could use his shoulder to hoist myself to a seated position. It was becoming a morning ritual, waking to find him staring at me and then offering his shoulder to help me get out of bed.

It felt like someone stabbed me with a hot poker as I rose, but it hurt a little less every day. I thanked Kurt and expected him to run off and play, but he continued to stand next to me.

"People say my lips flutter when I sleep," I said to him. "Like a little motorboat. Is that why you watch me?"

He shook his head. "You talk funny, and your face does weird things." He chuckled at the thought.

"I'm glad I provide you with a little entertainment. I guess you don't get much of that being stuck in this cabin."

"It's okay. My mom used to be really afraid and cried a lot. She's better now that we're here."

"Speaking of your mom—" I stopped. A car motor idled out front. No one had come in to finish me off, so that was good, but the presence left me uneasy.

"Who's in the car?" I asked Kurt.

He shrugged.

"Since you're standing there ..." I used his shoulder and the back of the wooden chair to slowly get to my feet. My entire torso throbbed, but it was tolerable. Kurt seemed to sense I was stable and went to the foot of the bed and brought me the walking stick Erika had fashioned from a tree branch.

I rubbed Kurt's hair as a thanks and gingerly hobbled over to the window. I stopped in the shadows and shifted to peer beyond the left curtain. The car was a good twenty yards from the cabin. Erika was standing by the driver's door and speaking to someone behind the wheel. Another person sat in the passenger's seat. The sky reflected off the windshield and obscured any details of the occupants, though their silhouettes indicated they were men.

By Erika's posture, I could tell she was nervous, if not scared. She appeared to have shrunk, her body rigid, her arms wrapped tightly around her chest. She glanced at the cabin with worry in her eyes. I shifted my weight to hide behind the curtain and bumped into Kurt, who was, again, standing next to me.

He hardly budged and remained glued to my leg. "What are you looking at?" he asked.

"I'm making sure your mom is okay. Do you know who

she's talking to?"

He raised his arms to me, and I lifted him and reoriented so he could see out the window. With one arm wrapped over my shoulders, he squinted in his mom's direction. Some of my tension eroded as I held this boy in my arms. He turned his head to me and didn't back away to put some distance between us, like he felt at ease being close to me.

"I can't see, but that's Uncle Ernst's car."

I stepped away from the window and lowered Kurt to the floor.

"You have an uncle?" I asked.

"He's not really my uncle. My mom told me to call him that."

I heard footsteps crunching in the snow and tried to get some distance from the window. The door opened a second later, and Erika entered. She spotted me and stopped.

"Were you spying on me?"

"He wanted to make sure you were okay," Kurt said to her.

"I got nervous when I heard the car engine," I said.

Erika was visibly upset and said nothing in return. She closed the door and headed for the kitchen. "You should eat." She ladled some soup into a bowl and set it on the small round table. "I'm sure you're getting tired of chicken soup, but it's all I have that's ready."

I hobbled toward the table, Kurt shadowing me. I sat, and Kurt stood at my side. "Were those some of your friends?" I asked her.

"That's none of your business." She laid out a spoon and napkin on the table in front of me and returned to the stove. "Kurt, stop bothering Herr Witt. Go outside and play while the sun is out."

"He's not bothering me," I said and immediately regretted butting in after receiving the sharp end of her glare.

Kurt protested and tried to sit next to me, but his mom jabbed her finger toward the front door. Kurt reluctantly obeyed and exited the house.

When the door clacked shut, I said, "He's good kid."

Erika ignored my comment and began to wash some dishes. I tackled the soup, and the cabin fell into silence. Over the last five days, after I emerged from the stupor of pain and fever, Erika had been polite and cared for me with patience. But every time I tried to broach the subject of her brother-in-law and her predicament, I received her wrath in return. It's not that she was cold; I'd witnessed her bottomless love and caring for Kurt. When it came to me and answering questions, I figured most of her silence came from fear. Maybe my presence was putting them both in danger, and she was too generous to say it.

"As soon as I'm on my feet, I'll be out of your way."

Erika stopped washing but kept her back to me. "That could be weeks yet."

"I know you're low on food, especially with one more mouth to feed."

"We'll make do," she said and started washing again.

"Couldn't your friends bring up more provisions?"

She spun around to glare at me. "Would you please stop trying to meddle in my affairs?"

"Uncle Ernst isn't really a friend, is he?" I asked, keeping my voice down so Kurt might not hear. "You're scared. That wasn't a friendly visit. If I'm to help you, I have to know what's going on."

"I didn't ask for your help."

"Your brother-in-law sacrificed his life to see you get to safety. He asked me to do it and died because of it. Once I'm fit enough to travel, I'm heading south. I can take you and Kurt with me."

"Leo acted on his own. It hurts when I think about him, but I didn't ask him to put his life in danger on my account. I told him I'd be fine—"

"Well, someone thinks finding you is important enough to send five gunmen to kidnap him and murder me."

"They only wanted to kidnap him? That means your interfering got him killed."

There might have been some truth to that, and it stung. "They didn't bring their guns just to have a friendly chat. If they'd grabbed him up, they would have tortured him to find out where you were, then dumped him in a shallow grave. It's that serious. It's that dangerous. Don't mess around with these guys. You might be cavalier with your own life, but you've got Kurt to think about."

"Don't you dare—" She stopped and turned away. She held herself and trembled.

I got up and took two steps toward her. She held up an open hand to stop me. The throbbing pain in my side flared as I stood there. But I put up with the discomfort and remained silent, allowing her to say something when she was ready. Kurt's whooping like an Indian in a western movie penetrated the cold silence inside.

"Who are you, really, Herr Witt?"

She said it with such earnestness and calm that I decided it was time to tell her. "My name is Mason Collins. I was a police detective in Chicago, and an army intelligence officer during the war, then a criminal investigator in Munich."

"That explains all your scars. Are you on an investigation, now?"

"I've been a civilian for almost two years."

"Then why are you still in Europe?"

"It's a long story."

"And you just happened to be in Sterzing when Leo went to you for help?"

"If you're asking why Leo picked me out of everyone in that town, I have no idea. But it's not the first time that's happened. I have a talent for stepping into hornet's nests. Or getting pushed into one."

Erika turned to face me and crossed her arms. "Why—"

"Hold on," I said, interrupting. "If you insist on asking more questions, then you have to answer a few yourself."

"I'll answer what I can."

"That's a start."

I had to sit down again or fall to the floor. I turned to the table, and my head spun. Erika helped me back to the table and to sit in the chair.

"You should lie down."

"I will. Go ahead and ask your question."

"So, what were you doing in Sterzing, and why are you trying to go through the pass in the middle of winter?"

"I'm trying to get south because the only woman I've ever loved asked me to join her in Naples." I decided to leave out the part about hunting Ziegler. I still wasn't sure which side she was on. "I was on foot because I was evading the police for putting a Brit official in the hospital."

"Am I harboring a fugitive?" she asked.

"The man was beating a woman. I didn't know he was some high-level guy in the British military government. I couldn't cross the border by car since my ID and travel papers aren't exactly legal. I took my chances crossing the pass on foot because my ex made it sound urgent."

"Is she your wife? Girlfriend?"

"She *was* my girlfriend."

Erika opened her mouth, presumably to ask another question, but I help up my hand to stop her. "My turn. Who are those men in town, and why do they want to get you so badly?"

"I don't know who they are. My guess is they were hired by my husband to bring me back to Germany."

I hadn't seen that one coming. "Your husband must have one hell of a grudge against you if he hired men with guns to bring you back."

Erika shrugged. "I left my husband because he's a violent man. And because I'm the one with the money—family money—and I put it all in a safe place before I ran away. He wants the money more than he wants me."

It all sounded plausible enough, but I wasn't going to buy into the whole story. I'd had enough practice reading people to sniff out a lie, but either she was very good at it, or she was telling just enough of the truth to keep an honest face.

"The men in town, did your husband hire them, or are they his associates?"

"I wouldn't know."

"If you had to guess. It takes good money to hire five gunmen, even these days. And all of them managed to get past British and Italian border guards."

"I don't like where this is going."

"I need to know who we're dealing with. How motivated are they? Hired hands will give up if things get too hot.

Professionals cost a lot of money, but they'll keep on until the job is done. If they're associates of your husband's, they may have a lot to lose, which makes them determined and desperate. And that could make them dangerous."

She paused a moment, and her gaze went elsewhere as if deep in thought. I suspected she was considering her response, which convinced me she knew a lot more than she was willing to tell me.

Finally, she said, "My husband kept me out of his affairs, business or otherwise, so I can't tell you how he arranged to have those men come after me."

"Who were those two men in the car?"

"One was the doctor who treated you, a Dr. Fleischman. The other was a friend of his. The doctor was kind enough to come all the way up to inquire about your recovery. And before you ask, he didn't come in to examine you because he's afraid. He saw all your scars while treating your bullet wound. And, of course, he heard about the gunfight in town. I didn't offer him an explanation, but I'm sure he put it all together."

"Do you trust him?"

"We traveled together and became friends. And he helped me when those armed men first tried to abduct me."

"You've already encountered those men?"

She nodded. "They tried to abduct me in Brenner. I was only able to get away because of Dr. Fleischman's quick thinking. We decided to hide out here, in the mountains, hoping they would give up, or they would assume we had continued and left the area."

"And why can't the doctor help you get to the south?"

"He's afraid those men will find him, so he came up here to

tell me he's leaving right away. He offered to take me and Kurt."

"You said no?"

Erika nodded.

"You saying no is not because of me, is it? Because I can take care of myself."

"No, you can't. There's almost no food left. What are you going to do? Walk down the mountain when I'm gone?" She looked down at her hands for a moment, then returned to the sink. "Besides, I think our chances are better if we go with you."

I stood up and shuffled over to the window. The clouds had dispersed, revealing a low winter sun that threw long shadows on the snow. Kurt threw snowballs at a barn of weathered boards and terra-cotta roof tiles.

"How did you end up here?" I asked.

"The man who owned this cabin was an Italian businessman and a fascist tied to Mussolini. I understand he's in prison somewhere."

"And you just happened upon it?" I asked with a tone of skepticism.

"Dr. Fleischman knew about it."

I had a battery of other questions, including ones about the resourceful Dr. Fleischman, but I decided to hold off. There was something I needed to address first. As I watched Kurt assault the barn, a new plan of action came to me.

I went over to my backpack, got on my knees, and started going through my stuff. I removed my pistol, laid it on the bed, and pulled the blanket over it.

"What are you doing?" Erika asked.

"I'm going to town tonight."

"That's ridiculous. You're in no shape to go anywhere. And it's too dangerous. What if we're seen?"

"We?" I shook my head. "No, just me."

"You can barely stand, much less drive."

I thought a moment and nodded. "You're right. You'll drive and stay by the car in a secluded place."

"What are you planning to go to town for in the first place?"

"We need provisions, right?"

"The stores won't be open—" She stopped. "You plan to steal food?"

"Yes, ma'am, I do." I reached back into my pack. My fingers touched what I was looking for and pulled it out. I held up the pocketknife-sized object. "No backpack should be without a set of lock-picking tools."

"Are you a cop or a thief?"

"A little of both," I said. "The lock-picking tools are for the store, and the other is for something else I want to do at the same time."

Erika was about to say something else, but Kurt entered and stared at us. "What are you doing on the floor?"

"Your mom knocked me down."

Kurt's eyes widened in shock and looked at his mom.

"Herr Witt is joking, honey."

"I think I have something for you," I said to Kurt. I found what I was looking for and pulled out a chocolate bar. I held it out for Kurt, who charged over and grabbed it out of my hand. I raised my arm to ask for Erika's assistance. She glared at me, clamped her mouth shut, and helped me to stand.

When I was up, I said to her in a hushed tone, "We go at midnight."

7

Erika parked Schwend's car behind a group of shops and storage buildings near Sterzing's train station. She doused the headlights, and we sat in silence a moment. So far, so good; the roads had been empty of cars and people. I had instructed Erika to take a roundabout way of getting where we were, by going south of town, then circumventing the center and going north again by following the railroad tracks and the Eisack river.

I looked to the back seat. Kurt lay underneath a pile of quilts with just his head sticking out. I said in a hushed tone, "He hasn't moved a muscle since we left."

"Traveling in the car in the middle of the night is old hat to him now. We've been on the road since late November."

I turned back to the front and said, "You'll get to a place where you won't have to be on the move anymore."

Erika formed a smile, but it turned melancholy. "Perhaps."

I slipped the strap of the backpack onto one arm, then removed my .45 from its holster underneath my coat and checked to see that everything was in order.

"I don't want you to take that," Erika said. "If you leave it here, you won't be tempted to use it."

"Showing this to someone usually means I don't have to," I said and pulled on the door handle. Before I could get out, Erika put her hand on my arm.

"Are you going to be okay? I wish you wouldn't do this."

"I'll be back in less than an hour," I said, but before I got out, another thought came to me. "If I'm not, get back to the cabin, pack your things, and get away from here."

I didn't wait for a response and hoisted myself out of the car and closed the door. A wave of dizziness hit me, and I had to use the car roof to stabilize myself. When the vertigo passed, I put on the emptied backpack and headed out.

My legs worked well enough, though I was unsure about getting very far in a foot race. My head and chest throbbed. The skin on my face was hot. The horizon tilted like I was on the deck of a ship in a storm. I pushed through it. I'd had enough practice at functioning through fevers and debilitating pain. It was a matter of conjuring up all I'd gone through in the past number of years: getting shot in the ass in the Hürtgen Forest, having the flu when I was captured behind enemy lines during the Battle of the Bulge, then tortured by a sadistic Gestapo captain, spending weeks in a Nazi extermination camp and months in prisoner-of-war camps, and topped off by a death march in artic conditions. This was child's play comparatively, though I was getting old before my time because of all the trauma.

As I decided which of the two streets I'd take that were swimming before my eyes, I thought of Laura, the love of my life and the reason I was traipsing across frozen Italy in the first place. I swore that one of these days I would settle down.

Swap trauma and mayhem for peace and solitude. Then again, my greatest talent seemed to be getting into trouble and having to fight my way out again.

After paralleling the train tracks going north, I turned left onto one of the small streets that would lead to the center of the old part of town. Erika had shown me a detailed map of Sterzing, so I knew where I was going.

A mom-and-pop grocery store was my first stop, which was a three-story building situated in the middle of the block of the small street. A dim light cast a glow on a curtain on the second floor. I figured the grocer lived above the shop. I knelt in front of the door and took out my lock-picking tool. I had double vision, and it was dark, but I could pick most locks in my sleep, so the old one securing the door was easy work. After entering and closing the door, I flicked on the flashlight I'd brought in my backpack and crept across the floor. I wove between the aisles and dropped cans and boxes of food into my backpack. There was little in the way of fresh fruit or vegetables, but I grabbed some potatoes and onions.

The floorboards above my head creaked as someone moved across the floor. I placed a 100-Swiss-franc note on the counter and turned off the flashlight. I turned to leave, but not before grabbing a handful of candies from a jar. I hurried out, not bothering to lock the door behind me. I'd be long gone before the grocer discovered the missing food and candies.

I headed for the main street and stopped at the corner, where the small street intersected with the main one. The main street was named Neustadt, meaning new city street, though this part of town looked just like the old one to me.

All was clear, and I turned right and headed north toward

the medieval clock tower. The clock indicated it was already 1:13 a.m., meaning I had no more than twenty minutes to do what I intended to do next and get back to the car before Erika drove away.

Two doors up, I came to the inn. There was one light in a third-floor window, but that appeared to be the only one. I checked my surroundings, then went to one of the front windows and peered in at a darkened interior. The proprietor had closed up for the evening. I knelt in front of the door and got out my lock-picking tools. Like the grocery store's lock, it gave way in moments. I opened the door, crept inside, and flicked on the flashlight. The odors of that night's cooked food and stale beer made my stomach grind. I'd had enough of chicken soup and was ready for a full plate of meat and potatoes.

I snuck across the room, got behind the inn's reception desk, and knelt down. The shift in my center of gravity made my head spin again. After a couple of deep breaths, I regained control and found the guest ledger.

Staying below the counter, I opened the ledger and leafed through the pages of names of those who'd checked in close to the current date. It took a few minutes, but I found the name and room number, put the ledger back and, this time, rose very slowly to my feet.

The fire in the wood-burning stove lit the way as I moved across the room. A few floorboards groaned under my footsteps, but I kept going. My leg muscles trembled with the effort of climbing the stairs. It was only because of the railing that I could prevent myself from stumbling. I would have to move fast, as I could feel my strength waning with each passing moment.

Fortunately for my faltering legs, the room I sought was on the second floor, two doors down the narrow hallway. I listened at the door and heard snoring. I knelt, removed my pistol from its holster and laid it on the floor while I worked on the lock. The bolt retracted with a click that sounded loud in the silence. I paused a moment to see if the noise had roused the occupant, but no one stirred within the room.

I lifted my pistol, pulled the sap from my left pocket, and slowly turned the doorknob. I nearly stumbled as I stood, and it took all my willpower to muster my remaining strength. I slipped into the dark room. All I could make out were darker shapes within shadows. The silhouette of the bed was highlighted by the dim light coming from the window.

My heart pounded so loud from the fever, I worried even my slumbering target might hear it. I stood next to the bed, ripped off the quilt, clamped my left hand on his mouth, and jammed the barrel of my .45 against the man's temple.

Kappler's body jerked as his eyes popped wide. He growled and struggled against my hand, but I dug the gun's barrel deeper into his temple and shushed him.

The man grunted in fear and anger, but he stopped resisting.

"That's better," I said softly. I got into his face. "You remember me, don't you? You killed my companion and tried to kill me."

Kappler's eyes pleaded for mercy, and he shook his head.

"I'd like nothing more than to spread your brains across the pillow, but I want information. You answer my questions to my satisfaction, and I might let you live. Do you understand?"

Kappler nodded.

"You cry out or make any sudden moves, and I'll pull the trigger. A .45 slug at this range does some really nasty damage."

The man nodded again.

I slowly shifted my left hand from his mouth to his throat.

"Look, I didn't—" he started to say in a normal voice.

I slammed my hand back onto his mouth and shook my head. "All I want from you is answers. Nothing else."

After his third nod, I moved my hand back to this throat. "Who do you work for?"

"I am a priest and under God's command."

It took me a moment to process this seemingly non sequitur response. "God commanded you to kill Leo Schwend and hunt down Erika Altmann?"

"I did not kill anyone. I was unarmed that night."

"That's still being an accessory to murder. Just as guilty as the one who pulled the trigger. Who told you and four other men to attack Schwend and me?"

"We decided on our own. Herr Schwend was a threat to our mission, but my intent was only to question him. Others in the group thought it was better to kill him than to see him escape."

"Your objective was to get information from Schwend so you could go after Frau Altmann."

Kappler flashed a smug smile, which tempted me to bash out a few of his teeth. "She is not who she claims to be. She is not to be trusted and is quite dangerous."

"You're dodging my questions, which is just pissing me off—"

A knock at the door stopped me.

"Friedrich, is everything all right?" a voice said behind the door.

"Help!" Kappler said.

I struck Kappler across his temple with the sap and spun around. The door burst open. Rudel, Kappler's bull, stood on the other side. He started to charge in, but I pulled back the hammer of my pistol. He stopped.

"Back away," I said. I jerked a dazed Kappler to his feet and used him as a shield. I advanced toward the door, forcing Rudel to back up.

When I came into the light of the hallway, Rudel's expression turned from shock to rage. "You!"

"That's right. Back away, and I won't put a bullet in his head, or yours."

Rudel obeyed, and I began to back down the stairs. By that time, more guests, and probably the owner, were out in the hallway. Some hurried back into the safety of their rooms, while a few seemed too frightened to move.

I walked backward, taking careful steps down the stairs with Kappler at my front, praying I wouldn't stumble. Rudel inched forward, as did two others I recognized from the shooting. One had his pistol at his side. I could keep control of the situation as long as I had my cannon pointed at them, but I had to figure out how to get to the car in one piece.

Rudel and his two companions started to descend the stairs. I took aim at them, and said, "Don't be stupid."

They stopped, but there would be a race once I got onto the street. Adrenaline had kept me alert and agile, but I only had so much in reserve. When it sputtered out, I'd be a gelatinous mess.

I got to the front door and opened it. I shoved Kappler to

the floor and fired three times, hitting the wall and stairs near the three men. They ducked and scrambled. I shot at the area one more time for good measure and bolted out the door. As I raced down the street, I listened for my pursuers. Lights in the surrounding buildings had come on, people peered out their windows.

I kept my head down and pushed my body to its limits. My lungs burned, and my heart slammed in my chest. I could feel my strength fading with each step. A shot rang out and zipped past my head just as I turned onto the small street where I'd broken into the grocery. I ran right into the front grill of a car idling in the middle of the street.

I jumped away and readied myself for a fight.

"Mason!" Erika said with her head sticking out the window. "Get in!"

I sped for the passenger's door and jumped into the Fiat. She threw the gear into reverse and hit the accelerator. The tires spun for a moment on the icy cobblestones, but then they found traction, and the car raced backward.

Rudel and his two companions turned the corner. The guy with the gun fired. A round took off the sideview mirror. Erika screamed, prompting Kurt to do the same. Still, she kept her eyes to the rear and drove the car in reverse like a pro. Two more bullets hit the hood.

We reached the end of the alley, and Erika steered the car to face north. She switched gears and hit the accelerator again, and the car raced up the street parallel to the train tracks.

I collapsed in the seat. Breathless, I managed to get out a raspy, "Thank you."

Kurt was jumping in the back seat and squealing with

excitement. He was either the bravest little boy I'd met, or he had a strange way of dealing with stress. Either way, I fell for that kid in that moment.

Erika was talking a mile a minute about how she couldn't face leaving me behind and drove up to the grocery to see if she could determine what had happened to me. But I was too exhausted to listen to much of it. Plus, as the town raced past my window, I could only think of Kappler's warning: she wasn't who she claimed to be and was dangerous. I promised myself to think about that further, but right then I closed my eyes and remembered nothing more.

8

I watched as Erika conducted a math lesson for Kurt. They sat at the kitchen table, Erika leaning into Kurt and trying to show him how to do simple additions. I sat on the bed, feeling better after two days of total rest. After the melee in town, it took me that much time to fully recover.

Erika and I had avoided any talk of that night. I wanted to wait until I had a clear head, and I presumed she wanted the same. Kurt had taken the whole thing in stride. He'd been pelting us both with questions and seemed satisfied with his mother's responses.

I found it hard to reconcile what Kappler had told me about her. Observing the patient and loving way she interacted with Kurt, and her diligent care of me, it would have been easy for me to chalk up Kappler's claims as a way to sow discord and doubt. But if there's anything I've learned from my years as a cop and an intelligence agent, people could have many faces. Even the most tender ones; they might have temperaments like the calm surface of a river that hides deadly currents.

She stole a few glances at me, smiling at first, but I must have advertised my troubling thoughts, because her expression turned dark, and she said to Kurt, "I think that's enough arithmetic for this morning. Why don't you go outside and play?"

Kurt didn't have to be told twice. He got off his chair and rushed to the door, but before exiting, he turned to me. "You want to come out and play with me?"

"Mason and I have some things to discuss, *mein Schatz*," Erika said.

Together we had told Kurt my real name a couple of days ago. Erika had told him to call me Mr. Collins, but Kurt insisted on Mason, which was what I preferred.

Kurt hesitated for a moment, opened the door, and went outside. Erika got up from the table and closed the door. She remained there, crossed her arms and glared at me. "As soon as you're well enough, I want you to leave. You put my son in danger by whatever recklessness you did in town."

"I did what I had to do. I told you to stay put or get out of there if I didn't show up."

"Are you trying to blame me for those men shooting at us?" she said, raising her voice.

I checked my anger. "No. What you did was brave, and you probably saved my life. And I have to say, that was some damn good driving."

Erika's taut face relaxed, but she stood firm at the door. "You were supposed to get the food and come back. Now you've probably enraged those men. They'll be desperate and bent on revenge."

"I couldn't pass up the opportunity to go after Kappler. I needed to know who we're dealing with."

Erika stood by the door a moment longer, and without a word, she turned and headed for the kitchen. "You must be hungry," she said flatly.

"You haven't asked what Kappler said."

The door burst open, startling me enough to reach for my pistol tucked under the mattress until I saw it was Kurt.

"There's a car, Mommy."

I leapt up from the bed, took Kurt's arm, and pulled him inside. I shut the door and went for the pistol. Shocked and frightened by my sudden moves, Kurt ran to his mother. With her arms wrapped around him, she backed into a corner.

I stepped up to the side of the window and shifted my weight just enough to look outside. There were, in fact, two cars, and they had stopped two hundred yards from the cabin.

"Who is it?" Erika asked.

"Too far away to see, but I have a good idea who they are."

"The men from town?"

I nodded. "My guess is they've been roaming around the surrounding area, searching for us. Or your doctor friend finally decided to give you up." I moved away from the window and looked at Erika. "Do they know what Kurt looks like?"

Erika said nothing as she stared at me with frightened eyes.

"Erika, do they know Kurt?"

She nodded.

"Now they know where we are." I peered out the window. The cars hadn't moved. "They're probably trying to figure out what to do next."

The cabin sat in the middle of an open field with the land in front sloping downhill at a shallow incline until about where the cars had stopped on the dirt road. It then dropped off rapidly toward the valley below. Behind the cabin, the field rose steeply for about one hundred yards until hitting the thick tree line. It would be tough to assault the cabin over open ground against me and my M1911 pistol waiting for them. But the terrain was also to our disadvantage: making a run for it over an open field would leave us vulnerable. And there was only one way off the mountain by car. Kappler and his men had cut us off.

One of the cars backed up, turned around, and headed downhill.

"What do you think they'll do?" Erika asked.

"They won't come now. One of the cars just left, probably to bring up more men. Then they'll wait until it's dark."

I moved away from the window and looked at Erika. She still stood in the corner. Her expression was one of defiance, not fear. "How many more men might be coming?"

"I don't know."

"Why are they so fanatical about going after you?"

"I don't know that either."

"You claim your husband wants your money, but it would have to be a fortune for these guys to work so hard."

I noticed Kurt hugging his mother harder. I wouldn't press her; the kid was obviously frightened, and interrogating Erika was making it worse.

"Is there any way off the mountain by car other than that road?" I asked her in a calm voice.

She shook her head. "Not that I know of."

I felt some of the weakness and lightheadedness return, but I refused to sit. Sitting was like surrendering, and I had no intention of doing that. I ran through the options. Trying to make a run for it with the car in the barn was a bad idea, especially with the kid. And waiting for them to get more guns and for night to fall was even worse. Escape on foot was out too …

"Do you know how to use a gun?" I asked.

Erika nodded. "I have pretty good aim, but I'm not sure I could shoot at a person."

"If things go the way I think they will, you won't have to. Just keep them pinned. I'll do the rest."

Erika nodded again, though this time there was fear in her eyes.

9

I stood by the cabin door with my hand on the knob. I looked to Erika, who knelt by the window with my .45 in her hand and the two spare magazines on the floor next to her. Kurt was under the spare bed that I used and was surrounded by pillows and a quilt.

"The only ammo I have is in that gun and those two magazines," I said to her. "Use only what you have to. If one of them goes after me, don't try to stop him."

"The quicker you do your part, the less ammo I'll need."

I gave her a quick nod, tensed my muscles, and threw open the door. I dashed for the back of the cabin. Just before I turned the corner of the cabin, three men scrambled out of the car. A bullet struck the cabin wall, followed by the crack of a pistol. As I ran along the side of the cabin, I heard the sound of breaking glass, then two shots from my .45.

I got behind the cabin and used it as cover while I ran for the tree line a hundred yards distant. Once I started climbing the slope, the cabin would no longer shield me. I only hoped the distance would reduce the accuracy of their pistols. If they had a rifle, that was a different matter.

Two more shots came from the cabin. I glanced back and saw the men had taken cover behind the car. Two of them were aiming in my direction, while the third continued to fire his pistol at the cabin. By my count, Erika had already expended four rounds. If I didn't get where I needed to be soon, she would run out of ammunition.

I poured on the speed. The wound felt like someone was turning a red-hot knife stuck between my ribs. The muscles in my legs were turning to lead, and my lungs burned. A bullet churned up the earth near my foot. Another roared past my head.

I penetrated the lead line of trees and entered the dense forest of pine. I took a second to catch my breath and looked back at the car. My hope was that the shooters would assume I'd made a run for it, leaving Erika and Kurt to fend for themselves. After three more deep breaths, I went deep into the trees and made a loop around to run in the opposite direction.

With the three shooters now concentrating on Erika, they could keep her pinned while one or more of them advanced. There was no time left. I leapt over logs and dodged trunks while keeping one eye on the clearing to maintain my trajectory. I had to cover the entire length of the field and come around behind the shooters.

My leg muscles locked up just as I reached a point perpendicular to the car. I cursed at my legs and urged myself to continue like a drill sergeant barking at green recruits. I looked out beyond the trees and saw that two of the men had made a move for the cabin. One would fire while the other raced forward, then hesitate and fire while the other caught up. The third man stayed at the car, covering them. And I could see the third man clearly enough now to recognize him. It was Rudel. Seeing him gave me that extra ounce of willpower to get up and continue running.

When my arc through the forest brought me behind the car, I burst out of the tree line. If Rudel heard my footsteps, it would be all over in an instant. Fortunately for me, the gunfire drowned out my charge.

I was within twenty feet of the car when Rudel turned toward me. His eyes widened in alarm, and he brought his pistol to bear on me, but he was too late. I slammed into him like a linebacker. The pain in my side was excruciating, but I ignored it as we collided into the side of the car. Though the wind had been knocked out of him, he put up a desperate fight. He swung his fists wildly and attempted to kick me, but I was in too close for his blows to be effective. I let loose with a series of punches to his stomach. He bent over in pain, and I kneed him in the face.

It took several more blows to his head, but he finally went down. I yanked the gun from his hand. A rage ran through me, and I had to suppress the urge to shoot him where he lay. In the end, I slammed the grip of the pistol into the back of his head, then an extra one for good measure. I didn't want him getting up again for a long time.

Another volley of gunshots brought my attention to the field in front of the cabin. One of the attackers was using the barn as cover while he fired. The other sprinted toward the cabin from the same position. Erika fired a shot. The guy cried out and fell to the ground. He held his leg and writhed in pain.

Erika fired again, but this time the bullet slammed into the car right next to me. I ducked and waved my arms, hoping she'd figure out it was me. But another bullet flew past my head.

"Erika, it's me," I yelled.

The attacker behind the barn turned to me and fired. I knew my yelling would get his attention and had aimed Rudel's Luger at him before calling out to Erika.

"Drop your weapon," I said to him.

The man ignored me and continued to shoot as he looked for cover. I fired three times, hitting him at least twice. The man crumpled to the ground.

"Erika, it's me, Mason." I held up my hands and stood up from my cover behind the car.

The cabin door opened, and Erika stuck her head out.

"Get the bags and head for the car," I said.

She went back inside the cabin. I opened the hood of the attackers' Maybach. Bullets had pierced the radiator in several places. Water and oil trickled from the bullet holes. No one was going to make use of the car anytime soon. Pity, as I would have preferred the superior Maybach to the aging Fiat.

I checked in the glovebox for any papers that might identify the shooters. There was nothing useful, though I did pocket two boxes of 9mm rounds for the Luger. By that time, Erika was heading for the Fiat in the barn. She had Kurt in tow and three large bags hanging from her shoulders. I rushed across the field and grabbed the three bags from her. Kurt had been cavalier during the escape in town, but this time his face was contorted in fear and trauma.

Erika raced ahead, unlocked the barn door, and pushed it open. She had to persuade Kurt to get in the back. I stuffed the bags in the back with him, so he could hide among them if he wanted.

I went around the side of the barn and took the Luger lying next to the dead shooter. I then crossed the field to check on the one Erika had shot in the leg. The man had attempted to crawl away and left a trail of blood. He was now still, his head down, groaning in pain. I picked up his gun and walked over to him. His pant leg was soaked red. The .45 slug had probably torn up his leg, and by the amount of blood, more than likely severed his femoral artery. He would be gone in moments.

I crouched near his head. His back heaved as he tried to take in air. His gaze looked upon something unseen. I didn't recognize him from the inn or the shoot-out in the street.

"There's not much I can do for you," I said to him in German.

"You can get me to a doctor," he said through gulps of air.

"Sure, that's something I could do, but first you have to tell me who you're working for."

"I hope you die like a dog." He turned his head to face the other way.

Erika honked the Fiat's horn. "Mason, let's go!"

"I hope you had a good reason to die alone in the middle of this field. Anything you want to share before I leave you?"

The man stopped moving. I checked the pulse in his neck. Nothing. Erika honked the horn again. I stood and walked to the car. I got behind the wheel, and Erika got into the front passenger's seat and reloaded the .45. I put two of the Lugers on the seat between us.

Erika looked down at the guns then up to me.

"We're not out of the woods yet," I said, started the car, and steered onto the dirt road.

10

As I raced down the switchback that would take us to Sterzing, Erika reloaded the Luger magazine. Kurt had disappeared into the pile of bags, building a kind of fortress. At points in the twisting road, I could see down the mountainside and spotted a car coming up the same road. The best I could tell, it was the same Mercedes that had stopped near the cabin. There was no other way down the mountain, making it inevitable that we'd meet somewhere on the narrow road. My hope was to surprise them and blow past without having to shoot our way out. But Erika was getting the Luger ready in case they tried to cut us off.

I glanced back to check on Kurt again, then took the fully loaded Luger and put it in my lap. Erika kept the .45 by her side, her finger on the trigger guard. There was determination in her eyes as she stared at the road. It made me wonder what kind of life she had before becoming a mother; she appeared barely rattled at being shot at and mortally wounding a man. If she were truly as dangerous as Kappler had claimed, then I was glad she was on my side—at least for the moment.

We made another hairpin turn and entered a short straightaway. The Mercedes completed a turn, bringing it directly in our path. The road was just wide enough for one car, with a sudden drop-off on the right, and the left side climbing uphill from the edge of the road.

The opposing car moved as if they were unsure who was coming at them. I accelerated, hoping to race past them on the right shoulder. Someone in the other car must have figured out who was in the Fiat, and it surged forward. Like a jousting match, we charged at each other, neither giving ground.

"Kurt, get on the floor," Erika said. "And hold on to something." She stuck her arm out the window and aimed the .45. She fired three times.

The surprise must have provoked the driver to go for cover, because he turned to his right, striking the hillside, slowing the car down. As I blew past them, the three men in the car opened fire. The front and back windows facing the shooters shattered. Kurt screamed, as did Erika. The left side of the car scraped along the side of our pursuers. I nearly lost control as the impact forced us to the edge of the cliff.

The tires spun on the graveled shoulder, but finally they got traction, and we sped away.

"Everyone okay?" I asked as I pushed the car into another turn.

Erika turned in her seat, got up on her knees, and leaned over the seat back to check on Kurt.

She spoke in a soft, comforting voice, which I took as a good sign. I checked the rearview mirror. The assailants' car was still motionless and wedged against the hillside. But it wouldn't be long before they recovered and continued the pursuit. Our best chance was to get down the mountain and put some distance between us and Sterzing as fast as possible.

Erika climbed into the back and got onto the floorboard to be with Kurt. I took the sharp turns as fast as the car and its tires would let me. The frigid air howled through the shattered side windows. I turned on the heater full blast, but it wouldn't be enough to fend off the cold. Plus, we'd be hard-pressed to explain the windows and bullet holes in the body to a curious cop. While the road was clear behind me, the pursuers could still catch up. Erika had advised me of another route that would bypass Sterzing to the west, avoiding the center of town. After one last turn on the switchback, I took a narrow road that cut an elevated path along the foothills and looked down upon the city and the valley floor.

Potholes and ice made the going tough and forced me to slow down. It was just wide enough for a single car, and I hoped I wouldn't encounter another car speeding in the opposite direction, or worse, a slow farm vehicle.

In minutes we entered a hamlet, and the road immediately became a tangle of narrow streets. I had only a vague idea of where we needed to go, but I knew that, south of the hamlet, the main valley took a turn to the east. That was enough for me to find a forested road that took me downhill. As I followed the curve around, I saw the south end of Sterzing. I eased off on the gas a little. We'd made it.

All I had to do was meet up with the main roadway taking us south, toward Bozen, and beyond. I came upon the intersection to the two-lane highway and slowed to turn.

Just as I made the turn, something impacted the hood with a loud bang. Another object hit the right rear fender. I looked frantically for the source and spotted a Horch parked on the side of the road just to the right of the intersection. Two men stood beside it with their guns aimed at us.

Kurt cried out in fear. Erika spoke rapidly to calm him, though there was panic in her tone. I hit the accelerator again. The car's rear end fishtailed, but I finally got it under control and took off down the highway. In the rearview mirror I saw the two men jump in their car and begin their pursuit.

"Damnit, who are these guys?" I yelled out to Erika. "How many more of them are there?"

I didn't expect an answer; my outburst was as much a way to vent my shock and frustration.

There were only a few cars on the road, which made it easier for me to pass them. I pushed the Fiat to its limits, but it was no match for the V8 engine in the Horch.

I called back to Erika, "Stay low. They're gaining on us."

I ran through the options in my mind, and none of them were any good. And not only was I pushing the engine to the top RPMs, the needle on the gas gauge was visibly dropping toward empty.

The Horch came right up on my tail and slammed into the Fiat. It took every trick I had to keep it on the road. Another car came up fast in the same lane. I zipped around it. The Horch followed, but instead of falling in behind me, it stayed in the opposing lane and came up next to us.

Two men, one in front and one in the rear, aimed their pistols through the open windows. I hit the brakes just as they opened fire. The driver hadn't expected this move and hurtled forward. The shooters' bullets hit the hood.

Smoke poured out from the Horch's back wheels, and the car decelerated. Only some split-second steering and braking kept us from colliding with the backend of the Horch. I raced past the pursuers.

Erika growled with fury and popped up from the back seat. She grabbed the Luger off the front seat and stuck her arm out the window. She shot at the Horch's windshield. The two shooters returned fire.

I knew we couldn't keep this up. The Horch had the horsepower to outmaneuver us. Either she or I was going to take a bullet.

Up ahead another passenger car cruised along in the same lane. Keeping the gas pedal to the floor, I switched lanes and got up beside the other car, a dated Alpha Romeo. A young man sat behind the wheel, and he was yelling and shaking his fist at me.

The Horch came up right behind us.

Enraged, the young man accelerated to cut me off. I nudged ahead of the Alpha Romeo until my back wheel was almost astride his front wheel. With a quick yank on the steering wheel, I clipped his front. The Alpha Romeo jerked to the right and spun, exposing its side to the oncoming Horch.

The Horch veered left and clipped the back end of the Alpha Romeo, causing them both to spin out of control on the icy road. The Horch had been going too fast, and the forward momentum caused it to flip over and tumble along the road.

I sped away.

11

I kept one eye on the gas gauge and the other on the road. We'd been driving for about an hour. Erika remained in the back. She'd managed to coax Kurt off the floorboard and had him nestled between two of the larger bags while he slept. So far, our pursuers were nowhere in sight, and the more distance we put between them and us, the better. The problem was, I'd yet to find a gas station open for business. It was late afternoon on a Sunday, and we'd passed several small towns, but everything was locked up tight, including the gas stations.

Up ahead was a larger town. A sign on the highway announced we'd be entering the town of Brixen, or Bressanone, depending on whether one preferred German or Italian.

I passed a battered sign advertising a petrol station saying it was three kilometers ahead and open on Sundays. By the looks of the sign, there was no telling if it was the case.

Erika stirred in back, and I looked at her in the rearview mirror.

"What if this one's closed?" Erika asked.

"Let's hope it's not. We're still too close to Sterzing, and I'm sure they know this is the only viable option for going south."

A loud clank coming from the front of the car startled us both. Erika drew in her breath. Kurt woke from his sleep and whined. Erika wrapped her hands around Kurt's head to protect him. But it wasn't a bullet that had struck us this time. Something had given out in the engine, and the oil pressure gauge dropped to zero. A moment later, the engine stuttered, and black smoke began boiling out from the seams of the hood.

"We're going to have to ditch the car," I said. "It's gone. Probably from one of the bullets the engine took back at that intersection."

"You don't think it could be fixed?"

"Maybe, but I'm not a mechanic. And even if we could find someone here who could fix it, we'd have to explain the half dozen bullet holes."

Erika said nothing in response. She seemed to shrink in her seat as she cradled Kurt.

I eased off on the gas pedal, letting the car drift in idle. Fifty yards ahead, a road veered off the highway. I steered the car onto the side road and immediately entered a group of dwellings surrounding a church—more than likely a hamlet on the outskirts of Brixen.

Just past the little town square was a short row of businesses, a bakery, and a pharmacy, now closed. I let the car drift as far as it could. With one final clatter of the pistons, the engine died beside the bakery, the last building in the row.

"Wait here," I said and got out. Like everywhere else we'd been on the road south, the buildings looked abandoned, and no one was in sight. I walked around the side of the bakery and saw a small parking lot in the rear. The snow had accumulated to about a foot, and there were no visible tire tracks.

I went back to the car, and Erika and I pushed it the hundred feet needed to get into the parking lot.

"It looks like no one has been in these buildings for some time," I said.

"They probably close up for the winter months."

"Finally, we get a small break: the car didn't conk out in the middle of nowhere, and we've found a quiet place to hide out."

"And we didn't die."

"Amen to that."

"I saw a sign for a guest room about a kilometer up the road," Erika said, pointing to the small road where the car had died. "Maybe they're open and have a vacancy."

"Then let's see if our string of luck will hold out."

I wiped the surfaces down for fingerprints as best I could, then removed the license plates and anything that could help trace us to the car. Erika gathered up Kurt, who was disturbingly silent and still. I picked up any shell casings I could find from the two guns, pocketed the .45 and one of the Lugers, then humped the bags onto my shoulder.

We headed up the street and away from the hamlet. Usually, a kilometer isn't far, but the icy road winding up a steep hill in the gloomy twilight made the going tough. Plus, I was drained from the day, and Erika appeared to be suffering from the same; her steps were slow and unsteady. She had that look of grim determination that comes from resorting to sheer willpower to keep moving.

We finally came to the two-story stone house advertised

on the road. A sign hung on the gate of a picket fence, saying a guest room was available. An elderly Frau Strobl met us, checked us in and showed us around. We registered under my alias of Witt and let the woman assume we were married. Whether she believed we were a couple or not, she seemed pleased to have the business. Her husband, on the other hand, eyed us with suspicion and said nothing as he followed us on the tour in his wheelchair.

Frau Strobl made us a dinner of sausage and sauerkraut accompanied by slices of thick bread. We inhaled the food, and I did the same with a bottle of beer. We then retired to our room on the second floor that consisted of a full bed and a single mattress, both on wooden frames. I sat on the single mattress and watched Erika as she laid Kurt on the full bed. He had already fallen asleep in Erika's arms on the way from the dining room and didn't move a muscle when his mother pulled the quilt up to his shoulders.

My full belly, the beer, and the relief that we were—at least temporarily—safe brought on the exhaustion. I looked upon Kurt with envy, but it was time for some answers. I waited patiently for Erika. She seemed to know what was on my mind, because she glanced at me with apprehension in her eyes. She fiddled nervously for a moment by the nightstand, then, as if resigned to the interrogation, she walked over and sat on the side of the bed opposite me.

"You know what I want to ask," I said. "So why don't you go ahead and save us both some time?"

She looked at her lap for a moment before raising her eyes to peer into mine. "Some of what I've told you is the truth. I come from a wealthy family." She looked at her hands, her fingers winding and unwinding. "I have familial connections to the Wittelsbach dynasty on my mother's side."

Wittelsbach sounded like a big deal, but I had no idea where they fit in with the rest of the royals of Europe.

She must have known what was behind my blank stare, because she said, "My immediate family has some connections to the House of Windsor in Britain." After a further pause on my part, she said, "Queen Victoria—"

"Yeah, I've heard of the House of Windsor." Which was true, though I was having trouble resolving her lofty connections with the woman before me, with the woman who was seemingly penniless, on the run, and shot her way out of the cabin.

She looked away as if embarrassed. I remained quiet and waited for her to continue.

"The part about my cruel and greedy husband is also true."

"Is he a royal?"

She shook her head. "Ludwig is the son of a banker. His father invested heavily in Hitler's regime and consequently lost most of his fortune with the collapse of the Third Reich."

"If I'm following you, he married you for your connection to the family fortune, and you married him for love."

Erika let out a bitter chuckle. "It was a marriage of expediency. My father was a royalist and against Hitler. But he'd seen what happened to the Crown Prince of Bavaria—a distant relative—who said Hitler was insane. He had to go into exile, and his wife and children were put in a concentration camp. My father wanted no part of any rebellion. In hindsight, I realized I was married off to keep the Nazis from knocking on our doors. But I also came to believe that he gave me control of a large portion of the money as compensation, or out of guilt, before he died."

"I assume the money is socked away somewhere safe."

Erika nodded. "That's why my husband wants me back, so he can force me to hand it over to him."

"Are the men who attacked us today working for your husband?"

Erika wrapped her arms around herself as if feeling a chill. "I don't know. I didn't recognize the men at the cabin."

"But you did recognize one or more of them in the car?"

She said nothing and looked away.

"Erika, answer me."

"Yes. A couple of them are friends of my husband's friends. The worst kind of Nazis." She looked at me. "I was afraid the truth might drive you away, but I see that keeping things from you might do the same."

"At this point, I'm committed. It'd have to be pretty despicable to drive me away. Despite what I might think after you tell me, I won't abandon Kurt."

Erika took a deep breath. "My husband is part of a group of influential men who are committed to helping Nazis wanted for war crimes—ex-SS members and high-level officials—escape prosecution."

"The ratlines."

"I've heard that term used. I think it's juvenile. These men committed atrocities. They're war criminals. Rats deserve better."

I couldn't help a little smile. "I presume you weren't a flag-waving Nazi, then."

My smile was met with an indignant frown. "I was one of them at the beginning."

Her admission left me cold. While I admired her courage to tell me the truth, I was still disappointed.

"I can see by your eyes you didn't like my little confession," Erika said. "Most Germans' hopes were raised with Hitler. The communists were threatening to take over, inflation was rampant—"

"I know the whole 'I wasn't a Nazi' song and dance."

She glared at me. "My father and I were among those foolish people who thought that Hitler and his brown shirts would just disappear in a couple of years. No one would take him seriously ..." She stopped. "I'm not making it any better, am I?"

I shook my head. "I've heard that same story over and over again."

"Yes, I was complacent. But I was also afraid for Kurt as well as myself. And I feared for my parents." She wiped a tear from her eye. "I'm done apologizing. I was not even fifteen when Hitler came to power. How aware were you as a teenager?"

"I was an ignorant pain in the ass. I only snapped out of it because my grandmother would kick my ass every time I got out of line."

Erika smiled, though it faded in an instant.

"How much do you know about the group your husband belongs to?"

"From what I understand, it's loosely organized: politicians, bankers, industrialists who've hidden their Nazi pasts from the Allied authorities. What unites them is one goal: to help their fascist comrades to escape justice. Some believe they can unite to form a new Reich in some place like Argentina. Some are simply ardent fascists who don't want to see their fellow believers thrown in prison or executed. Some are so fervently anti-communist that they see the Nazis as crusaders and martyrs who tried to stop the red tide."

We fell silent for a moment. Erika stepped over to a sleeping Kurt to check on him while I processed her information. There was a lot at stake for the group. Erika's information on the group might not stop every effort, but it could slow them down, and many would risk arrest. Which meant that while we might have stymied the first team coming after Erika, more would surely follow.

Erika returned to her spot on the bed and reached for her purse.

"What do you know about Kappler?" I asked.

Blood seemed to drain from her face. "Kappler?" She got up and moved to the opposite side of the room. "I didn't know he was with them."

"Of the men I've encountered, he appears to be the one in charge. That's who I went to see after the grocery store."

She said nothing and lit a cigarette with shaking hands.

"He claims he's a priest," I said, "and you're not who you claim to be. That you're dangerous."

Still, she said nothing.

"Erika…"

"He's not a real priest. Maybe he was at one point. I don't know. He was an SS captain and one of the chief administrators of the Lodz ghetto in Poland. Even his men called him Satan's priest. He used to recite passages from the Bible while executing Jews. He'd pick his victims at random, fabricate an infraction, and shoot them."

I'd heard so many stories of atrocities, but it still sickened and enraged me. "Too bad I didn't shoot him at the inn. But you didn't answer my question. Why did he say you're dangerous?"

"I have no idea. Probably to convince you to turn against me."

"It sounds like he knows you."

"My husband spent time in Poland on some assignment, and he and Kappler became friends. I despised him, and he knew it."

"And it was your husband who put him in charge of the group?"

"I don't know, but I suspect it's Kappler who brought my husband along. You see, Kappler is likely the leader because he has strong connections to some high-level priests at the Vatican."

"What does the Vatican have to do with escaping Nazis?"

"Those Vatican priests are facilitating the ratline in Italy. They're providing support and safe havens. They see that the men get displaced-person passports under false names, then help arrange issuance of visas to countries like Argentina."

I felt shocked and confused. I found it hard to swallow that the Vatican would help Nazi war criminals escape justice. "How could these supposed men of God raise even a finger to help them?"

"Mason, those ..." She appeared to search for the word. "... *priests* have the wealth and power of the Vatican behind them. And they'll be determined to keep the Holy See's involvement a secret at any cost."

"I just trying to absorb this. My mother, grandmother, and all the family were devout Catholics. My grandmother went every Sunday and Wednesday. My mother did when she was sober. Even though I stopped going to mass by the age of eleven, the idea that the pope is God's representative on earth was pounded into my brain from an early age. I stopped buying into that stuff, but I'm finding it hard to believe that the Holy See would help Nazi war criminals escape justice."

Erika sat on the bed across from me. "I'm *still* a Catholic, but if you know much about the history of the popes and the Vatican, you'd realize that these men can be as petty and political and selfish as anyone else. I imagine the church is terrified of communism and would support anyone fighting against its spread."

"Do you have proof?"

"Of course not. I don't have *proof* of anything. Just what I've overheard and seen in some of the papers my husband had in his office. But Kappler being the group's leader is pretty close to proving the church's involvement."

"And are you willing to divulge what you know to American intelligence?"

She let out a heavy sigh. "I was hoping ..." She paused, then said, "Yes."

"Good. One of my best friends is in the Counter Intelligence Corps. He's a good man, and I trust him. We should get word to him as soon as possible."

"Not before we get to a safe place."

"And where is that? Where in Italy would be safe if they're that desperate to stop you? If we get the CIC combing Austria and northern Italy, your husband's group would have to crawl back into the woodwork. They won't be able to move, and we can get you safely south."

"Mason, you don't understand. There are countless ex-Nazis holed up in the towns and mountains around this area. And many more still are local sympathizers and helpers.

There's a smuggling network throughout this whole region, and those ex-Nazis are just waiting for their opportunity to make good on their escape. If we stay here, they'll find us. I can't risk that. For all we know, there are some fugitives or their collaborators in this town."

This revelation gave me pause. Most of the people of South Tyrol identifying as Austrian made for a potential network of local spies. If we stayed, chances were good we'd be found. If we moved, chances were we'd be spotted and reported. And the thought of us being holed up in this bed-and-breakfast in what appeared to be, by all intents and purposes, hostile territory left me with a feeling of being cornered. I'd compromised our safety by assuming we'd escaped the worst of it. But I'd just moved the pieces and had failed to get us anywhere near off the board.

I still hadn't recovered all my strength, and the strains of the day had left me completely drained. Despite this, I had to find a way to get us out of our predicament. Which involved going out into the cold night.

12

I forced myself to my feet and pulled on my overcoat.

"Where are you going?" Erika asked, which sounded more like an accusation than a question.

"I'm not running out on you, if that's what you're thinking." I retrieved the Luger from my backpack, since there was more ammunition for it than my .45. And if Erika had to use the bigger gun, one round could stop an attacker. I checked the Luger's magazine to make sure it was full and popped it back into the grip.

"I'm going to see if I can acquire a car in the town," I said. I pocketed the second magazine and belted the pistol. "If I'm successful, I want to get out of here fast. So be ready to go when I get back."

I exited the room and closed the door as quietly as I could. Our room was among two others on the upper floor. Light glowed from underneath the owners' bedroom door, and I'd have to pass that and another before getting to the stairs. Floorboards squeaked under my feet. Stealth was out of the question.

I got to the top of the staircase without either of them popping their head out. A soft orange glow emanated from the living room below. Probably the wood-burning stove, as I could feel the cloud of warm air accumulating in the staircase. The dim light was enough to see where I was going, and I landed on the ground floor. A short hallway led to the living room and dining room on opposite sides, with the front door ahead of me.

I quickened my pace, aiming straight for the exit, but as I passed the living room, someone cleared their throat to get my attention. I looked in the direction of the noise. Herr Strobl glared at me from his wheelchair situated in front of the wood-burning stove.

"Leaving the young lady alone?" he asked in German with a stern tone. "Shame on you."

"I'll be back, old man."

"Good thing we asked you to pay in advance."

"I said I'll be back."

"Do me a favor and don't."

I snapped open the deadbolt and exited the house. I turned left on the single-lane road. It quickly leveled off and curved to the right. After a couple of miles, I began to grow concerned, as I hadn't encountered any cars to steal. The hamlet consisted mostly of secondary residences for the well-to-do, probably for the skiing, as well as a few houses converted to shops, a clinic, and a car repair place.

Finally, I reached a bridge that spanned the highway. Once I crossed over it, I entered the outskirts of town. There was a scattering of cars parked on the main road, but I preferred to steal one that appeared to be in good enough shape and with a decent engine—just in case we ended up in a high-speed chase. The main road led to the center of town, and I could see the double onion-domed towers of a church in the distance. It being only about eleven p.m., there was the occasional car or pedestrian. I had to find a quiet street.

I checked my watch and realized I'd been gone for over an hour. I suddenly felt a sense of urgency. I had nothing to go on, but I'd learned to trust my instincts and quickened my pace. I passed two side streets before spotting a pre-war Alpha Romeo that had seen better days. With the minutes ticking by, I took a left and strode down the narrow street of two-story buildings with businesses on the ground floor and apartments above them.

I slipped off my overcoat and used it to mask the noise of breaking glass. That done, I got in, got on the floorboard under the steering wheel and found the correct wires. I was about to cross the ignition wires to the battery wires when I heard footsteps.

Someone started shouting at me in Italian. I didn't understand, but I had a good idea what he was saying. I ignored his shouting and his presence by the car and crossed the wires. The engine started up, and I stood up on the sidewalk. The man shouting looked middle-aged, not too small, not too big. I glared at him and pointed my index finger to a spot behind him. I was ready for a fight, but that would take up more time and attract too much attention.

Luckily for me, my menacing look and aggressive finger pointing were enough to persuade the man to retreat.

I got in the car and took off, leaving the guy standing on the streets as he continued to yell.

Now it was doubly vital that we get out of town before the

police or the operators of the ratlines showed up and spoiled our voyage south.

~

THERE WERE no lights on in the house when I parked the car in front. I got out and looked toward the house. The front door was wide open. A groan of alarm escaped my throat as I ran for the entrance while pulling out my pistol and loading a bullet into the chamber.

I knew someone might be waiting in the dark in ambush, but I didn't care. I charged into the living room. The wood-burning stove still glowed, giving me enough light to find the stairs. I took the steps two at a time, raced down the hallway, and into the bedroom.

I growled in frustration and rage. Erika and Kurt were gone. All their bags, including my backpack, still lay on the floor and a chair. The only items that appeared to be missing were their winter coats. A spark of hope flickered within me; maybe something happened that spurred Erika to grab Kurt and make a run for it.

I raced to the window and looked outside. It was too dark to see much, but I could make out a clump of trees at the rear of the house that was about a hundred yards deep, then an open field. Moonlight reflected off the snow-covered field just enough to see it was empty.

The only way the men hunting Erika would know about our location this quickly would be because of the owners. I left the room and stomped down the hallway, gun at my side. I kicked in the couple's bedroom door. Frau Strobl lay in her bed as if asleep. Blood had soaked the pillow where someone shot her in the head, then put one in her chest.

Back out in the hallway, I sprinted down the stairs and entered the living room. Herr Strobl lay on the floor in front of his wheelchair. He, too, had one in the head and one in the chest. Strobl had asked me when I might be back. I should have guessed then that he had already called the hunters to report us and hoped I'd be here when they arrived. This was his reward.

More than ever, it appeared these men were not only determined to stop Erika, they were also ruthless enough to kill the people who'd reported us. I could only guess what would become of her and Kurt.

13

I pushed the stolen car to its limits as I hurtled down the highway in the dark. I had no way of knowing which direction the hunters would take. I tried not to think about the possibility that they would simply execute Erika and Kurt and dump their bodies in a remote area. If that turned out to be the case, I swore I would track them down and kill them all.

But I had to find them first. And it appeared the only option was to go back to Sterzing and hope I could pick up their trail.

The traffic thickened about fifteen miles out of town, and soon I saw why: the ambulances and investigative cops had left hours ago, but the tow truck and road crews were still there to clean up the mess I'd left from the previous encounter. The car belonging to the bystander sat upright and looked banged up, but not as bad as the assailants' vehicle, which was still on its roof and crushed in on three sides.

I kept my head down as I passed a couple of cops directing traffic. Once I was free of the congestion, I made good time and arrived in the outskirts of Sterzing. Since the hunters had missed me in the abduction, there was a good possibility that they'd be on high alert, so I watched carefully for lookouts and took the road along the south perimeter of the town.

If, by chance, they used Sterzing as their base, the inn would be guarded. There was one place, however, they might have neglected, and that was the hospital. With Rudel seriously wounded from the beating I gave him at the cabin, I was betting on them being treated locally. I'd seen a sign for the *Krankenhaus*, or hospital, when I'd driven south to escape Sterzing with Erika, and remembered it was somewhere on the southeastern end of town.

It took only a short while to find *Das Deutschhaus*, a compound bordered by a street-side high wall and anchored by a small hexagonal church. Fortunately, there were few other buildings in the immediate area aside from another larger church further west. The street was quiet and devoid of pedestrians. I went a block up the street and pulled to the curb alongside a park.

Walking back toward the hospital, I could see the hodge-podge of buildings that made up the compound, each a different size and shape and all linked together. I could have gone around back in hopes of breaking in through one of the windows on the ground floor, but then I'd have the impossible task of searching every room. Best to walk straight in the front door.

The pedestrian entrance appeared to be accessed through an arched gate in the wall. There was no one on the street guarding the gate, no cars with lookouts, but I wasn't taking any chances; there could still be a lookout somewhere on the property. I stopped just outside the iron gates and peered around the corner. The church and collection of buildings formed a rectangular courtyard of gravel with a small garden next to the church. Each building had its own entrance, and the one for the hospital was located at the building furthest away from where I stood. A man paced next to the double doors, with his overcoat pulled tight over his chest against the cold. He smoked a cigarette and had his hat pulled low on his brow. He glanced toward the gate, then went back to his cigarette.

Someone guarding the hospital complicated things, but at least it confirmed that Rudel was being treated inside. The downside was that I'd have to cross sixty yards of open ground before making it to the entrance.

I spied another option: the enclosed property had a parking lot, which was simply an area of gravel marked out with short wooden posts. And beyond the hospital building was a larger gate for cars and ambulances. It was closed up for the night, and probably locked, but if I could get in through that gate, it was a matter of yards to the hospital's entrance and the lookout.

The guard turned away from me. I zipped past the pedestrian entrance and hurried along the street-side wall. I turned right and down the driveway between a cemetery and the wall's western leg and came up to the pair of heavy wooden doors. There was an old pin tumbler lock in the center. I kneeled by the lock, pulled out my lock-picking tools, and found the pins. The old lock turned reluctantly but finally gave way. The bolt clacked back with the sound echoing in the courtyard. I pushed the left gate door open just a crack, then stepped back and readied my pistol.

Footsteps crunched on the gravel. I put my back to the

opposite door and mumbled curses about dropping my key in German just loud enough for him to hear. The crunching stopped.

"Who's there?" the man said.

"I dropped my key and can't find it in the dark," I said in a frustrated tone. "How stupid of me."

The gate's hinges groaned as the man slowly opened the door. His gun came out first—something I was hoping for.

I grabbed his pistol with one hand and his wrist with the other. In a twisting move, I seized the gun from his grasp. The man charged out of the gate and rammed into me before I could bring up the gun to aim. He tried to knee me and strike my head with his free hand. I was too occupied with holding on to the gun to strike back. Instead, I twisted my body and kicked his foot at the same time.

He fell hard onto his back, but his hold on me was too tight to break free. I went down on top of him. Even though I still had possession of the gun, it was lodged against both our stomachs. I was afraid it might go off, and there was a fifty-fifty chance I'd be on the wrong end of the barrel.

I slammed my forehead into the bridge of his nose repeatedly. Stunned, the man's grip on me weakened. I pulled away and hit him several times using the pistol like a pair of brass knuckles. He barely moved, but I was left with the problem of what to do with him while I explored the hospital. Plus, I might want to question him later.

I cursed myself for not planning this out properly. My fear for Erika and Kurt's survival had clouded my judgment.

I jumped to my feet and ran toward the street. The only alternative I could come up with in that instant was to go for the car and hope that the guy would be too out of it to move. I sprinted up the sidewalk and got into the car, started it up, and made a U-turn. In seconds, I raced down the short alley and stopped in front of the bloodied guard.

He was trying to crawl back toward the gate. I bounded out of the car and opened the trunk. The guy made guttural sounds as he slithered along the graveled driveway. When I got up to him, I saw why he hadn't called out for help: I'd broken and dislocated his jaw.

I grabbed his feet and dragged him toward the open trunk. He grabbed at the gravel as he made a kind of barking noise. I got him to the trunk and hoisted him to the lip and dropped him in. He banged his head on the way down and immediately stopped putting up a fight. I closed the trunk lid.

The whole episode had left me drained. My chest heaved to take in air. The wound in my side burned like fire. Adrenaline and rage were the only things that kept me going. I took a deep breath and walked through the gate, turned the corner, and faced the hospital's main entrance. Through the glass doors I could see the small reception area was empty, with two desk lamps forming pools of light in an otherwise dark space.

I'd expected the doors to be locked, but I tried one because I didn't feel like making the effort of getting on my knees again. It was unlocked, and I stepped inside. There was a line of chairs against one wall opposite the reception counter. Off to the left was a corridor, and at the end of that was a nurses' station in another pool of light. One nurse stood at the station's counter writing something.

I slid around behind the reception counter and searched the shelves until I found what I was looking for: a register of admitted patients. Rudel would have been brought in that afternoon, so I turned to the last page of entries and found his name. No contact information, no room number, but at least it confirmed he was there. Now, I had to find his room.

I straightened my overcoat, patted down my disheveled hair, and came out from behind the reception counter. I marched down the corridor like I owned the place. The nurse looked up with a start and backed away from the nurses' station counter. I simply nodded as I approached.

"There's been a change of circumstances," I said in German. "We need to move Herr Rudel to Bozen."

The nurse, whose name badge said Nurse Posch, glanced toward the entrance, presumably to see if the guard was there to confirm the request. "He has a severe bruise on his spine and several broken ribs. He also suffered a concussion. Moving him could worsen his condition."

"Lady, I just do what I'm told. And my instructions are to see that he's ready to be moved. My partners will be here in a quarter hour."

"At this time of night? Without consulting the doctor or the head nurse?" She shook her head. "I can't allow it." She tried to give me a stern expression, but her voice trembled.

I made a theatrical sigh and adjusted my hat as if pondering what to do next. "I tell you what, let me have a look at him. If it looks like that's a bad idea, I'll say something to my superiors."

"Take a look at him? What's that going to tell you? Do you presume to know better than the medical staff of this hospital?"

I leaned on the counter with both elbows and furrowed my brows, causing Nurse Posch to back up farther. "I'm trying to be nice, okay?" I said. "Believe me, you do not want to cross my superiors. If they come in here and find out that you won't even let me see Herr Rudel, let alone refused my request, they won't be nice at all."

Posch thought a moment and glanced toward the entrance again. "I guess you looking in on him won't hurt anything."

I smiled and acted relieved. "That's better. I don't like to be mean. Not to young ladies, at least."

"Room 131."

I gave her a slight bow. "Thank you. And I would like you to come with me."

"Me?" she asked, her eyes wide. She took another step back, and her back hit the wall. "Why?"

"We can't have you making any phone calls to the wrong people, now can we?"

"I won't make any—"

I hit the counter with my fist. She jumped along with several items on the counter. "You see? I don't like to get mad, but I get that way when I'm frustrated." I paused for effect. "Please." I waved my hand for her to accompany me.

She moved around the counter while trying to keep her distance like I might lash out at her at any moment. I wasn't going to say anything to make her more comfortable; fear would keep her in line. We moved down the corridor, her ahead of me by a yard. She kept looking around as if searching for an escape. I didn't want her to bolt. She had an athletic form and was in her mid-twenties, and I wasn't sure I had it in me to chase her down.

"This will be over in a few minutes," I said. "I got to see for myself before I talk to my bosses. You understand?"

She gave me a weak nod and stopped at a door with 131 on it. After one more glance in both directions, she opened

the door, and I followed her in. Rudel occupied a single room
—nothing but the best for the group's henchmen. A miniscule
lamp mounted over the bed provided the only illumination.
Rudel was out cold. He had a bandage around his head and a
cast on his arm. The rest of the damage I inflicted on him was
hidden by the bed covers.

I pointed for Nurse Posch to stand on the far side of the
bed, making it difficult for her to escape. I was going to
have to get results fast and knew I'd have to use force to
coerce Rudel. I didn't want to have to worry about the
young nurse making a dash for the exit while I persuaded
her patient.

She complied with my command and went further than
my request by cozying up to the corner of the room. It
seemed she had an idea what was about to happen and
wanted the wall for support. I approached the bed. The son of
a bitch looked so peaceful—aside from his skull wrapped in a
bandage and the purple bruises on his face.

I looked at the nurse and put my index finger against my
lips. I clamped my hand on Rudel's mouth. He jerked awake,
and Nurse Posch sucked in her breath. When he saw me, he
attempted to scream through my hands. I showed him my
knife and placed the blade under his chin. He pulled back his
head as far as the pillow would allow. Nurse Posch covered
her face with her hands and suppressed a scream.

I leaned in close to Rudel's face. "I'd try to calm down, if I
were you. No telling what too much excitement might do to
your damaged brain. Or my knife hand."

Rudel's eyes bounced around in their sockets, which I took
for him desperately searching for a way to fight back and
escape. For good measure, I pushed the blade into his neck,

drawing a little blood. He stiffened, and his eyes concentrated on me.

"That's better," I said. "I'm going to lift my hand only for you to answer my questions. You try to cry out for help or raise your voice, and I'll cut your vocal cords. Nod if you understand."

Rudel's eyes had changed from shock to rage, but he nodded all the same.

"Your buddies abducted Frau Altmann, along with her boy. What are they planning to do with them? Murder them? Take them somewhere?"

I raised my hand a few inches away from the man's face.

His mouth now free, Rudel used the opportunity to sneer at me. "It's up to her husband what happens to that bitch."

"Show more respect, or I'll cut more than your vocal cords." To illustrate the point, I used my free hand to grab his balls through the thin sheet and blanket.

He grimaced in pain and moved to rise, but my blade cut him a little deeper. He growled in frustration and became still. I glanced at Nurse Posch to see if she might make a run for it. She stayed in her corner, still covering her mouth, but she seemed to have focused her fear and anger away from me and now onto her patient.

"Are they taking Erika and her boy to her husband?" I asked.

"How am I supposed to know? I wasn't there. You put me out of action, remember?"

"What was the original plan?"

Rudel clamped his mouth shut. I squeezed his groin harder. His body jolted from the pain, and the blade went deeper.

"What were you supposed to do once you got Frau Altmann?" I said with more force. "You're starting to soak the sheets with your blood. I'm tempted to slice you open, right here and now. One less Nazi in the world."

"Yes, the plan was to take her to her husband."

"Where's the husband now?"

Rudel growled and pounded the bed with his fists. "Meran. We were to meet him in Meran."

"Meran's a big town. Where precisely?"

"An inn called Tante Anna."

I released his groin but kept my knife at his neck. I said to Nurse Posch, "Is there a spare sheet in this room?" Upon her nod, I said, "Get it and tear off a strip about thirty centimeters wide."

Posch slid across the wall to the opposite corner and opened a drawer in a small cabinet. She took out a sheet and tore off the strip as instructed, then threw it to me.

I nodded my thanks and said, "He tried to murder a woman and child. Patch up his neck if you want, but maybe you'd like to let him bleed. It doesn't matter to me." Using the blanket, I wiped the blood off the knife and put it back in my boot.

As I was twisting the strip of sheet, Rudel said, "Altmann is not that woman's real name. She's been playing you for a fool." With that he formed a cruel smile.

I jammed a balled-up piece of the sheet into his mouth, forced his head up and gagged him with the rest. He couldn't go very far in his condition, so I backed off and nodded at Nurse Posch before turning on my heels and rushing out of the hospital.

14

The smell of overheated brakes and tires filled my nostrils as I took the hundredth hairpin turn on the road to Meran. After leaving the hospital in Sterzing and depositing the stunned guard on a desolate section of the road, I'd been faced with a choice: There were two routes that formed a circle from Sterzing to Bozen. The left, or eastern portion, led back to Brixen, while my road map indicated that the most direct route to Meran was to take the western portion of the circle. I should have paid attention to the squiggly lines representing the more direct route to Meran, because it quickly became a series of switchbacks that climbed high into the mountains. The car jolted when I hit another pothole. The clouds covered the moon, making the way pitch black. And the narrow road hadn't seen a mainte-nance crew since Julius Caesar crossed the Rubicon—not ideal for running the car like a bat out of hell.

I figured it was around three a.m. when I caught sight of Meran far below me on the valley floor. The road descended rapidly, bringing me finally onto flat ground and straighter roads. I took the left fork where a sign pointed to the center of town and the police station. I was dog-tired but still had to locate Aunt Anna's inn. I'd have to ask someone where it was, and at that time of night, or morning depending on your perspective, there'd only be the bums, drunks, and cops.

It wasn't long before I reached the old part of town, and as I got within a block of the police headquarters, I spotted a pole plastered with signs for a dozen hotels. In among the signs was one for the Pension Tante Anna.

I turned left and crossed the bridge over the Passer river. The road took me through more of the surrounding suburbs until I saw the rather subtle sign for the inn out in front of a large mansion on a sprawling piece of property. Despite the early morning hour, I wanted to avoid any attention, so I rolled past the place and didn't stop until I was a good two blocks away.

I'd had some long days in my various careers, but this one seemed like I'd folded four days into one: a shoot-out, a car chase, a brawl, one interrogation, and five hours of perilous driving. A guy has only so much adrenaline, and my mind and body threatened to shut down at any moment. But when I thought of Erika and Kurt, and what might be happening to them, raw energy returned, and I launched myself out of the car.

Once I had my overcoat on and my .45 tucked in my belt, I walked back toward the inn on the opposite side of the street. I passed grand houses and a scattering of shops before coming abreast of the inn. I kept going while stealing glances at the two-story house. It was more Victorian than Alpine, built of wood, and graced with delicate latticework. It didn't look at all like a Nazi hangout, except that there were two men standing guard on either side of the front door. Another man stood on the second-floor balcony. Even at that distance, I could tell they were hiding rifles or submachine guns under their overcoats.

This display of armed men hanging out in the middle of the night in the freezing cold could only be for one reason: there was a bevy of Nazi VIPs holed up there for the night.

I'd already risked getting their attention just by walking past, so I kept going until reaching a side street on my left. I turned and passed a small shop with a rear parking lot. It offered a clear view of the inn, yet was still far enough away to avoid suspicion.

I circled back by taking a parallel street and hurried to the car. I got in, started it up, and navigated the same roundabout path. I doused the headlights before turning into the shop's parking lot. Once I got into position, I shut off the engine and peered at the inn. The car's engine noise hadn't seemed to attract their attention, as they seemed more interested in stomping their feet to stay warm and smoking their cigarettes.

"Now what?" I said to myself. Sneaking into the inn was out of the question. My only course of action seemed to be to wait until the Nazi group made a move. If *they* were even in there, and if Erika and Kurt were with them … and still alive.

A lot of ifs and no good options at the end of it.

A SHARP RAPPING next to my ear jolted me from sleep. Imminent danger blasted my brain with adrenaline. I jerked in my seat and couldn't remember where I was.

I reached for my pistol, when another rap hard enough to break the glass stopped me. I looked toward the sound. Two men in overcoats stood at my driver's window with pistols pointed in my direction. One of them shook his head when my hand finally found the pistol grip.

I was so disoriented that it took me a second to register everything. I was still in the Alpha Romeo in the shop's parking lot. Beyond exhausted, I had committed the detective's cardinal sin of falling asleep during the stakeout. It couldn't have been too long because it was still dark out.

The tapping started again, and one of them made a motion for me to roll down my window. And that was when it hit me: I recognized them both. I'd half expected Kappler or one of the other shooters from Sterzing, but it was the two guys I'd seen executing a man and tossing him off the bridge. Either way, I was probably a dead man.

I lifted my hand off the pistol grip, though I kept my hand close enough to grab it in case they started plugging me with holes.

The handsome guy with the glasses said, "Roll it down or we start shooting." He spoke in a quiet tone, but the words got through to me all the same.

With more clarity, I realized that if they'd really wanted me dead, they could have shot me while I slept. I cranked the window down. "What's a guy gotta do to get some sleep around here?"

"Hello, again," the one with the scarred face said. "Or should I say *Guten Abend*?"

"Look—"

I stopped when both of them jammed the barrels of their pistols against my forehead.

"No more talking," the one with the glasses said. "Hand over the pistol."

While still looking at them, I extended the fingers of my left hand and slowly reached for the .45. I made sure they saw I was using two fingers to pluck the gun out of its holster that was wedged between my hip and the seat. I lifted it carefully and brought it up to the window.

The one with the glasses nabbed it and said, "Get out of the car."

I pulled the lever and opened the door. I pivoted to bring my legs out, but they refused to cooperate, as if the blood had frozen in my veins. I resorted to lifting them with my hands, then pulling my body up and out.

The guy with the glasses waved the barrel of his pistol vaguely in the direction of another car.

"Where are we going?" I asked, more to buy time so my blood would start flowing again.

Both of my captors grabbed my arms and pulled me away from the car. My feet tingled, and the frostbite scars screamed in agony. I managed to stay standing as they forced me across the parking lot. Every part of my body ached from the shoulders down, and I wondered if I might have died from hypothermia while I slept if my executioners hadn't come along.

One of them threw me onto the hood of a car. "Could one of you get my backpack?" I asked. Erika's and Kurt's bags were also in the back of the car, but asking for them would have been a request too far.

The wearer of glasses got in my face. "Where you're going, you're not going to need it." He turned to look in the distance and hissed at his companion, "What are you doing? We've got to get out of here."

"I'm getting his backpack," the other one said.

While the guy with the glasses bound my hands behind my back, I heard his companion's footsteps on the frozen snow, then a car door open and the backpack get thrown inside their car.

"I put your pistol inside. Wouldn't want one of the locals to see it and call the cops."

"Thanks," I said.

"Shut up," the glasses man said, then hoisted me up and shoved me toward the back of the car.

The two of them pushed me in the back with my pack, and the glasses guy got in next to me, cursing as he shoved me to move over and make room. Feeling started to come back to my body, which set off a burning pain in my arms and hands.

My seatmate yanked a hood over my head. "You don't move, you don't speak," he said. "Do that, and I might not kill you when we get to our destination."

15

Being driven around with a hood pulled over my head reminded me of the several times that occurred to me in Vienna. And it seemed absurd to me that, while being blind and in a tight spot, I'd be thinking of Laura. I missed her and wondered what had been important enough to contact Forester to urge me to come to Naples. And I imagined her waiting for me for my already late arrival, that I'd let her down again, and she had become so pissed that she would leave me permanently for parts unknown.

Simultaneously, I tried to keep track of our direction and speed, and figured we were heading south, out of town. The car took a moderate incline, and about eight minutes later it made a sharp turn and stopped.

The car's springs bounced as the men got out, then hands grabbed me, dragged me out, and let me fall hard to the ground.

I managed to sit up. "Now, is that any way to treat a guest?"

More heavy handling and more dragging ensued until we

passed through a door and into the warmth of a room. They stripped off my coat and dropped me onto a chair. While one of them tied my hands, the other bound my feet and torso to the chair.

Finally, someone pulled the hood off my face. I winced against the bright light until my sight adjusted. I was in a living room, next to a small round table with a lamp sitting in the middle. With the immaculate sofa and chairs in embroidered upholstery, the castle-sized fireplace, the wood-paneled walls and ceiling, and the lack of little personal decorative touches, I figured we were in an upscale Alpine cabin for wealthy skiers.

The two men finished the web of ropes, took off their overcoats, and sat at the table across from me. When I'd first seen them on the bridge, they were in British Army uniforms. This time they wore wool pants and thick sweaters. While the atmosphere was cozy, they resumed training their guns on me.

"We are going to ask you a few questions," the one with the scar said. "And your survival depends on your responses."

I wasn't about to speak until given permission; I had the feeling the one with the glasses was looking for any excuse to inflict some pain. But my silence just angered him more. The one with the scar glanced at his sneering partner, looked at him disapprovingly, and returned his attention back to me.

"Imagine our surprise when we saw you parked in front of a Nazi hideout. That tells us you're not who you said you were at the bridge."

He stopped, but I said nothing. That got the one with the glasses gritting his teeth and seething in place.

"Am I allowed to speak now?" I asked.

"Who are you, really?"

"I told you the truth. I'm an American who has a way of stepping in piles of manure everywhere I go."

"You have five seconds to give us a straight answer," the one with the glasses said. "Try to convince me you're not working for those Nazis. Or you're not one of them yourself. Otherwise, I'll enjoy shooting you in the gut and watching you die in agony."

"David, that's enough," the one with the scar said. He sucked in a breath and looked at me as if he'd accidently given away a name.

I said, "I was an intelligence officer for the U.S. Army's G-2 during the war because I speak fluent German. After the war I was an investigator for the U.S. Army's criminal investigation division in Bavaria. I left the army—"

"But you stayed in Europe?" David, the one with the glasses, said with a skeptic tone.

I shrugged. "It's a long story."

"We have nothing else to do for the moment. Entertain us."

"The short version is, after I left the army, I got waylaid by assassins for busting up a criminal enterprise, then wound up in Vienna to kill the man who was contracting the killers. In the meantime, I met the love of my life, but she left me. I wandered around while figuring out my options until I got the message that she needed me to meet her in Naples—"

"Now, if that doesn't sound like a load of bullshit, I don't know what does," glasses man said.

"It's all I got. You want another story, turn on the radio."

Mr. Glasses had steam coming out of his ears, but Mr. Scar seemed amused by his buddy's frustration.

Mr. Scar said in a calming voice, which I figured was more

for his partner than me, "None of that explains what you were doing in that car tonight."

"After having the displeasure of running into you guys at the bridge, I nearly got killed helping out a guy in Sterzing." I then proceeded to tell them about Schwend getting killed and his sister-in-law nursing me back to health. Then about the Nazis coming to kill her and her son, that we got away, but not far enough, because those same Nazis abducted the woman and boy in Brixen. "The only lead I got was that her husband is there, in that inn."

Mr. Scar leaned back in his chair and chuckled. "That's so outrageous, I have to believe it."

"I told you I have the annoying tendency to step in manure, and this one's a big, stinking pile."

Mr. Scar returned the hammer of his Walther pistol to its resting place and slipped it into his shoulder holster. "My name is Arie Feldman. My hot-headed partner is David Hazan." He furrowed his brow when he noticed his partner still had his pistol pointed at my chest. "Put it down, David."

Hazan glared at Feldman, then gave me a menacing smile before uncocking the gun. He put it on the table but made sure the barrel was still pointed in my direction.

"We heard about the shooting in Sterzing about a week ago," Feldman said. "Was that you?"

I nodded. "That's when this guy asked me to help his sister-in-law. They tried to grab him, and I got in their way."

"I heard one dead."

"I wouldn't know. But it was two if you count the brother-in-law. They killed him in the shoot-out, and I took a bullet fragment in the side." I told them about my drive up to the cabin, then Frau Altmann nursing me back to health. "I'd agreed to take her and her son south to safety, but we were attacked twice before they managed to abduct them in Brixen. I persuaded one of the shooters I put in the hospital to tell me where they might be headed. And that led me here. Now, if it's all the same to you, I'd like to get back to trying to free her and the boy."

"Typical American," Hazan said. "You think you can single-handedly take on ten to twelve armed men. You've done a nice job so far, haven't you? Losing the woman and falling asleep in your car."

"If you've got a problem with me, then maybe you can untie me, and we can settle it without you hiding behind that gun."

Hazan shot to his feet. Feldman did the same and held out his hand to block his partner from going any further. "That's enough from both of you."

When Hazan took his seat, Feldman came around to the back of my chair and began untying the knots. "You're not curious at all about us?"

I pulled off the loose ropes and tossed them on the floor. "The less I know, the better. I wouldn't want to give your partner an excuse to toss *me* off a bridge."

Hazan got up, slower this time, and said to no one in particular, "I don't have to listen to this." As he walked toward the back of the house, he said to Arie, "I don't trust him, and I think the others would agree with me. You do what you want, but that'll be on you."

Feldman pulled my coat off the back of the sofa and tossed it to me. "I'll drive you to your car."

I pulled on my coat and followed Feldman out the door. It was still dark out, but the sounds of the town stirring to life reverberated up the hill. We got into Feldman's car, and he started it up and pulled out onto the street.

"You guys were army, I can tell that much," I said. "But you're not now, and you're not from the U.K."

Feldman gave me a smile of satisfaction. "Curiosity finally got the better of you, huh? We're from Eretz Yisrael. Mandatory Palestine to you."

"You're mighty far from home. You and your buddy are Jewish, I presume. Why would you two ever want to stay another minute in Europe, let alone a place like South Tyrol? On a map it might be in Italy, but it still feels like Little Naziland."

"David and I are on a mission. Once we feel we've done all we can do, we'll go back home. The fight is now with the British to allow more European Jewish refugees to immigrate to our rightful homeland."

"If you want to fight the Brits, then what were you doing in their army's uniforms and using their trucks?"

"*Tilhas Tizig Gesheften.*"

"What kind of business?"

"The first word is Arabic, the second is Yiddish, and the third German. Loosely translated as 'lick-my-ass business.' We're part of a group formed from soldiers in the Jewish Brigade, which was part of the British Army."

"You talk like I should know something about that brigade."

"After a lot of handwringing, the British government decided to allow the formation of three army regiments and one artillery regiment of Jews, mostly from Palestine. It was called the Jewish Brigade. They brought us to Italy to fight the Nazis in the fall of '44. When we were disbanded in '46, many of us decided to stay. One of our leaders noticed how easy it would be to move around in British uniforms and trucks, so we borrowed them. And he formed the TTG."

"There's more than the two of you?" I exaggerated my shock for comic effect, but the idea still unnerved me.

Feldman chuckled. "I don't know how many for sure. Three dozen, maybe. We answer to a couple of men at the top, but we work in independent cells. That way, if one group gets caught, they can't identify the others."

"Your mission is to hunt Nazis."

Feldman said nothing as he steered the car into town.

"That man on the bridge," I said.

"An SS officer who carried out deportations of Italian Jews."

I sat back in my seat. I believed that the principal Nazis deserved to be hanged, but still not before being convicted in a court of law. The guy sitting next to me carried out vigilante executions, and he appeared nonchalant about it. Of course, I'd killed men when I had to, and was often was tempted to carry out my own justice—particularly killing the man who'd ordered assassins to go after me, my friends and associates, and the love of my life—but I always stopped short.

"It seems I've shocked you," Feldman said. "After shooting those men in Sterzing, I expected you'd understand."

"I was trying to stay alive," I said, almost yelling. I calmed myself. "Look, I get the urge for revenge after what the Nazis did in the holocaust. But those bastards should be tried in a court of law. What if your information is wrong? Or an informer rats on an innocent guy? What if I hadn't answered your questions to your satisfaction, and you or your hot-headed partner had shot me in cold blood?"

"What a vivid imagination, you have. You're quite impassioned about justice."

"And I've noticed how dispassionately you've dealt with your prey."

Feldman pounded the steering wheel. "Our passions are what guide us. Maybe I don't let you see what I'm feeling inside, but it is there. My aunts and uncles, my cousins all perished because of those evil men. David's entire family, outside his parents and siblings, were murdered in the camps or perished in the ghettos. Six million Jews. The perpetrators should all be executed without remorse or mercy."

"You hunt enough men and you'll lose your soul. Believe me, I've come close, and sometimes I wonder if it's already too late."

Feldman took an unexpected turn south, away from town.

"The inn is back the other way," I said. "Turn around, now, before I get nasty."

"I want to show you something. It will only take a moment. It's just six thirty. Your Nazis aren't going anywhere anytime soon. Please. I need to show you this."

The man—boy really—had such sincerity in his voice that I sat back in my seat and let him take his detour. "You've got thirty minutes."

16

In ten minutes, Feldman pulled off the road and onto a gravel drive that led to a large group of warehouses lining the opposite side of the Adige river from town. Most of the wood and corrugated-tin buildings appeared empty and forgotten.

"Do you keep your Nazi victims locked up in one of these?" I asked.

"A little patience, please," Feldman said as he drove past the cluster of buildings. He continued on the gravel road, the stones popping under the tires, until reaching a structure set away from the others and triple their size. I could only see the tips of three sloped roofs. The rest of the building was hidden by a high wooden fence topped with barbwire. Someone got out of a car parked at the solid doors of the gate and stood at the entrance. He wore a British Army uniform and held a STEN submachine gun slung on his shoulder. He raised his hand for us to stop.

Feldman pulled up to within a few feet of the man and rolled down the window. "Shimon, it's me."

Shimon walked up to the driver's window and peered in. He looked to be in his late thirties and had that look in his eyes I'd seen so often when men had experienced the savagery of war. "Who is that?" he asked in German and tried to give me a tough-guy sneer.

"He's fine," Feldman said in English. "He's with me."

Shimon raised the barrel of his submachine gun slightly and said, "Show me your hands."

"I'll do that when you lower your STEN," I said.

"American?" Shimon said. "I don't like Americans."

"Good for you."

"Mason, please," Feldman said. "He's just following orders."

I raised my hands and put them on the windshield. That seemed to satisfy him that I wasn't forcing my way in at gunpoint.

"Do you really trust this man?" he asked Feldman.

Feldman glanced at me before turning back to him. "I do."

"Oscar won't like this."

"He's not here, is he? That makes me in charge."

After a final glare at me, Shimon walked over to the doors, removed a chain, and pushed them open. Feldman drove through the gap and entered a spacious lot. Parked to one side were three troop transport trucks in olive drab with an Allied star painted on the door panel, though the other markings on the fenders were distinctly British. There were also two jeeps and a black sedan. A dozen or so people in civilian clothes wandered the yard. Some were skinny to bone-thin, with gaunt faces and sunken eyes, but others appeared healthy and smiled as they played with their children.

Feldman parked his car in front of the sedan. "Come with me."

"Fifteen minutes left."

"This will take five. Please."

"What is this place? Who are these people?"

"You'll see."

My curiosity piqued, I got out of the car and followed Feldman across the yard. A few of the people smiled and waved when they saw him. I had a handful of questions, but I stayed silent; it was his show, so I'd let him do the explaining.

We walked toward the building of about a hundred and fifty feet at its longest. It was constructed of steel and cement and looked to have been built sometime in the 1920s. It was already showing its age, or a lack of maintenance. Italy was still in economic and political shambles after the end of the war, I knew that much, but aside from the occasional bomb damage, this run-down area of abandoned warehouses was the first physical sign I'd seen of Italy's troubles.

We stopped at a standard-sized door in the center of the building. He opened it without knocking, and I followed him inside. I stopped and took a step back in surprise. The sprawling interior had been turned into a kind of refugee camp, with tents and lean-tos made from found material. There must have been seventy people spread out in the space. At the far end was a larger tent of white cloth with an open front. Inside, a handful of nurses and doctors cared for patients.

"This is what I wanted you to see," Feldman said. "These people are just a small sample of the countless thousands of Jews with no place to go. Like so many others in camps in Germany, Austria, or here in Italy, these people all are desperate to get to Eretz Yisrael."

"I know about the camps for surviving Jews," I said. "You're not showing me anything I haven't seen."

"Most of the non-Jewish displaced persons have made it home. But not the people who have suffered and died the most at the hands of the Nazis."

"A fair point, but I still don't see why you thought it was important to bring me here."

"Hunting Nazis isn't our only mission. We also help displaced Jews from all over Europe get to Mandatory Palestine. The Brits have imposed draconian quotas on Jews admitted into their mandated territory. My homeland. The homeland of the Jews for thousands of years. The people here, the countless Jews in refugee camps, are herded into camps while they wait. With the quotas, it could take decades before everyone who wants to go is allowed to immigrate."

"So your group's idea is to smuggle thousands of Jews through Italy, across the Mediterranean, and into British-controlled territory? Good luck with that."

"We've already had some success, with ships leaving every few months."

"Have any the ships gotten through a British blockade?"

"A few. But that still counts as success."

"I'm still waiting for you to tell me why you're showing me this."

"I think we could help each other."

That was so unexpected that I turned to look at him just to see if he was kidding. He looked dead serious.

"You want me to smuggle people to Palestine?" I shook my head. "I'm definitely the wrong guy for the job. I'm in trouble with the Brits, I have a forged ID and an expired U.S. travel pass. Plus, I'm committed to another mission, which you're keeping me from as we speak."

"There are one hundred and five people in here, though a good many are too sick to make the journey. And I fear this may be the last run before we have to go back to Palestine. It will be a tight squeeze, but we can get the seventy who are able into those three trucks outside. The problem is, we only have two drivers. We need a third. You. In exchange, we can help you track the men who have the woman and boy. And we can help you get them back. At the same time, my associates and I get to hunt a few more high-level Nazis. There's a ship leaving for Palestine in two weeks …" He paused as if for dramatic effect. "And it's departing from Naples."

That bit of news did make things more interesting. "How do you know the Nazi captors are going south. I don't know that."

"Of course they are. To get to Argentina, or whichever rock they've chosen to crawl under, their first stop will probably be Rome."

"Because the Vatican is helping them?"

Feldman nodded. "But that's just the waypoint. Usually there they get Red Cross displaced persons IDs, which then allows them to apply for refugee status in order to get visas for South America or the Middle East. That can take a while, so they sit tight in Rome until they can get passage on a ship bound for South America—or, you know, another rock—and for a majority of those ships the port of departure is Genoa."

"But they use other ports?"

"They've been known to use other ports, and wouldn't that add a sad touch of irony if these Nazis departed from Naples?" Feldman said. "The port apparently depends on what the Vatican can arrange. If we can't get to the Nazi group beforehand, we'll get them in Rome. Then we'll go on to Naples." He turned to face me. "How does my proposition sound?"

"How does it sound? Crazy. Too many unknowns. Too many moving parts. And too many people tagging along for me to be nimble if our quarry makes unexpected moves. And why do you think I'm the right guy for the job, anyway? Aside from us tracking the same quarry, we have completely different objectives."

"You're not going to get close to that group. And even if you manage it, you'll more than likely wind up dead."

"Watch me," I said. "Your time is up."

Feldman's friendly demeanor vanished, though, to his credit, he kept his anger to himself. He motioned for me to follow him out the door. We were silent on the way to the car. We got in, and Feldman guided the car to the gates. Another guard opened them, and Feldman exited the compound. He connected with the paved road and steered toward the bridge that crossed the Adige river.

"To answer your question from before," Feldman said, "I asked you because of your training, your skills, you speak fluent German, and you're an American. Plus, you seem like an honorable man. Stubborn, foolhardy, annoying, with that typical American cowboy bravado, but honorable."

"You forgot that the woman and child I swore to protect are being held by some Nazis in that inn. Getting them out before they're tortured or murdered is my sole objective. Right now, doing that, and me staying alive, are the only things I can consider."

Feldman pulled into the parking lot behind the row of

stores and stopped next to my car. Everything was still closed up tight, and the same three men still guarded the inn.

Feldman turned in his seat to look at me. "If you change your mind, or find yourself in a bind, you know where to go. If I'm not there, someone always knows how to get in touch with me."

He held out his hand. As I shook it, I noticed someone emerging from the inn. It was a man and woman, both middle-aged and well dressed. Another man, who looked like the hotel's bellhop, came out carrying a heavy suitcase.

Feldman turned to see where my attention had been drawn. He reached in the glovebox and pulled out a pair of binoculars and trained them on the front of the inn. We both watched as the small entourage crossed the front lawn and passed through the wrought-iron gate. A Horch limo waited for them at the curb. The couple got into the back of the limo, while the hotel employee loaded the suitcase in the extended trunk attached to the rear.

Feldman shook his head. "They're not part of the group as far as I know. Normal guests, probably."

"You know what the Nazis in that inn look like?" I asked with a tone of skepticism.

Feldman looked at me. "We've been tracking this group for some time now. Most of the information we have on them is from witnesses. Plus, one of our TTG members has had access to Brit Intelligence Corps records. I should know if that couple is a target or not."

Suddenly it became clear that these guys were miles ahead of me in terms of knowing who I was hunting.

He held out the binoculars in my direction. "Look at the fellow who just came out of the front door."

I took the binoculars, put them to my eyes, and aimed them at the front door. A tall man stood just outside it. He had the heart-throbbing good looks of a '30s movie star topped by a curly mop of blond hair.

"That's Gustav Wagner," Feldman said. "An SS staff sergeant and an ex-deputy commander of the Sobibor death camp. A sadistic man that the inmates called 'the Beast.'"

As the man smiled and waved at the occupants of the Horch, I struggled to resolve the man's cruelty with his mama's-boy looks. But then it was just a matter of conjuring up the memories of my investigation into the murderer in Munich. I'd learned about many mama's boys who carried out unspeakable cruelty in the camps.

"I assume he's part of the group you've been tracking," I said.

"Indeed. We believe he's traveling with Franz Stangl, the former commander of Sobibor. What I wouldn't give to get my hands on either of them."

"Why don't you get all your buddies together and storm the place? I'll even help."

"Are you really suggesting that we do that? Just shoot everyone indiscriminately? You're not a fool."

"No, you're right. It just makes my blood boil that those bastards are walking around and might escape justice."

"Our mission is to execute them, not die at the end of ropes," Feldman said and nodded at the inn. "You see what you're up against if you do this alone?"

"I'm not going to get it done as a truck driver in a convoy."

Feldman looked away. "Suit yourself."

I grabbed the backpack out of the rear seat and put my

hand on the door handle. "Good luck with getting those people into Palestine."

Feldman nodded his thanks. I got out of the car and stepped behind the building to remain concealed from the guards diagonally across the street. As I watched Feldman drive away, I had the unexpected feeling of being stranded. I usually preferred working cases on my own or with a partner whom I trust. Even so, I wondered if I might be truly in over my head this time. Following Feldman's plan seemed ludicrous, but this one was going to be a tough nut to crack on my own.

I shrugged off my doubts; I'd been in over my head before and found a way. And this time the only solution seemed to be a direct assault. I laid my backpack on the seat of the Alpha Romeo and pulled out the two pistols. After belting them, I shoved one spare magazine for each in my pockets and moved out.

17

I went to the far end of the strip of shops, snuck up to the front corner, and poked my head out to observe the inn. It was situated on sprawling park-like grounds, which were surrounded by a high brick wall. A row of hedges about eight feet high ran along the wall on the neighbor's side.

The three guards were still at their posts at the front of the building. Boredom and the cold had obviously set in; they appeared less interested in the street than their cigarettes. Still, a frontal assault would be a bad idea, meaning the only option was to scale the wall from the neighboring property.

I stepped out onto the sidewalk. In case one of the guards decided to pay attention to the street, I turned away from the inn and walked in the opposite direction. Once I had gone a block, I crossed the street, entered the adjacent property, and jogged up to the hedge row. Using the tangle of branches, I got within chest range of the top of the wall. I leaned forward, planted my elbows into the cement top, and hoisted myself up to peek over the wall.

The property was dotted with copses of trees, now bare of

leaves, with raised stone flower beds fabricated to form various geometric shapes, and then the whole thing was laced with graveled footpaths. To my left, a paved driveway came from the street and led to a parking lot along the side of the building. There were about two dozen cars parked in the lot, a mix of old and new, expensive and cheap.

Two men strolled along a path on the far end of the property. They talked and smoked pipes as they walked. No lookouts or saber-toothed guard dogs that I was able to see.

I heaved with both arms firmly planted on the top and got my legs up. The wound gave me a jolt of pain, but I ignored it and kicked my legs up and over. I landed on the hard ground and squatted behind a shrub, with my hand on the butt of the Luger. Except for the two strollers, all was clear. The back of the inn was visible through a stand of trees. The rear side of the three-story structure repeated the balcony theme of the front. Ten doors along each floor afforded access to the balconies, so I figured there were about twenty rooms per floor, making a maximum of forty.

On the opposite end of the ground floor there was a glassed-in terrace extending out from the back. The interior lamps had been turned on to counter the dim morning light. Dining tables lined the glass wall, though the few early risers ate breakfast at tables closer to the fire in a stone fireplace.

I kept close to the wall and crept forward. Just to my left, there was a door for what appeared to be a service entrance. It was situated at the near corner and stood open slightly, which I figured was an effort to reduce the heat in the kitchen. An idea came to me.

I stopped at the edge of the parking lot. One row of cars was parked head-in and against the building. Above, lamps had been attached to the inn's wall to illuminate the lot, and the electrical wires feeding them were simply strung along in a series. The lamps were dark, meaning no electricity ran to them.

I stood on the bumper of the second car from the end and yanked the wire leading to the first lamp. That gave me the length I needed. I jumped off the bumper and squatted between the two cars. I wound the hot and neutral wires together and shifted over to the gas filler cap of the last car—a dowdy Mercedes 230. With the cap off, I inserted the wire into the tank until I figured it was touching the gasoline.

After one last check that all was clear, I straightened and moved toward the service entrance. I kept my Luger by my side as I stopped just outside the entrance door. Two people conversed over the noise of a sizzling pan and clacking plates. My stomach quivered, and my mouth watered when the smell of cooking bread hit my nose.

The switch for the parking lot lamps was next to the door. If I switched on the electricity and the gas tank was close to empty, it would likely explode. That would alert everyone too soon. Instead, I hoped the hot wire would ignite the gas, creating a fire that would give me enough time to get situated. I mentally crossed my fingers and flipped the switch. The lamp just above the door came on for a few seconds, then it flickered and went out again.

I let out my breath. No explosion. The electrical short likely blew the fuse, but not before the wire inside the gas tank sparked. I heard a crackle and fizz, like a firecracker dud, then a muffled roar.

I slipped inside. The two cooks were too busy with preparing food to notice me. There were two other doors: a swinging door giving access to the dining room and another that I presumed led toward a service corridor.

With my Luger hand in my pocket, I pulled my fedora down onto my forehead and moved for the second door.

My movement alerted them to my presence.

"What are you doing in here?" the older cook asked.

"Sorry, I just parked my car. I guess I used the wrong door."

The older one grunted and gestured toward the swinging door with a knife in his hand. I ignored him and made a beeline for the door opposite.

"Hey, not that one," the older cook said. "You've got to go through the dining room."

"Sorry," I said again as I pushed through the forbidden door.

It was, indeed, an exit to a long service corridor. The door opened behind me. I glanced behind to see the older cook glaring at me as I marched for another door at the end of the corridor. The younger one said something with urgency in his voice, and the older cook ducked back inside the kitchen.

If the younger cook had noticed the car fire, things would move pretty quickly. I had to get in place before alarms were raised. I exited the corridor and entered a small sitting room. The chairs sat empty, the only sound an ornate clock ticking on the table by a tall window. It said the time was 6:37.

To my left was a narrow staircase for the hotel staff. Beyond that, a door stood open offering a clear view of the lobby. The lobby consisted of a registration area and a bar/lounge at the far end. A broad marble staircase began just outside the sitting room's door. The registration desk faced the front entrance. Two people stood behind it, one woman and one man, both in black and looking more like funeral directors than cheery hosts. A couple sat in the lounge. Otherwise, it was quiet.

A man I didn't recognize stepped off the stairs and entered the lobby. I tucked back behind the door and watched him through the gap between the door and doorjamb. He wore a gray wool suit that looked tailor made. After a few steps, he turned left into what I assumed was a hallway hidden from my sight.

I shifted slightly to have a view of the row of tall windows overlooking the porch. I could see two of the guards standing outside on the porch. I kept an eye on them to see what they would do when word of a fire reached them.

Someone outside near the parking lot shouted, *"Feuer!"*

The two guards stiffened with alarm and dashed for the parking lot.

The third guard came running down the porch and popped his head in the door. "There's a car on fire in the parking lot, and it's spreading fast," he said in German. "Call the fire department and get the guests outside."

The guard went out again and ran in the direction of the parking lot. The woman behind the registration desk picked up the phone and dialed, while the man came racing my way. I tucked behind the door and watched him bolt up the stairs.

Pounding footsteps in the service corridor prompted me to pull the door closed enough to hide. The door to the service corridor burst open, and the two cooks ran across the sitting room and out into the lobby.

The older cook yelled, "Fire in the kitchen!"

"Get anyone in the dining room outside," the receptionist said with alarm in her voice.

I opened the door and shifted my position enough to watch as the two cooks raced down the hallway out of my field of view. Excited voices and rushing footsteps came like a flood down the stairs. Guests from the upper floors, some clothed, some in pajamas and robes, hurried across the lobby for the front doors.

I watched their faces as they passed. I recognized the cherubic mass murderer who Feldman had pointed out, but no one else in that first wave of evacuees. A handful of others from the dining room joined the stream, and among them, I spotted Kappler and one of the other men in the car we avoided when escaping the cabin.

A second wave of people rolled off the stairs. That was when I spotted Kurt, since he was the easiest to pick out among the adults. He held tight to Erika's hand, with two men flanking her, both with a hand clasped around her arms. The two men were partially dressed, though Erika and Kurt were in pajamas and robes. Then I noticed they were shoeless, probably because the men guarding her knew they'd have a tougher time making a run for it over ice and snow. It was a cruel precaution, and one that made my blood turn hot.

18

I'd seen enough. I raced for the service door and dashed down the corridor. The door to the kitchen was open, allowing smoke to roil out and begin to fill the narrow space. I had to lean forward to stay below the black cloud. The closer I got to the kitchen, the more the temperature rose. When I breached the kitchen door, I had to shield my face against the heat. To my left, the main part of the kitchen was engulfed in flames, and if I'd been any later, there would have been no way to exit the service door.

I coughed from the smoke and felt the hairs on my left hand begin to singe. I blew out the back door, coughing and trying to catch my breath. A small crowd of guests stood away from the building in a group and were wide-eyed with shock as they looked at me. With my head low and my hat pulled down on my forehead, I made a sharp turn into the parking lot. The three guards looked helplessly at the now three cars in flames. I covered my face with my hands as I coughed. One of them made a move to help me, but I waved him off and kept running for the front of the inn.

Once I was at the front, I slowed my pace and kept my face covered. There were close to a hundred people gathered along the fence. A few looked my way as I moved toward the street, but most stared at the inn with concern on their faces.

Two firetrucks came racing up and stopped in the middle of the street. They were dated, pre-war models. One had a ladder mounted on top, and both towed tanks of water. The firemen leapt off the bench seats situated on either side and went into action. I circled around behind the trucks, then moved between them and stopped near the rear line of the guests.

The fire had spread to the front sitting room where I had observed the lobby, and smoke came out of the extreme left room on the second floor. Plus, a fourth car had caught fire by this time. It didn't care about the inn, considering the owners knowingly harbored escaping Nazis, but I regretted causing a beautiful Mercedes Roadster to go up in flames.

With everyone's attention fixed on the inn, I surveyed the crowd. I picked out Kappler and the deputy commander of Sobibor. The others were unknown to me, and it was frustrating to think that I must have been within killing range of a number of mass-murdering Nazis. The problem was, I didn't see Erika or Kurt in the crowd.

My worry growing, I quickly scanned the crowd again. There were several women with children, but not Erika or Kurt. The men guarding her must have taken them somewhere away from the crowd in case she tried to call for help. I checked both extremes of the property, then spotted them with the two men who now held them tight to their bodies. There was another man with a long leather coat draped over his pajamas. He had handsome, aging tennis-star looks, with a black mustache and hair slicked back, and stood with a rigid spine. Her husband, perhaps, but I noticed the boy clung to his mother, and the man had neglected to offer Erika or the boy his overcoat, while they shivered in the cold.

I turned away from the inn and the crowd and took quick strides in another circling maneuver, crossing the street, then turning back toward the inn. I skimmed the storefronts to avoid detection. Erika's group stood on the sidewalk in front of the house on the southern side of the inn.

Continuing my fast pace, I got around behind them. With my .45 in my right hand and the sap in my left, I came up on the biggest of the two men holding Erika and struck him in the back of the head with the sap. He staggered forward. Erika sucked in her breath, turned and let out a guttural moan from fear. The elegant man with her spun around, wide-eyed with shock.

The other guard was my main concern. He had good reflexes and immediately went for his gun. I punched him in the neck, then kicked his feet out from under him. I turned back to the first guard and landed several blows to his head with the sap. As he went down, the man, who I assumed was her husband, took several steps back, then spun on his heels and ran for the main group, calling for help.

I grabbed a still-shocked Erika by the wrist and pulled her in the direction of my car.

She yanked her hand away. "What are you doing?"

"I'm getting you and Kurt out of here."

"If I go with you, they'll kill us."

She turned toward the inn and started to go, but I grabbed

her again and started dragging her. She fought and groaned. Kurt clung to his mother and whimpered.

By that time, the presumed husband reached the larger group and alerted some of the men of what was transpiring. Plus, the two guards were recovering quickly.

"Don't be a fool," I said. "They'll kill you as soon as they have what they want. I can get you to safety."

She stopped her struggle and looked into my eyes. I released her and started running for the parking lot and my car. At this point, she'd either follow me or go back to her captors. As I ran, I heard her footsteps right behind me. I slowed and scooped up Kurt into my arms, and we ran as fast as we could for the car.

I heard more than saw several men in pursuit. I was reluctant to use my pistol with Kurt in my hands, but I had to do something to slow them down. I turned as I ran and fired several shots at the group. Kurt covered his ears and screamed. My intention was not to hit one of them but to make them go for cover—which they did by splitting up or going to ground.

None of them returned fire, which I assumed meant Erika was too valuable to risk killing.

We made it to the car. I opened the doors and let them get inside, while I trained my pistol on our pursuers. Several of them had split off. I figured that meant they were trying to flank me while others headed for the parking lot to get their cars.

Someone threw shots at me. A bullet screamed past my head. Another struck the hood of the car. I dived into the car and jammed the ignition key into the switch, but when I turned the key, the engine refused to turn over. It groaned and sputtered.

I cursed at it as I tried the key several times. My frustration rose when I saw three cars exit the inn's parking lot. Two more bullets hit the engine hood. They were trying to disable the car.

From the back seat, Erika began slapping my shoulder. "We have to get out of here."

"I'm trying." I turned the switch and pumped the accelerator. "The engine's cold."

The engine finally started up with a roar just as one of the cars from the inn turned into the parking lot behind me. I gunned the engine and slammed the gear shift. The Alpha jerked forward, and I drove it over the raised flower bed and the curb. Several more bullets impacted the car's hood and around the fender.

I hit the accelerator and raced down the side street. As I turned right and onto a larger road, I glanced in the rearview mirror. The three vehicles from the inn jumped the same curb in pursuit.

"There are three cars coming after us," Erika said with fear in her voice.

"I see that."

"Of all the stupid things to do," Erika yelled. "You endangered my son without any thought of how to safely get away from them."

"It was the only option. I wasn't even sure if you were—" I stopped, not wanting to voice the obvious in front of Kurt. "I wasn't sure how long they'd hold you, or what they might do to you two while in their hands. And if I'd waited for a better opportunity, I could have lost you."

The lead pursuing car was almost on my bumper. One car, I might be able to evade or put out of action. But only the luckiest guy in the world could take on three. I was going south and knew I'd be out of the city in a matter of minutes. The open road would be worse.

Up ahead, the light turned red. I gunned it and blew through the light. Erika cried out in alarm. A car nearly struck us, but hit its brakes at the last minute, fishtailing as it skidded to a stop. The lead car was still right on my tail, but the near accident had held up the other two—at least it would for a few seconds.

A shooter leaned out of the lead car and shot at the tires. It sounded like someone was banging the car with a sledge-hammer as bullets hit the bumper and fender. Erika tried to calm Kurt, who was close to hysterics.

Then the tire blew. The car fishtailed. The metal wheel ground into the pavement and spewed out sparks. At sixty miles per hour, I could no longer control the car. I had to let off of the accelerator. All the while, I quickly ran through my options. None of them were any good. Closer to downright dangerous.

Something huge came hurtling at us out of the corner of my eye. It was just a blur, but I knew it was the grill of a truck towering over us. It headed straight for the side of our car. In that split second of realization, I flashed to another truck that slammed into the car I was driving, killing a person precious to me in Garmisch.

But to my utter surprise, this truck missed us and rammed into the pursuers' car behind. It was as if a giant had crushed the car and tossed it aside. The car rolled over several times before coming to a stop.

I hit the brakes, and the car wobbled to a stop. The traffic ahead had stopped. A couple of people got out of their cars and looked on in shock. Then I remembered the other two cars pursuing us. I grabbed my .45 and charged out of the car, ready to fight or die.

But down the street, another of the pursuers' cars had suffered a same fate: another truck had broadsided that one too, and the third car had turned around and was fleeing in the opposite direction.

I tried to resolve the scene in front of me.

"What is going on?" Erika asked from the open side window.

I shook my head.

The truck had stopped at the point of impact. The driver got out and came around the front. I found it hard to find words ...

It was Feldman. He made sharp gestures for me to hurry and come to him.

"We've got to go," I said as I opened the back door.

"Where are we going?"

"To safety." I pointed at Feldman. "Hurry. Get Kurt and go."

She didn't question me. She helped Kurt out of the back, hoisted him into her arms, and approached the truck. I got my backpack out of the front, and Erika's and Kurt's bags out of the back. I then belted the two pistols and caught up with her.

Feldman opened the passenger's door and yelled to us, "Hurry up. We've got to get out of here before the police arrive."

I helped Erika into the cab and lifted Kurt up to her, then threw the bags in after them. While I did so, Feldman rushed up to the crushed pursuit sedan and, what I thought was odd, leaned into the broken front passenger's window and appeared to take photographs with a small camera. Then I understood what he was doing. Police sirens sounded in the distance. I got in and shut the door just as Feldman climbed behind the steering wheel, jammed the truck into gear, and gassed it.

19

"I thought we had a deal to go our separate ways," I said to Feldman as he raced toward the Adige river.

"You're welcome," he said.

"Okay, yeah, thanks," I said and waved my hands to cut him off. "That's not the point."

"I think it is," Erika said and touched Feldman's arm. "Thank you for helping me and my son."

Feldman looked at me. "That's how you show your gratitude."

I pulled off my overcoat and draped it over Erika and Kurt. I said to Feldman, "The only way you knew where to ambush these guys was if you'd been watching me."

"It's a good thing we were, no? But you forget, we have as much—no, more—interest in those people than you."

"Who are you?" Erika asked.

Feldman looked at me as if warning me not to say too much.

"Who is he?" Erika asked me with growing impatience.

I scratched my head as I tried to come up with an answer. "A colleague."

She turned to Feldman. "British intelligence?"

Feldman glanced at me before saying, "Yes."

"So, neither of you is really interested in me. You've been stalking ex-Nazis, and I'm just an inconvenient byproduct." She glared at me. "And you've been using me to get to them."

"I was just trying to mind my own business until your brother-in-law came along. You saved my life, and I promised to get you and Kurt to safety. That's all there is to it."

"That's not all there is. You two are after someone, and I want to know who and why."

"We are not working together," I said. "I'm here for you and Kurt. If I take down a few Nazis in the process, I'm fine with that. An added bonus."

Erika turned to Feldman. "And who are you after?"

Feldman said nothing as he negotiated several sharp turns to cross the Adige river.

"My name is Arie Feldman, by the way."

"Erika Altmann," she said, and they shook hands.

Kurt's shock must have worn off because he started to cry and hug Erika tighter. Erika tried to comfort him with assuring words and a soft tone. For the sake of the kid, we all fell into silence. Erika opened one of her bags and fished out a spare pair of shoes for both her and Kurt.

Feldman took the same route back to the warehouse complex. I could see his partner in the other truck was close behind.

When we came to a stop at the gate, Feldman said to Erika, "I'm trusting that you won't disclose what you see here or the location."

"That would depend on what you're doing," Erika said.

"It's for good," I said. "He and his colleagues are giving hope to people who had none."

Erika looked at the closed gate for a moment, then said, "I promise."

I nodded to Feldman that she was good for her word. Shimon, the same guard, came up to the driver's window and showed his displeasure at seeing another stranger. He kept his mouth closed and opened the gates to let the two trucks enter the compound.

The activity in the compound was pretty much as before, with couples or small groups circulating in the yard.

Feldman parked the truck so the back was to the warehouse. The second truck did the same. Hazan was behind the wheel of the second vehicle. He didn't miss an opportunity to glare at me before getting out of the cab. Feldman climbed out and stood by the open door with his hand out to help Erika.

Erika stayed where she was and held Kurt just a little tighter. "What is this place? Who are these people?"

"Those people are Jews trying to get out of Europe," I said. "Arie and his colleagues plan to smuggle them to Palestine."

Erika fixed her gaze on the people. "Were they from the concentration camps?" she asked with what I could only describe as awe.

"Some of them. Others came out of hiding after the war, and others were forced out of countries all over Eastern Europe."

"Where are they going?"

"This is their last stop before being taken to a port for embarkation. Naples in this instance."

Erika seemed riveted as she looked on. There was some

deep emotion going on behind her eyes that I couldn't quite resolve.

"Unless you're going with us, it's time to get out of the truck," Feldman said.

Erika snapped out of it when I opened my door and climbed down. I lifted out my backpack and Erika's bags and put them on the ground, then I took Kurt from her arms. He whined and tried to free himself from of my grasp. Erika had to hurry to the ground and take him from me before he lost control.

Feldman came around the truck with Hazan, who scrutinized Erika before turning his attention to me. "I was hoping to never see you again, and now you've brought a Nazi whore with you?" Hazan said with a tone of disgust.

I balled my fists and advanced on him. Feldman stepped in between us and held us both back. His big mouth, his sneering, had raised my hackles, and I wanted to shut him up for good. I knew he'd experienced the horrors of battle and lost so many of his extended family at the hands of the Nazis. I knew he'd suffered and was angry. And I saw a younger version of myself in him. Maybe that was why I wanted to break his jaw so much. It'd be like giving myself a solid wake-up call and get past it.

"One of these days we're going to get into it," I said.

"I think now's a good time," Hazan said and tried to get around Feldman.

Feldman grabbed both of Hazan's arms and pushed him back. That left me open to charge. Which I did until Erika got in front of me while still holding Kurt.

"They may have saved our lives," she said. "Be the bigger

man and let it go. Plus, I've been called worse. And by my own countrymen."

She was right, and I let her stop me without putting up a fight. Hazan ceased struggling with Feldman, and we stared at each other for a few seconds before we all moved toward the warehouse. Hazan said something to Feldman I couldn't hear and quickened his pace to get to the entrance before us. The rest of us were silent on the walk across the lot.

"We need to find you two some coats," I said to Erika.

"I'm sure we have plenty," Feldman said. "They're clean, though definitely not the height of fashion."

"As long as they're warm, we won't mind," Erika said.

Feldman nodded. He entered the warehouse ahead of us. Erika averted her eyes from the people milling around the grounds and slowed the closer we got to the warehouse door. I couldn't tell if it was from shame or empathy.

We stepped through the door and stopped a few paces into the room. The majority of the refugees were busy packing their meager belongings and taking down the tents. The place was abuzz with excitement and cheery conversation. Some of the doctors and nurses still went about caring for twenty or so patients in the medical tent, while a couple of others were boxing supplies. One of the women refugees came up to Erika and Kurt and offered to help them find some coats at an area set aside for Red Cross clothing.

I watched as Erika and Kurt followed the women to several racks of coats, dresses, piles of shoes. They picked out some coats and entered a tent with their bags. I turned my attention to Feldman, who had joined Hazan and four other men, including the guy who declared his dislike for Ameri-

158 | JOHN A. CONNELL

cans, Shimon. They talked heatedly, which I figured had to do with Erika and me.

A few moments later, Erika and Kurt emerged from an area closed off with blankets. They were now dressed in clothes from their packed bags and wore overcoats. With the ill-fitting, oversized coats, dirty faces, and disheveled hair, they both looked like so many displaced persons that I'd seen since the end of the war.

They came over to me. Kurt grinned at his "big boy" overcoat, and Erika self-consciously tried to fix her hair. Feldman joined us and shrugged an apology for their hand-me-down attire.

"Are you planning on moving out soon?" I asked Feldman.

"Yes. This evening. We'll travel at night. Our hope is to get to Rome in two days." He lowered his eyebrows and peered into my eyes. "We still need a third driver."

"I'm grateful to you guys for getting us out of a jam, but driving one of your trucks is not in our plans."

"What is in your plan besides getting to Naples?" Feldman asked.

"Get Frau Altmann and her son south, to safety."

"Which is where, exactly?" Hazan said as he strode up to us.

I realized I hadn't actually asked Erika where she considered a safe place other than southern Italy. I looked at her to prompt an answer.

"I have a friend in Mykonos—"

"Greece?" Hazan said. He looked at me and laughed. "I bet that's further south than you thought."

It definitely wasn't what I'd expected, and it left me at a loss for a response.

"My plan is to get to Brindisi," Erika said. "My friend is waiting for me there." She turned to me. "But if you get me to Naples, I can get to Brindisi. You see? You can drive the truck and get to Naples at the same time. Everyone's happy."

"Not a chance," I said. "A convoy of three British Army trucks is going to attract the wrong kind of attention. We could get stopped by an Italian patrol, or worse. We'll also be easy to track by the men after you. We've got to be stealthy and quick if we're going to make it there undetected. And these guys want to stop in Rome so they can ..." I stopped before revealing Feldman and Hazan's mission of assassination.

"So they can what?" Erika asked.

"We have other business there," Feldman said. "Just leave it at that."

Erika looked between Feldman, Hazan, and me as if trying to deduce the reason. If my expression was anything like Feldman's and Hazan's, then she could tell it was something bad. A tick of unease crossed her face, but she covered it in an instant and looked at me. "Whatever the reason, I want you to drive that truck and get these poor people to Naples."

"I told you why that's a bad idea."

"Can we talk alone?" Erika asked Feldman and Hazan.

With a nod from Feldman, Erika took my arm and led me and Kurt to a quiet spot far enough away from the two Israelis to be out of hearing range. Her expression was firm, though her touch was light. Kurt took a few steps over to an empty tent and looked inside.

"I'm overwhelmed by your concern," Erika said. "I think you've been incredible, and I admire your determination to stick to your promise."

"But?"

"Helping these people is an opportunity to do something good." She looked away as if summoning her courage. She watched Kurt for a moment, then turned back to me. "I did nothing when Hitler was rounding up the Jews. I did nothing when we heard rumors of the death camps. I was a coward and in denial. I opted for my own security and comfort instead of speaking out."

She was voicing everything that made me angry with every German I'd ever encountered. Yet, when I looked into her eyes and listened to her words, I found myself defending her. I wasn't sure why, but I had my suspicions. "You had Kurt to think about. And the Gestapo would have put you in a camp or executed you." I lowered my voice and said, "And no telling what they would have done with Kurt if that had happened."

"That's not good enough. If those who were against Hitler —and there were many of us—had spoken out in the beginning, if we'd opened our eyes to the acts of violence and done something to stop it, maybe things would have been different."

"So you want to risk your life, Kurt's life, to assuage some of that guilt? That's just another form of conceit. The world doesn't revolve around you."

"I don't care what others think. This is for Kurt. When he's old enough to understand, I want to look him in the eyes and tell him his mother tried to do the right thing—at least once in my life." She crossed her arms and furrowed her brows. "You're risking your life for a woman and child who you barely know. Why? I think it comes from the same kind of conceit. For whatever reason, you feel you have to make up for your sins. And driving that truck could go a long way in doing just that. If you refuse, then leave. I can't go with you if you're using Kurt and me as an excuse to turn your back on these people."

Her determined expression meant she wouldn't change her mind. The whole thing felt like a bad idea, but I had to admit that helping those people escape the past horrors of Europe was the right thing to do. And she was right on another count: I was as guilty of conceit as Erika was. My actions wouldn't bring back Hana, the girl I failed to protect in Czechoslovakia, or Adelle in Garmisch-Partenkirchen, or Tazim in Tangier, or Dave Lupin in Chicago, or any of the other victims.

I stepped away from Erika and walked over to Feldman and Hazan. "All right. I'll go, but I take the woman and boy with me. It's that or nothing."

Feldman smiled. "I'm glad. And I have no problem with you taking them along." He looked at Hazan, who signaled that we should walk a little farther away from Erika.

We went twenty paces to an empty part of the warehouse.

Feldman said, "She can't know what else we're planning to do on this trip. Not even a hint. She can't be anywhere near our hunting expeditions. Is that understood?"

I nodded. "That's okay by me." I wasn't about to tell them I had the feeling she already suspected their other purpose. Neither was I going to tell them she might have information on the other Nazis traveling in the same group. I'd keep that as our get-out-of-jail card in case Hazan tried to renege on the deal and get rid of her.

Hazan said, "After Arie's stupid idea to rescue you, the

police are probably on the lookout for the trucks. Meaning we'll have to take back roads."

"It's going to slow our progress, but we hope to arrive near Florence by daybreak," Feldman said. "We'll take the staff car and lead the way."

"Is the car for your hunting expeditions?"

"That's not your concern," Hazan said.

Feldman shot Hazan an impatient glare, and said to me, "With the car, we can go for supplies, scout ahead, split off in case of emergencies," Feldman said.

That made sense, though I figured the main purpose was to give them freedom of movement. "Have you got a list?"

"What do you mean?" Hazan asked.

"I saw you taking photos of the dead men in the cars. Was that to check them off a list of your targets?"

Feldman looked around as if to make sure we weren't being overheard. "We try to take photos to show to our commander.

"Proof of death," Hazan said.

"How are you going to hunt while simultaneously leading a convoy of refugees?" I asked.

"That's none of your concern either," Hazan said.

"It is if I'm going to be a part of this enterprise. I want to know we all can rely on you two not abandoning the convoy or doing something that gets us deeper in hot water than we already are."

Hazan took one big stride to get in my face. "You just do your job."

Feldman stepped in between us. "We have a long night ahead of us, so I suggest we all get something to eat and some rest. Okay?"

"Just keep me in the loop," I said. "If we're delayed or up to our necks in police, I reserve the right to bail."

I walked off and joined Erika and Kurt, who were sitting on a blanket laid out on the floor. Kurt was already asleep with his head next to her thigh. She stared in the distance as she stroked his hair. I got on the floor next to Erika.

"I take it you agreed to drive one of the trucks," Erika said.

I nodded.

She put a hand on my knee and said, "Thank you."

"It's still a bad idea. And if we have too many delays or run into trouble, we're bailing."

She gave me a quick smile as if appeasing me and had no intention of listening. She got to her feet and said, "I'll get us something to eat. Would you stay with Kurt?"

I nodded again and slid over to be closer to the boy. He stirred and put his head against my thigh. It was a simple act, but it felt good to think I was his protector and comforter. And it made me want to protect this boy, save him from a cold and cruel father. I would do whatever it took to make sure that happened.

20

I was dreaming of wandering in a black void when a sharp jolt to my foot woke me. I jerked up to a seated position and instinctively grabbed for my sidearm—which wasn't there. It took a moment for the fog to clear before realizing I was still in the warehouse, though the light had dimmed and lamps had come on. Then I noticed Erika standing over me with a tray in her hands.

She lowered the tray to me. I took it, and she sat next to me. Kurt was still asleep and nestled up against my leg. We'd all taken a long nap while waiting for nightfall.

Most of the refugees had finished packing and taken down the tents, and were now in two chow lines or putting the final touches on their bundles for the trip south.

Erika took one of the sandwiches and a bowl of soup off the tray and set them aside. "I'll let Kurt rest until the last moment," she said. I nodded, and she helped herself to some food. "Kurt has really taken to you."

"And I to him," I said and drank the soup from the bowl.

"I think you'd make a good father."

"The idea scares me. I never knew my real father, but my stepdad was a cruel bastard. And my grandfather on my mother's side had a heart made of stone. My mother was loving but drunk most of the time. I wonder how much of that has rubbed off on me."

"And your grandmother?"

"Tough exterior but a softy on the inside. She's the one who really raised me, and even when she kicked my ass, I knew, deep down, there was always love there. She's one of the finest women I've ever known."

She squinted at me and gave me a faint smile. "I can see your grandmother's same faults and qualities in you. There's hope for you."

Kurt groaned and his body twitched as he slept.

"His bad dreams, are they a new thing?" I asked.

"They're not new, but more frequent and more intense. This has all been so hard on him. He acts like he knows what's going on, but he doesn't really understand why we had to leave home, why his father is so terrible, or why people are shooting at us."

"What happened when they grabbed you in Brixen?"

"About fifteen minutes after you left, I heard a key in the lock. They'd locked us inside. I pounded on the door and yelled at them. They ignored me, and Kurt became hysterical. There was nothing much I could do. The door was too thick and the window too high. Forty minutes later, I heard several gunshots, then several men burst in and dragged us to their car. My husband didn't even have the courage to come with them or see that Kurt would be treated gently."

"I missed you by about thirty minutes."

She looked away for a moment. "I'd started to think you weren't coming back."

"Was your husband at Tante Anna's?"

She nodded. "He was the one who ran when you attacked the guards."

"Who else was there?" I asked.

She put her head in her hands as if suddenly exhausted. "Dr. Fleischman."

"The doctor who treated me at the cabin?"

She nodded. "He turned on me when they offered him money. Then I learned that he was involved with the Aktion T4 program, euthanizing the mentally ill and children. When that program was shut down, he went on to help with the first experiments in gassing the Jews. My skin crawls thinking about how I shared a car with him, that I befriended him."

"Who else was there?"

"Why do you need to know? Are you looking for targets?"

"I need to know who we're up against."

"It was the middle of the night, and we were taken directly to my husband and locked up until you started the fire."

"How about when you were evacuated for the fire? Did you see anyone out in the yard?"

"Gustav Wagner and Franz Stangl. I wasn't sure, but I think I saw Rudolf Lange."

"It's a pity I didn't do a better job burning the place down," I said more to myself than to her. But then I saw the look of shock on her face. "That's not what I meant."

"Then don't say things like that. That would have been murder many times over. They're monsters, but they deserve their day in court. Otherwise, you'd be no different from them."

"Did you overhear any of their plans? Like who's going and when? Who's in charge?"

"There's no one giving out orders, though with so many megalomaniacs, there have been clashes. Kappler is managing everything. Trying to manage."

"Because he has the Vatican behind him?"

She nodded. "But I got the impression that he's barely keeping them together. There seem to be two factions traveling in tandem, though with separate agendas."

Feldman, Hazan, and four others in their group started circulating among the crowds, speaking to the people and pointing at the door. Feldman then came over to me with two of his companions.

"It's time," Feldman said to me.

I got up, while Erika turned her attention to Kurt. Feldman pointed to two of the men and introduced them as Aaron and Moishe, the other two drivers. Both were young. Aaron was short and thin, wore a sparse beard and glasses, and flashed a big smile. Moishe towered over Aaron and me. He had red hair and what seemed to be a permanent look of boredom or indifference. He looked over my shoulder when he shook my hand with an iron grip.

The refugees had formed an orderly line and filed out the door. It took only a few minutes to get everyone outside. Hazan, Feldman, and the two other drivers grabbed up several equipment bags and headed for the door. I went over to Erika. She corralled Kurt and joined me, and we fell in behind the others. Feldman yelled out something in Yiddish to the doctors and nurses in the tent and waved good-bye.

Outside, the passengers had split up into thirds, with each group climbing into the backs of the trucks. Aaron and

Moishe joined three other men and helped the women and children get into the back of the trucks. Once everyone was loaded, three of the men each chose a truck and stood at the back, waiting for orders to move. Feldman and Hazan spoke to the fourth man. They shook hands and patted shoulders.

Feldman walked Erika and me over to the back of the third truck and held out his hand to the waiting man. "This is Henri. He'll be riding with the passengers in your truck. If there's a problem, he'll be the one to let you know."

Henri shook our hands. He had blond hair cut to the scalp and an elongated face that stretched even more with his big grin as he said, "*Enchantez*" to Erika and me, then "Pleased to meet you," in French-accented English. He ruffled Kurt's hair, then jumped in the back. I closed the gate, and Henri pulled down the top flaps.

Feldman pointed to Shimon. "He'll be riding in the back of Moishe's truck. He's the old man of the outfit—almost forty. He's from Poland and our newest member."

Shimon walked over with his hand out. I got a better look at him this time. He had dark, curly hair, with cow eyes and chiseled features. He barely looked at me when we shook hands. His attention was more on Erika, and he flashed her a big, flirtatious smile even as he walked back to his truck and climbed in the back. I arched an eyebrow at Erika, who dismissed me by clicking her tongue.

"Are you going to have a problem with an American driving one of your trucks?" I asked Shimon.

"If it was up to me, you wouldn't be here. Americans are spoiled and rich."

That elicited a burst of laughter from me.

"Enough of that, Shimon," Feldman said. "Get back to your truck."

Shimon complied, and Feldman turned to me. "You have to excuse him. The Nazis took everything away from him. His family was wealthy before the war, but now all he has left is the coat on his back."

"I don't have a problem with him," I said.

"If we get separated, just keep heading for Rome. We'll find you."

I collected my backpack, walked up to the back lip of the cargo area, and checked to see if the passengers were all settled in. These people were now my responsibility, their lives in my hands. They smiled and nodded and looked content to be finally on the road despite the discomfort of being crammed in the back of a cold and dark space. I smiled back at them, patted Henri on the arm, then walked around to the driver's side of the cab and threw the pack in. Erika helped Kurt into the passenger's side and climbed in next to him. I situated the backpack between me and Kurt, and their bags on the floorboard under Erika's feet.

I pointed to her oxford shoes and said, "We'll try to pick up some warmer ones for you on the way."

Erika nodded, but Kurt was only interested in trying to get a better view out the windshield.

"Are you ready for a road trip?" I asked Kurt.

"Yay!" was all he said, and he started to jump on the seat.

The February sun was already setting behind the mountains by the time I started up the engine. I pulled out behind the other two trucks driven by Aaron and Moishe, with Hazan and Feldman riding in a British Humber Super Snipe staff car painted olive drab—all very official looking. It amazed me how fast Kurt had recovered from the earlier trauma; he cheered when we hit the road and began the descent into the valley.

Erika was as reserved as I was, and I was sure she shared the same notion.

It was going to be a long and perilous journey.

I strained to see past the snow swirling in the headlight beams. The windshield wipers struggled to keep up with the accumulation of snow on the glass, which didn't make navigating the narrow, twisting road any easier. Feldman had said we'd be taking back roads, but I hadn't expected we'd be driving on cow paths that hugged the mountain slopes five hundred feet above the valley floor—at least they seemed like cow paths to me. Even though they were paved and connected villages, the potholes outnumbered the flat spots, and the snow erased any visual signs differentiating road from field, or worse, the road from the drop-off on the left side.

Kurt stood on the seat, while Erika held him steady. "I don't want the snow anymore," Kurt said.

"Me neither," I said.

"And I don't want the cold."

"You and me both. Things should be warmer when we get further south."

"How long is that?"

"At this rate, a couple of days."

"Is my dad going to be there when we get to the south?"

"Do you miss him, *mein Schatz*?" Erika asked him.

He shook his head. "He's mean. Mason can be my new daddy."

He said it so matter-of-factly that it made me chuckle.

"Mason has a girlfriend," Erika said.

The truck ahead of me jolted, and the brake lights came on as the tail end spun off the road and came to a halt. I braced Kurt with my right hand and slammed on the brakes. The people in back cried out, and several hit the back of the cab. I had to steer left and right to keep from fishtailing. Our truck slid forward and came to a stop a few yards from the rear of the other truck.

"Everyone okay?" I asked and checked Erika and Kurt.

Erika nodded as she clung to Kurt.

Aaron was driving the truck ahead of mine, and he tried to nudge it forward, but the right back tire just spun in deep mud. The truck would inch forward then settle back into the same position. He was stuck.

Aaron got out of his cab, and I did the same. I went to the back of my truck and met Henri, who had jumped down.

"Everyone okay back here?" I asked.

He nodded. "Maybe some bruises, but no one's hurt."

He instructed everyone to stay in the truck and followed me to the front. Aaron's truck sat leaning to the right with the right back tire sunk deep in mud. We joined Aaron and Shimon, who were checking on his passengers.

Aaron turned and said to us, "I hit that last pothole so hard that it almost yanked the steering wheel out of my hands. Then I hit a patch of ice, and the rear wheels lost traction."

"At least you didn't spin out the other way," I said, pointing to the drop-off.

Aaron glanced at the edge of the drop-off and took a deep breath.

After inspecting the right rear wheel, Shimon said, "We should be able to push it back on the road, but everyone is going to have to get out."

Aaron and Shimon started calling for the passengers to come off the truck and helping everyone to the ground. Henri pitched in, while I walked over to my truck and met Erika as she climbed down from the cab.

"Our first big delay," I said.

"Where are we?"

"We passed a sign for Trento not long ago."

I walked to the other side of the road. Erika followed me, and we looked out past the tree line. The valley floor appeared as a black chasm, and mountains on the other side were shades of charcoal gray outlined by the stormy sky. Beyond the snow and mist, there were lights of a decent-sized town visible far below us.

I scanned the valley for some indication of our position, and that was when I noticed the headlights of two vehicles that had stopped on the road where it bent back around a portion of the mountain that jutted out toward the center of the valley.

I motioned for Erika to look in the same direction.

"Do you think they're following us?" Erika asked.

"I'm sure of it. They're keeping their distance. There are too many of us to handle."

"Like wolves waiting for one of us to fall behind."

"And we take up the rear. If it's anyone, we'll be the ones to stray from the herd."

A car engine racing toward us from the opposite direction got our attention. It was the staff car weaving around the disabled truck and coming to a halt. Feldman and Hazan got out and spoke to Aaron. We met them by the car.

Feldman said, "Moishe didn't even notice you guys had fallen behind until we were a couple of miles ahead."

"At this rate, we're not going to make it to Florence by daybreak," I said.

Feldman nodded. "We have an alternative stopping point if that's the case. In the meantime, we push."

Aaron had enlisted the help of a dozen of the men from the passengers to help push. A couple of others took some planks from a wooden fence and jammed them under the right wheel. Aaron got behind the wheel, while I joined Feldman, Hazan, Shimon, Henri, and the rest of the men and got ready to push.

Aaron revved the engine and tried to nudge the truck forward. It took several tries, but the wheel finally climbed out of the hole, and the truck was able to get back onto the road. The passengers cheered and began to climb into the back.

Erika and I followed Feldman and Hazan back to their car. I pointed out the two cars still stationary at the bend in the road. "They must have picked us up not far from Meran."

"There's nothing we can do about them now," Hazan said. "We'll take care of them once we get out of the mountains."

"We're in the rear, so tell Moishe to keep an eye out for us so we don't get separated."

"You just keep up, and there won't be any problems," Hazan said as he got into the staff car.

Feldman shrugged as an apology and got in the passenger's seat. The two turned the car around and headed for the front of the convoy. I glanced back at the cars waiting for us before walking back to our truck.

I doubted the wolves would wait until we got out of the mountains to make a move. The question was when.

I RUBBED the tiredness from my eyes, then glanced at my watch: 4:40 a.m. We still weren't out of the mountains, though the road had descended to around a hundred feet above the valley floor. The prospect of getting into the flatlands would have raised my spirits, but we were proceeding even slower than before because the wind and snow had picked up in intensity, taking the visibility down to yards. The only way I knew we were still with the convoy was the faint red taillights of the truck in front of me.

Erika remained awake despite the tedious journey, either to make sure I didn't fall asleep or from fear of knowing the wolves were stalking us. Kurt slept through the bumps and jerks of the truck on the rough roads with his head on Erika's lap. She stroked his hair and sang a German lullaby. Her voice, though just above a whisper, was soothing, which might have put me to sleep if it weren't for the idea of crashing or getting lost.

"The sun will be up in about three hours," I said. "We should press on even in daylight."

"Won't that be too much of a risk? I noticed the towns and signs are all in Italian. We must be out of South Tyrol."

"Yeah, it's a little risky. But at this rate, it could take us another three days to get to Naples."

"If the Italian police or British Army become interested in us, the chances are we won't get there at all."

"At least we're almost out of the mountains," I said in hopes of calming her fears. "Things will be smoother after that."

One minute the snow seemed to be slowing, then we ran right into a heavy curtain of it. The road disappeared. The headlights revealed nothing but snowflakes swirling in the wind. Visibility was now down to feet.

Red taillights came out of nowhere. I hit the brakes and almost ran into the back of Aaron's truck. He had obviously slowed to a crawl because of the blizzard. I backed off on our speed, then Aaron's truck seemed to be swallowed up by the snow again.

I rubbed my eyes again and strained to see the road ahead.

Someone pounded on the wall between the cab and the cargo space. At first, I thought it might be that someone had fallen against the wall, or maybe they had had enough of the rough bone-chilling ride and were taking it out on the truck.

The pounding erupted, more frantically this time.

"We have to stop," Erika said.

I flashed my high beams at the truck ahead and honked the horn several times as I slowed and eased the truck off the road. With one more flash and honk, I shut off the engine. Kurt woke up and fired worried questions at his mother. I secured my overcoat and opened the door.

A blast of frigid air hit me as I climbed down. Henri was already on the ground when I came around.

"We have a man who's suffering from a heart attack," he said. "Elazar Berg, a rabbi."

"How bad is he?"

"There's a doctor among the passengers, and he says that if the man doesn't get to a hospital, he'll die. We also have a pregnant woman who's not doing well."

I glanced at the road ahead—or what little I could see of it —hoping the others had realized we'd stopped and someone was coming back to help. There was nothing but snow and darkness.

"We can't go any faster in this storm," I said. "I'm afraid they'll just have to hang on."

Erika joined me and asked what was going on. I let Henri fill her in while I glanced at the road once again. In this blizzard, there was no telling when Aaron would notice we were no longer behind him. He'd then have to get the attention of Moishe, and so on. I mentally kicked myself for not asking about where the alternative rendezvous point would be in case of an emergency. More than likely we were on our own for hours.

That idea prompted me to glance back the way we'd come. The snow was too dense, the night too dark, to see if our trackers had stopped behind us. Then my stomach constricted. A pair of headlights appeared in the darkness, and it looked like they were getting closer.

"Erika," I said, interrupting her and Henri, "get back to the truck and hide. Henri, get in the back. We might have to get out of here in a hurry."

Erika followed my gaze and sucked in her breath. I led her

by the shoulders back to the cab. She went around to the passenger's side and got in, while I opened the driver's door, stood on the step and rifled through my bag. Erika coaxed Kurt to get on the floorboard. I found my .45, jumped down, and closed the door.

I readied my pistol, went to the front of the truck, and got behind the left fender to use it as a shield.

Then I waited.

22

The car continued to creep forward. It was about fifty yards away when I could make out the hood and windshield. The occupants were still invisible, but I could see enough of the side of the car to know that no one was hanging out the window with their gun aiming in my direction.

The Opel sedan rolled past the tail end of the truck without pausing, then slowed even further when it came up to the cab. The driver must have spotted me behind the high fender and stopped.

I refrained from aiming my pistol, but my finger was poised near the trigger. Every muscle tensed when the window rolled down. I was surprised to see an attractive blonde in her early thirties sitting in the passenger's seat, while the driver was only visible from the waist down. There were two passengers in the back seat, but the reflections off the rear windows obscured my view.

The woman spoke Italian—at least I assumed it was Italian.

When I shook my head, she said in German, "Is everything okay? Can we help?"

"We're fine."

"We've been following you because we were afraid to try to pass you in this terrible weather."

The appearance of a woman and her speaking Italian had thrown me, but I wasn't about to let my guard down. I simply nodded that I'd heard and understood.

"Are you sure we can't offer any assistance?"

The men in the back seat said something I couldn't hear to the woman. They looked like they were going for their door handles.

I raised my pistol with more intent. "I said we're fine."

"Well, good luck," she said.

She rolled the window up, while the rest of the passengers stared at me. The driver put the car in gear and drove off at a crawl. The rear passenger on the right side turned his head at the last minute to glance at me and the truck. I didn't recognize him, but he certainly looked more like a hostile observer than a casual traveler. And I could tell by the way he looked at me that he knew who I was and that he wanted nothing more than to have a piece of me. I made sure he saw me ease the hammer to its resting position.

It wasn't until the car was long out of sight that I returned to the cab and opened the door. "All clear."

Erika rose from a lying position. She checked on Kurt, who appeared to be in a deep sleep on the floorboard of the truck. She freed her legs from Kurt's body and climbed down. She went around the front and met me as I closed the door as quietly as I could.

She had her arms wrapped around her torso. "I recognized

the woman's voice. It was Greta Schweiger. She's Franz Stangl's mistress and a viper if there ever was one."

I glanced at the road ahead. "Could be they're going ahead of us to set up an ambush." I looked in the opposite direction. "And their friends will stay back to attack from the rear."

Henri came up to us. "Did you ask if those people could help us get Elazar to a hospital?"

"They're part of the wolf pack that's been following us."

"Wolf pack?"

"We're being stalked."

All our heads turned to lights moving toward us from the road ahead.

"Get back inside," I said to Erika.

She answered by getting the Luger out of her overcoat and taking a position at the rear fender.

"Have you got a gun?" I asked Henri.

"In my bag in back," he said, though he stayed where he was and concentrated on the road.

"Then go get it," I said to him.

He hurried toward the back just as the sound of the engine became audible over the blasts of wind. I ducked behind the truck next to Erika and waited. Henri joined us a moment later. Then Feldman and Hazan's staff car came out of the shadows. Erika, Henri, and I stepped out to meet them.

Hazan jumped out of the car and marched up to me. "Damnit, what's the problem now? We can't afford to keep stopping like this."

I stared him down and said, "Got a passenger who's having a heart attack. Also a pregnant woman who's pretty sick."

Feldman came up to us and wedged himself between Hazan and me again.

"It's Rabbi Berg. He's in bad shape," Henri said. "And Rachel Baumann is sick. The doctor thinks it could be severe dehydration. Maybe worse."

Feldman and Henri stepped over to the back of the truck, looked inside, and conversed with the doctor. Erika got into the cab to be with Kurt, while Hazan stayed with me.

"Did an Opel pass you going south on the way here?" I asked.

"Yes, about halfway. I take it they weren't simple travelers."

"That Opel and another car have been shadowing us for miles. My guess is, the Opel's occupants wanted to scope out an ambush. Maybe use the pretense of helping us to get the draw on us. Erika was hiding in the cab but heard the woman who talked to me. Stangl's mistress."

That seemed to take Hazan by surprise.

"He on your list?" I asked him.

Hazan nodded. "But I didn't think he was part of the group in Meran." He thought a moment. "I hope he and the others try something. It'd be nice to get a crack at that bastard. He was the commandant of the Sobibor and Treblinka death camps."

"They won't attack us as a group," I said. "They're waiting for a stray. My bet is the only reason they didn't go after us this time was that the storm would make it too difficult."

Feldman called for Hazan, and the two of us walked over to the back of the truck. Feldman and Henri were trying to lift the limp body of the rabbi out of the truck. Hazan gave them a hand while I helped the doctor get the pregnant woman down to the ground.

The five of us got the rabbi into the back seat of the staff car and helped the pregnant woman into the front.

"We'll be at a DP camp near a town called Dolcé about twenty-five miles south of Rovereto," Feldman said to me. "It's run by a United Nations group and has a clinic with some good doctors."

"If the rabbi survives the trip," Henri said, visibly upset.

Feldman put a hand on Henri's shoulder. "We'll do the best we can." He said to me, "Henri knows where the camp is. Aaron and Moishe do too. They're about two miles up the road. They'll be waiting for you. Good luck."

Hazan was already behind the wheel, and when Feldman got in beside the pregnant woman, Hazan made a three-point turn and raced south.

Henri said to me, "If we get separated again, just follow the signs for Rovereto. That should be in about an hour. Less if this storm eases up. Once you get south of the town, I'll come up front to direct you to the camp. In the meantime, I'll be in the back to comfort the passengers. The rabbi means a lot to everyone."

He and the doctor got into the back, and I hoisted myself into the cab and got behind the wheel. Erika stared out the windshield and cradled the Luger in her lap.

"We're going to a DP camp," I said in hopes of easing her worries. "Not too far. We can all get some rest and food."

"What if they're waiting for us between here and the camp?"

"Then we'll deal with them," I told her with false confidence.

23

The storm had passed by the time the DP camp was in sight. The skies were clear of clouds, and the mountains to the east were silhouetted in orange with the moon setting behind the ridge to the west. We'd come down out of the mountains onto the flat terrain of the valley. While seeing the camp in the distance raised my spirits, the blizzard and the constant threat of an ambush had sapped my mind and body.

The United Nations Relief and Rehabilitation Administration DP Camp #23 was south of the small town of Dolcé. The organization ran camps for DPs, or displaced persons, of every background and from every country devastated by the Nazis, though it served mostly the needs of the countless Jewish DPs coming from all over war-torn Europe.

Moishe was still in the lead truck, with Aaron next, and me taking up the rear. I was surprised our pursuers hadn't taken advantage of the twisting roads and blinding snow to carry out an attack, but I was sure they hadn't given up. They were dogging us and just waiting for us to be at our most vulnerable.

Erika had slumped to the seat a while ago and fallen asleep. The stress and wakeful vigilance had sapped her, and I decided to not wake her or Kurt with the news of our arrival.

From my distance of five hundred yards, the camp looked eerily like a prison camp, with bright lights around the high fence that delineated the sprawling grounds. That conjured up some nightmarish memories of the time I spent in several camps, including a stint in the Buchenwald satellite camp of Berga. Adding to this illusion was the array of single-story buildings in regular rows within the fence line.

But as we got closer, the differences became obvious: the gates for this camp were wide open with an arched sign across the top declaring it a UNRRA facility with "Welcome" across the bottom, and the whole thing was decorated with wreaths and pine garlands. There were no train tracks leading up to the entrance, and despite the early hour, a handful of kids played in the snow while their mothers looked on.

As we came up to the gates, my stomach churned at the sight of two Italian policemen guarding the entrance. There was probably another squad of police for security, mostly to guard against unauthorized intruders. I hoped that was all they were interested in as I drove past the guards at the gate.

I followed the other trucks around the compound of buildings and into a dirt parking lot on the north side of the camp. Passengers were already getting out of the two other trucks when I pulled up and shut off the engine.

Erika stirred, sat up, and rubbed her eyes.

"We're here," I said.

"Thank God. Sorry I fell asleep."

"You needed the rest."

"You do too."

"I'm used to pulling all-nighters."

She touched my arm as a thanks and urged Kurt awake. I climbed out of the cab and went around to the back.

Henri was helping the passengers to the ground. Every couple of moments he said, "There's a cafeteria around front. There's also an infirmary if anyone is sick or needs medical assistance."

I pitched in helping people get down. Most of them had a hard time moving from being crammed in the back and in the cold for so long. Everyone looked pale, and some could barely stand. The odor of an open sewer emanated from the interior.

"We ran out of water and food a while ago," Henri said.

We got the rest of the people out of the back. The other two trucks had already discharged their passengers, and everyone was making the slow trek to the camp's central courtyard to seek out the canteen. I walked around to the passenger's side and opened the cab door. Kurt ambushed me by jumping out of the cab. Fortunately, my instincts were more awake than my brain, and I caught him.

I said, "Whoa, for a minute there, I thought you were a leopard."

I moved to put him down, but he clung to me. I straightened and hoisted him onto my hip.

"Are we there yet?" Kurt asked me.

"No," Erika said, smiling and pretending to pinch his leg. "You asked me that two minutes ago, silly."

"We're somewhere," I said. "And that's a big deal since they have food. I bet you're hungry."

Kurt nodded as we rounded the side of the compound and

entered the courtyard. At that same moment, I saw Feldman and Hazan in their car, driving toward the front gate. I put Kurt down and said to Erika, "Get some food. I'll be back in a moment."

Hazan was behind the wheel and driving slowly to avoid the crowd of people streaming for the courtyard. I broke into a sprint, ran in front of the car and waved my arms to make them stop. I had a flash of doubt about the wisdom of doing this, as Hazan was driving but, fortunately, he stopped the car.

I marched around to the driver's side, and Hazan rolled down the window. I grabbed onto the door and bent low to look at them.

"I should have run you over," Hazan said.

"Where are you going?"

"We have some business to attend to in a town on the other side of the river."

"There are plenty of towns on this side of the river to get supplies—" I stopped. "This business wouldn't have anything to do with a Nazi would it? Someone on your list?"

I looked between Hazan and Feldman. Hazan betrayed nothing in his expression, but Feldman looked like he wanted to tell the truth.

"That's none of your business," Hazan said.

"Your first responsibility is getting these people to Naples."

"Says the man who didn't care about that until the lady forced you."

"The people need to eat and rest before we start up again," Feldman said.

"We've already lost way too much time," I said. "We have to get back on the road."

"We'll be back in time."

"Tracking a man down and doing what you want to do to him takes time. And more often than not, things get complicated. Things go wrong."

Feldman opened his mouth to speak, but Hazan hit the accelerator, ripping my hands off the car door. The car raced for the gate, and the tires squealed as Hazan turned too fast onto the highway.

As I watched the car disappear around a curve, another car drove past the guards at the gate without being checked. In fact, the guards seemed more interested in chatting over cigarettes than controlling access to the camp. I didn't recognize the car's occupants, but that wasn't much of a comfort considering we'd been dogged by at least two cars most of the journey.

They had to be out there, somewhere.

I turned on my heels and marched toward the courtyard. Feldman or Hazan must have advised the camp administrators we were coming, because they'd set up an overflow tent to feed the influx of people. Erika and Kurt were still near the back of the line waiting to be served when I walked up to them.

Kurt was bouncing around and ignoring Erika's attempts to control him. She smiled at me as I approached, though her expression turned serious when she looked into my eyes.

"Where were Feldman and Hazan going?" she asked.

"They wouldn't tell me, but I don't expect them back for a while."

"Their other mission?"

I heard the bitterness in her tone, but I was too busy watching for suspicious characters or signs of danger.

"What's wrong?" she asked.

"Nothing concrete. I saw that the guards at the gate aren't doing much in the way of security."

Erika's face turned pale. "Those two cars."

I nodded. "Come with me."

"We're going to do something, darling," she said to Kurt and tried to pull him out of line, but he resisted.

"But I'm hungry."

I squatted and took Kurt by his arms. "I'll get the food, okay? But I want you and your mom to go find a place to rest." I leaned in and talked out of the corner of my mouth, as if conspiring. "All these people ahead of us are going to get all the best places to sit down to eat."

He sighed but took his mother's hand and let her lead him away from the line. I took them back around to our truck, where I climbed into the cab enough to open my backpack and get out my .45 and the Luger. I stuffed the .45 in my belt and jumped back down. I slipped the Luger into Erika's coat pocket. She nodded and put her hand into her pocket where I'd left the gun.

"Find someplace safe while I look around and get some food," I said.

"Henri and Shimon told me building number three is a community center. It's about halfway up the courtyard on the left. I'll wait for you there."

I touched her arm. "Don't worry, okay? I just want to be cautious."

She nodded and coaxed Kurt to go with her toward the courtyard. I scanned the surroundings. The parking lot was just a leveled area of dirt and gravel and was about half full with vehicles: our three trucks and two others with hard shells; a handful of sedans; then a van and four squads cars

WHERE THE WICKED TREAD | 193

belonging to the Italian police. The sedan I'd seen enter was empty, though it had official-looking documents inside.

Beyond the lot was an open field a hundred yards wide that butted up to the perimeter fence. Goal posts at either end had been erected on the lot for a soccer field, and two basketball hoops stood at the edge of the lot. The early hour and bitter cold explained why they were empty at the moment. All looked quiet, and I headed for the courtyard and the south end of the camp.

There were two rows of single-story buildings forming the courtyard, with an administrative building at the far end capping off the rectangular space. The buildings were all the same, probably constructed that way simply to save money, and were intended only for temporary use—how temporary was anybody's guess. I was sure some of the "residents" had been there for a year or more. I figured there were another four hundred people in addition to our passengers.

On the other side were four other outbuildings for showers and toilets, with a larger structure beyond those, which served as the hospital. There was some foot traffic to and from the toilets and showers and the hospital. Everything seemed as it should be, making me feel comfortable enough to get in the food line in the central courtyard. There were maybe thirty people in front of me, and the line moved at a snail's pace. Just standing there allowed the fatigue to creep in along with the cold that started in my feet and slowly moved up my legs. No food and no sleep were taking their toll, and I knew I'd have to get some rest if I wanted to stay awake for the rest of the trip.

I was counting on Erika to find a safe spot so I could close my eyes for a couple of hours before we had to head out again. I glanced at building three up near the administrative building, my mind subconsciously plotting my course before it went into autopilot.

An electrical shock blasted through me. Two men were pulling Erika along toward the back of the administrative building. One appeared to have a pistol trained on her concealed under his coat, while a third man had Kurt planted against his chest, his hand wrapped around the boy's mouth.

I took off running up the courtyard, hoping to encounter one or more of the Italian police to give me assistance, but I didn't see any of them. The three men with Erika and Kurt disappeared around the back of the building.

As I got close to the administrative building, I ran through my possible actions. Taking on three armed men, with two ready to shoot down Erika and Kurt, would take some finesse and a lot of luck.

I reached the side of the administrative building and pulled out my pistol. I raised the gun into the air and fired twice. The firing sounded like a cannon in the cold stillness. I heard people screaming behind me, and heavy footsteps and yelling coming from inside the building. Maybe now I'd gotten the attention of the right people.

I made it to the back and saw the group halfway across an open field. Two cars were waiting for them on a dirt road outside the fence, where a hole had been cut for their escape.

The booming of my pistol had also alerted the abductors. One man took a shooting stance, while the other two walked backward with the barrels of their pistols against Erika's and Kurt's heads. Two other people waited outside the fence, with their guns drawn. One of them was the woman who'd questioned me from the car. Seeing the other one sent shock waves through me.

It was Ziegler!

I brought down my pistol, then stopped when I saw Kappler holding his gun to Kurt's head.

"Put your gun down or I shoot the boy," Kappler said.

Three guns were pointed my way. With Erika and Kurt in danger, I had little choice. The only thing I could do was stall for time. I kept ahold of my pistol, though I pointed it at the sky.

The abductors made slow progress toward the hole in the fence. It wasn't easy walking backward uphill and on rough terrain while holding their hostages.

"Put it down," Kappler yelled with a hint of desperation in his voice.

I slowly lowered my gun, but at that moment all eyes shifted to the building behind me. I heard running footsteps, then yelling in Italian. By the sound of their voices, the policemen had stopped just a couple of yards behind me.

Erika shoved her captor's gun arm up, over her head. The gun went off. She grabbed his arm and twisted it while kicking his legs out from under him.

Then hell broke loose behind me: the nervous police opened fire. Erika dropped to the ground but managed to wrench the pistol out of her captor's hand. She released him, and he made a dash for the cars. One of the cops hit him in the shoulder, but he kept running and finally got to the cars. Erika pointed her gun at Kappler and yelled something I couldn't hear over the gunfire.

I ignored the bullets screaming past my head, as I shot at Ziegler. I could only watch in fury as he dived into the car.

Then I realized I'd better duck before one of the Italian cops hit me.

The man in the shooting stance returned fire, and one of the Italian cops cried out in pain.

I took careful aim and fired three times, hitting the shooter in the chest.

In a panic, Kappler released the boy and raced back toward the cars. Despite the rounds flying everywhere, Erika tackled Kurt and covered him with her body.

I didn't have a clean shot at Kappler, and the last thing I wanted was to shoot a man in the back in front of the cops. However, Erika had him in the clear, and though she kept her aim on him, she didn't fire. Whatever her reasoning, I was glad she refrained from gunning him down.

The Italian police, however, continued to fire, and their bullets impacted the cars.

I turned and waved my arms for them to stop; Kurt and Erika were still between the cops and the getaway cars. But they kept on shooting, even reloading and firing again.

The would-be abductors dived into the cars under a hail of bullets and drove off.

The man who had taken a shooting stance lay still on the ground. The police stopped firing, and I ran for Erika and Kurt. Both of them were crying when I got there. I dropped to my knees and put my arms around them.

"It's all over," I said, though I knew that would bring little comfort.

Three of the Italian cops came running up to us and yelled. I didn't understand what they were saying, but I got the gist by their gestures. I raised my hands and remained on my knees. Erika continued to hold Kurt and gave them a defiant look.

They holstered their pistols and motioned for us to go with them. I stood and helped Erika to her feet, while Kurt clung to her body. We followed them down the hill.

Dozens of people stood at the corner of the administration building and looked on as we descended. Aaron, Shimon, and Henri were among them. The crowd parted as we accompanied the police around the building and into the courtyard.

The policemen separated us, and as I watched Erika being taken away, I recalled the skill with which she had taken down her captor. It also deepened the mystery around the woman: Who was she, really?

But what really burned in my stomach was seeing Ziegler. He'd almost been in my sights and got away. I could only temper my rage by knowing he was out there, he was part of the group of Nazi fugitives, and I would do anything in my power to track him down and put an end to him.

24

The sound of a door bursting open startled me awake. I figured I must have dozed off. The only space available for the Italian police to confine me was an office on the second floor of the administration building, where I'd lain down on a ratty sofa to rest my eyes.

I sat up as two Italian policemen came into the room, followed by a man in a rumpled suit. He was in his forties and wore wire-rimmed glasses perched on his nose. He had the tired look of an overworked administrator.

"I'm Eric Phillips, the camp director," he said in a southern American accent. "I'm sorry this took so long. Paperwork, you see?"

I found that last statement odd, since it felt like I'd just fallen asleep. I looked at the clock on a desk in the corner of the room. It was 3:30 p.m. I hadn't dozed but passed out for five solid hours.

"What paperwork?" I asked, still in a stupor.

"Your release. Since no one can determine who fired the shots that killed the intruder, you're off the hook. And since you're an American, discharging your firearm will be over-looked. Nevertheless, I want you off these premises as soon as you gather your things. We'll have no more hooliganism around here."

"I'll leave with the convoy I came with."

"Then that's convenient for you, since they're getting ready to depart." He said something in Italian to one of the cops and left the room. That cop dropped my .45 on the table, and they both turned on their heels and walked out.

I waited a few moments, then got up, exited the room, and walked out of the building. The sun had sunk behind the mountains, and the temperature had already dropped ten degrees.

As I walked across the compound, there were two things churning in my brain. Seeing Zeigler and missing an opportunity, and the new mystery surrounding Erika. Both of them were burning a hole in my stomach.

I entered the parking area. The convoy passengers were slowly gathering to get into the backs of the trucks. When I saw Erika and Kurt standing by the truck, I stopped. She was talking with Henri, while Kurt repeatedly kicked one of the truck tires almost as tall as he was. The two adults appeared to be having a pleasant conversation, both of them smiling, Erika occasionally chuckling. She had such an open manner and tender expression that it put into doubt some of my worst suspicions. I'd spent enough time with her to believe she was a good person—just one with dark and dangerous secrets.

Another realization surprised me, which aggravated the heartburn: seeing her and Kurt had created a glow in my chest and brought a smile to my face. I loved Laura, but this woman and her son had touched me in unexpected ways. I would have to make sure my feelings wouldn't betray my better judgment. No telling what lay concealed behind her charms.

Erika noticed me standing at a distance, and she smiled, but the longer I remained at a distance, the more strained it became. I forced a smile of my own and walked toward her. Kurt noticed me and sprinted my way. A moment earlier he'd had a dark expression, but now he smiled and collided with my thigh and wrapped his arms tightly around me. A warmth ran through me, and my anger dissipated.

I continued toward Erika with Kurt clamped to my leg. I lifted him with each step, making him giggle. Erika still smiled, but her eyes had narrowed as if trying to divine my thoughts.

She touched my arm and said, "Thank you for coming to my rescue."

"Remind me to ask you where you learned those moves."

She glanced away, obviously not wanting to talk about it.

Erika coaxed Kurt off my leg, and he ran over to a group of kids waiting to board the trucks. Erika told him to stay in sight and turned back to me. "He kept asking me when you'd come out of that building."

"He keeps surprising me at how quickly he can recover. Almost being abducted. In the middle of a shoot-out."

"He hasn't recovered. Not really. I'm sure there's a lot of hurt he's not showing, and that worries me more. I think being around you is what's keeping him strong."

I nodded.

"What's wrong?" she asked.

I didn't know how to answer that and fell into an awkward silence.

I was saved when someone behind me said, "Now we can finally get underway."

I turned to see Feldman and Hazan stepping up to me. Both appeared downcast; gone were their usual cocky grins.

Seeing them reminded me of what else I was pissed off about. "You had no business leaving us in a lurch."

"Everything was in order when we left," Hazan said. "If it wasn't for you and your lady friend, this would have been a routine trip."

I got in Hazan's face. "You have a problem with us, then get someone else to drive. I don't have to listen to your griping."

Hazan grabbed my overcoat lapels and tried to shove me against the truck. I twisted out of his grasp and swung my body, turning him in the process. I pinned him against the truck. Hazan grimaced in pain as I held him there.

Feldman forced himself between us. "You can break each other's bones when we get to Naples. But in the meantime, we have to finish this mission."

I released Hazan and said to both of them, "Before I drive this truck another foot, we have to talk. In private."

I stepped away, and Feldman and Hazan followed. When we were out of hearing range, I turned and said, "Who were you after?"

"That doesn't concern you," Hazan said.

"By the looks of things, you failed. That's when it concerns me."

"It was Eduard Roschmann," Feldman said. "He was the SS commandant of the Riga ghetto and had his hand in murdering countless Jews. He was arrested twice and managed to escape from the Dachau camp."

"You missed him."

Feldman nodded.

"He and two other thugs seemed to know we were coming. It was a trap."

"Then it's lucky you got out of it."

"Someone must have tipped him off," Hazan said. "Maybe your lady friend is working for them."

"And how would she have done that?" I said. "Think before you spout off any more of your crap."

Hazan bristled, but Feldman put his hand on the man's arm.

"You two have to put me in the loop next time you think of going out there on the hunt," I said.

"Now you want to go out after criticizing us for doing it?" Hazan said.

"What I'm saying is, we pick the right times, and we pick our battles."

"What's changed your mind?" Feldman said.

"I saw the Gestapo commander, Ziegler, I told you about. He's with the group."

"The group that wants your lady friend?" Hazan asked.

"Erika Altmann is her name. And, yes, the same group."

Hazan and Feldman glanced at each other with what I surmised to be a conspiratorial exchange.

Feldman tilted his head toward the trucks. "We should get out of here. The sun will be down soon. We're almost out of the mountains, meaning we should have some smooth sailing after that."

I let Feldman and Hazan get ahead of me before I walked back to Erika.

"What was all that about?" she asked.

"I wanted to set them straight about leaving the convoy."

She looked skeptical. "You could have said that in front of me. What was it really about?"

"They got into trouble in some town. Don't ask me to tell you any more than that."

I stepped around her and went to the back. I felt her staring at me as I joined Henri. I got on the opposite side of the cargo area and helped people climb into the back. Henri teased me about charging like a cowboy toward the kidnappers, while some of the passengers looked at me with a mixture of unease and admiration.

"How's the rabbi?" I asked Henri.

"He didn't make it."

"I'm sorry to hear that."

"He was the spiritual leader of the group, so he'll be missed."

"And the pregnant woman? Mrs. Baumann?"

"She'll be fine, though she and her husband have to stay behind."

Ours was the last to be loaded. Henri got in, and I closed the tailgate. I looked to Feldman and Hazan, who stood by their command car. Feldman give a hand signal. Moishe and Aaron climbed into their trucks, and I did the same. Erika was already in her seat and gave me a look that I figured was disappointment. Kurt sat in the middle on top of our bags so he could look out the windshield.

I started up the engine and followed Aaron's and Moishe's trucks out of the parking lot and onto the highway. Some of the passengers in the back of the other trucks waved at a group of people gathered to see them off. Everyone seemed to be excited to get underway again, despite many more hours of being cramped inside a freezing truck.

Once we were out on the highway, Erika asked me, "Are those two really British intelligence?"

I figured she was referring to Feldman and Hazan. "That's what they told me," I said, lying.

"You don't believe that any more than I do."

I said nothing in response.

"They left the camp and went to a town to go after an ex-Nazi, didn't they?"

I didn't have a good rebuttal for that, so I said they did. "Things went wrong, and the man escaped."

"Children playing a dangerous game."

"Those children and millions more like them were asked to kill and sacrifice their lives for the ultimate dangerous game. I can't blame them for doing what they were trained to do."

She turned in her seat and looked at me. "I despise what those men did in the name of Hitler, but executing them without a trial is despicable."

I didn't have an answer for that one either, since I planned to do the same thing myself if I ever caught up with Ziegler.

The truck in front of ours came to an abrupt halt, forcing me to hit my brakes in turn. I used my right arm to brace Kurt and Erika as we came to a stop.

"What's happening?" Kurt asked with panic in his voice, then buried his face in Erika's chest.

"Maybe a deer or something," I said to calm him.

I started to get out of the cab when two British MP motorcycles and two army sedans came up behind and stopped with their lights flashing. One of the motorcycles and a sedan stopped opposite my door, while the others went ahead and did the same thing by Moishe's truck.

Erika and I exchanged a look of dread. The Nazis hadn't stopped us, but the British military police had. Illegal possession of three British Army trucks and a sedan, plus Feldman and Hazan in Brit uniforms wasn't life-threatening, but it ended our journey all the same.

25

A red-capped British MP with a bushy mustache stood at my door and hollered for us to get out, hands up. Kurt tried to hide on the floorboard, but Erika coaxed him out, saying the men meant no harm. I showed the MP my hands before opening the door.

When I saw that the MP had his hand on the butt of his pistol, I said, "Take it easy. There's a woman and a kid in here."

"Shut up and get down."

I complied, then took Kurt from Erika while she climbed down to the tarmac.

"Corporal!" the MP yelled. A younger uniformed man ran up to his superior officer. The mustached MP said to him, "Take this man and put him in the Bedford."

The corporal took my arm, but I pulled away and said to the mustached man, "Wait a minute. The woman and child are with me."

"All DPs will be returned together. Drivers to the Bedford. If there aren't any issues, you'll be reunited."

Erika had to hold Kurt back as I was dragged one way and

then the other. Henri, who was wearing a British Army uniform, was trying to convince the mustached sergeant of something when he was also dragged in my direction.

The corporal opened the back door of the Bedford. He and another MP shoved me inside. I was the first to be put in the back, as my truck was the closest. Henri tumbled inside a moment later thanks to the MPs. He took a seat on the bench next to me.

"I should have never agreed to wear this uniform," he said.

"Were you in the Brit army?"

He nodded. "Two years."

"Then relax. There's not much they can do."

Moishe and Aaron were pushed in next. Both looked dejected; this was probably the end of the mission to smuggle out one last group of Jewish DPs to Palestine. After an audible scuffle outside the truck, Feldman and Hazan were thrown in. Hazan landed on Feldman as they both hit the deck.

I could hear yelling and screaming coming from the area of the trucks. "What are they going to do with them?" I asked Feldman.

"The only thing the staff sergeant would tell me is that we're all going to the same camp."

"Which is?"

"How should I know? Wherever it is, it looks like we're done."

~

I'D BEEN DOING TOO much of it lately—walking out of yet another detention. Only this time, I'd spent no more than fifteen minutes under guard by a pair of British MPs. I was supposed to have been in the custody of the CIC and Major Forester in Vienna—that was the first mark against me. Then traveling under false or expired travel passes in Italy, and driving a misappropriated Brit military truck with a load of unsanctioned DPs, all had me in plenty of hot water.

I couldn't figure out why they'd just released me.

I checked my watch, which I had to recuperate from a grumpy MP. It was 10:40 p.m. The camp the MPs had taken us to was in a bowl formed by rolling hills about ten miles north of Florence. It dwarfed the one we'd stopped at that morning. There were three rows of two-story structures, and two buildings that appeared to have been small hangars, making me think it had once been a military training base.

A few couples and families moved in the courtyards formed by the buildings. There were a handful of MPs patrolling the grounds, but that was the only activity at that time of night. An MP told me the convoy passengers were all being housed temporarily in one of the former hangars, so I descended the porch steps of the administration office to head in that direction.

I got just three paces when the car doors of a Mercedes opened in front of me. Two men got out. Both wore trench coats and fedoras. One had the build of a football player and was in his mid-thirties, and the other looked like a long-distance runner—a sort of Laurel and Hardy with grim expressions. There was something different about their mannerisms, and I pegged them for Americans even before the bigger guy opened his mouth to speak.

"Mason Collins?" the bigger man said. He showed me his leather holder with his badge and ID. "We're with the CIC. I'm

Agent Barker, and this is Agent Tilsit," he said, pointing to his thinner partner. "Would you please get in the car?"

"CIC?" I said. I remembered being duped before by guys posing as U.S. officials, so I plucked the ID from his hands and examined it carefully. It seemed legitimate, but I was in possession of an excellent forged ID myself. "Who sent you?"

"Major Forester," Barker said. "The Italian police at the Dolcé camp called Major Forester inquiring about your expired travel pass, and Forester called us. Then we heard about the Brit military police diverting the convoy. We got here as soon as we could."

"I have business to attend to, so I'll pass on the lift."

"We weren't planning to take you anywhere you didn't want to go," Barker said. "We just have a few questions." He opened the rear passenger's door. "Please."

I wanted nothing to do with CIC agents I didn't know, and I was about to object, but it occurred to me that they might have been the reason I got off so easily. I looked at the back seat and noticed my backpack. I felt like it was being used as an enticement. Despite my misgivings, I got in anyway.

Barker and Tilsit got in front and turned in their seats to look at me.

"First of all, Major Forester is pretty steamed you haven't checked in," Barker said.

"Tell him I've had my hands full."

"We can see that," Tilsit said. "We're the ones who had to get you out of this jam."

I said nothing.

"Can you bring us up to speed?" Barker said.

I took a moment to weigh what to say and what to leave out. "I'm following leads."

"That confrontation this morning, for instance," Tilsit said.

"About five people tried to kidnap a woman and child. I, and the squad of Italian police, managed to stop them from carrying it out."

"Shooting and killing one in the process."

"It's unclear whether that was me or one of the Italian cops," I said, lying. "No loss, either way."

"Because you believe they're ex-Nazis trying to escape justice," Barker said.

"They're part of a group I've been investigating," I said.

Tilsit gave me a skeptical look. "What about that woman and child?"

"That woman is the best lead I have at getting information. There are several big fish who are supposedly members of the group, including the guy both Mike—uh, Major Forester—and I are trying to track down. A Gestapo commander named Ziegler."

"Who are some of those big fish?" Barker asked.

Both agents leaned toward me, in anticipation of my answer.

I wasn't sure why, but I felt giving them some of the bigger names would give these agents, and the CIC in general, too much of an incentive to interfere and, consequently, screw things up. There were a lot of politics messing with CIC's mission, including their recruiting ex-Nazi scientists and former Nazi intelligence officers to work for the U.S., looking the other way on their crimes in the name of fighting the Reds. Then there were the stories of Germans, sympathetic to the Soviet cause, infiltrating American intelligence as double agents.

"A Dr. Fleischman, Friedrich Kappler, and Anton Rudel," I said.

Barker turned away slightly as if disappointed with the news, but Tilsit leaned in further and commenced to stare me down.

"This woman, how does she know so much?"

"One of the men in the group is her husband."

"What has she told you about her background?"

I hesitated. I could tell by their expressions they knew more than they were saying. And this was beginning to feel more like an interrogation than a fact-finding mission. Their game was to hint at information to get me to talk, a game I'd played often when interrogating someone.

"That she's from minor royalty and trying to escape her sadistic husband."

Barker and Tilsit exchanged a look, then Barker said, "Her last name's not Altmann, but Klarsfeld. She has family connections to German royals, that part is true, but her husband is Ludwig Klarsfeld. His father helped bankroll Hitler's regime—"

"Yeah, she told me."

"What she may not have told you is that her husband was Waffen-SS and held the rank of colonel, or Standartenführer. And I'm sure she didn't tell you he was a member of staff for Hans Frank, the governor-general of occupied Poland. Among other atrocities, Frank oversaw rounding up and sending Polish Jews to the extermination camps. He was hanged, but his aides disappeared."

That revelation left me cold. I tried to control my disappointment, to temper it by using the worn notion that being married to the guy didn't make her guilty, but it wasn't working. Still, my gut was telling me different. I'd had enough experience gauging people as an intelligence agent and detective, and while I knew she was tainted by association, I felt she was trying to redeem herself.

And something else was gnawing at me: These guys were here telling me this for more than an intelligence briefing. They had another agenda.

"Did you think I was keeping her safe out of the goodness of my heart?" I said. "She's the bait that brings me the fish. The group's failed attempt today just proves that. And the farther south we go, the more desperate they'll get."

After another glance at Barker, Tilsit said, "All right, we arranged for her and her kid to be released into your care. Proceed with your plan, but we'll be keeping an eye on you. The only reason we're not detaining her or putting you on the first plane out of here is that we want those names, a good location to grab them up, and the nature and location of Frau Klarsfeld's cash."

I hadn't mentioned Erika's money. Somehow they knew about it. I kept a neutral expression, though now I suspected there was more to their agenda than intelligence gathering.

Barker said, "Regardless of what she told you about the money's origins, it could still be SS money, all of which is to be confiscated by the U.S. authorities."

"By you two, for example."

Tilsit's face twisted into a snarl, and he opened his mouth to say something when Barker put a hand on his arm to shut him up.

"That's not your concern," Barker said.

I paused to show them I wasn't buying what they were

selling. "The convoy's not going anywhere anytime soon. I need to make arrangements for a car."

"There's a black Opel sedan in the motor pool for you," Barker said. "It's got military government plates, so you shouldn't have any trouble getting past checkpoints and the like." He held out a card, which I took. His name and phone number were printed on it. There was also another phone number scribbled on the back. "That's the local number where we're staying. If you have any trouble reaching us, you can call the CIC detachment number in Milan and leave a message."

Tilsit tilted his head at the door. "Beat it." As I grabbed my backpack off the seat, he said, "Get some results, and call us directly when you have anything. No need to report in to Major Forester. We'll relay any pertinent information. You got that."

I said nothing as I got out. I closed the door, and they drove off.

The inside of the hangar seemed colder than the outside, and the entire group of sixty-five passengers were bundled up, either standing in line for some hot food or eating in small groups. Some were sleeping on cots or conversing in hushed tones.

I spotted Erika and Kurt sitting alone on a cot in one corner, isolated from the rest. Feldman, Hazan, the other two drivers, Henri, and Shimon sat huddled on cots arranged to form a circle. I would deal with them later.

As I walked toward Erika, the odors of hot food and coffee reached my nose, and my stomach urged me to make a beeline for the food, but I wouldn't have an appetite before I was able to confront Erika about the information on her husband.

She was reading the same book she'd read to Kurt many times, about a bunny brother and sister going to bunny school. How the kid could listen to it hundreds of times without finally growing tired with it was beyond me, but he sat riveted each time his mother read it to him. Seeing them there together, him on her lap and her reading by candlelight, eased my anger, but only some of my suspicion.

I had to find a way to get her away from Kurt long enough to grill her about her past. Was she the loyal Nazi wife until he'd resorted to beating her and Kurt? Or was it only after the war that she'd grown a conscience? What other sins had she committed for her own survival? Was the origin of the money really her family, or did she lift it from a cache of SS blood money?

I laid my backpack on the concrete floor and crouched, facing them. Kurt looked half-asleep when he climbed off his mother's lap and hugged me. After a moment, he took his place back on his mother's lap. Erika must have seen the anxiety in my face, because she said to Kurt, "It's time for you to go to sleep."

He whined a little before crawling onto the cot and curling into a ball. "Good night, Mason," he said and closed his eyes.

We waited in awkward silence until Kurt's breathing became slow and steady. Erika rose from the cot as gently as she could. I stood and faced her.

"We have to talk, yes?" she said.

I nodded, and we walked a few yards away from Kurt. Since the cot was at the far end of the line, we were alone in the shadows. She said nothing and gave me an expectant look.

"I couldn't figure out why the British MPs let me go so easily until I ran into two American intelligence agents outside the administration building."

Even in the shadows I could see Erika's face blanch. "You've been working for American intelligence all this time?"

"No, I told you the truth. The Italian cops at the camp called my agent friend in Vienna about the expired pass he issued me, and then he called two local agents to come get me out of trouble. I didn't ask for their help, but without them I'd still be under guard and more than likely sent back to a British jail in Graz."

"Why are you telling me this?"

"When you told me your life's story you left out the fact that your husband was an SS Standartenführer. That he worked for Hans Frank in Poland, who was hanged for his part in the mass execution of Jews."

Erika froze. I couldn't tell if she was even breathing. Dim candlelight reflected off the tears in her eyes.

"My father arranged the marriage when I was eighteen, and Ludwig was just a low-level bureaucrat in the Nazi party. He started rising in the ranks after Kurt was born."

I stared at her as I weighed what to do from that moment.

"I see the contempt in your eyes," she said. "Why don't you leave? I wouldn't be able to stand that look, your judgment."

"I want to trust you, but omitting something like this isn't helping."

"It may not matter to you now, but I never lived with Ludwig in Poland. By that time, I despised him and what he'd become. I would only visit out of obligation, to put up appearances. I refused to ever stay more than a week at a time, which prompted him to start beating me and being cruel to Kurt. That's when I decided to smuggle the family money out of Germany. And when Ludwig was arrested after the war, I used that opportunity to run. If this news bothers you that much, then leave."

"I made a promise, and I intend to keep it. But you have to be honest with me."

"How do you know that whatever I tell you isn't another lie?"

"Why? What else do you have to hide?"

Erika said nothing.

"Get your things," I said. "We're leaving."

"What?"

"Yes. The CIC agents arranged for your and Kurt's release, but only under my supervision."

"What about everyone else?"

I shook my head. "Just you and Kurt. So get your stuff. You've got five minutes."

"I'm not leaving these people. You have to find a way to get them released, too."

"I don't have any power with the Brits, and I doubt that, even if the CIC agents could convince the Brit police to release everyone, they'd agree to do it."

"Then I'm staying. Go, if you want. You really didn't care about these people anyway. I release you from your promise. Kurt and I will be better off without you."

She stepped around me and went back to Kurt. I didn't know what to think. My attachment to them kept my feet planted. Finally, I passed by the cot without a word or a glance, snatched up the backpack, and headed for the door.

A flurry of emotions coursed through my mind: anger at her evasiveness and putting Kurt in further danger to allay her guilt; anger at myself for my stubbornness; anger at the abandonment of my morals to hunt down Ziegler, even to the point of using Erika and her boy as bait; and regret and guilt for contemplating walking out on these people.

But I kept walking, and I exited the building. I got some distance from the door and stopped. I lacked any kind of plan on how to pick up their trail, let alone go up against a gang of well-armed and desperate ex-Nazis.

I hoisted the backpack onto my back and walked toward the camp's motor pool.

~

It turned out the camp had been built in the middle of an area of vineyards planted on the surrounding slopes. I had parked the black sedan the CIC agents had given me diagonally across the road from the camp's entrance on a small dirt road most likely used by a grape farmer to access one of his fields. As far as I could tell by the light of a half-moon, there was little snow; a misty rain had taken care of whatever had accumulated. And though it wasn't freezing like it had been in the mountains, the cold dampness was creeping into my bones.

The camp was surrounded by a high cement wall, with a steel gate in the center. Lampposts and the roofs of several buildings were visible poking above the wall. A guard's kiosk was situated at the main gate, with two MPs inside huddled over something I assumed was an electric heater. Although the camp was sponsored by the United Nations refugee organization, it was also a shared posting for American and British military police, meaning it would be much harder for the Nazi gang to gain entry.

The trick for me now was to stay awake and ignore the growling in my stomach. The hope was that I might catch Erika's hunters nosing around the camp for a way in or to post lookouts to watch for her release. Nothing so far, and it was creeping past midnight. Still, I was as certain of my hunch as the cold in my bones.

A battered Horch sedan came up from the south and slowly cruised past the gate. That in and of itself was not unusual, as I'd seen a dozen cars and small trucks using the road. But this one was going no more than twenty miles an hour. It rolled to a stop fifty yards further down, near the northern corner of the perimeter wall.

No one got out; it just sat there. It was too far away and too dark to see the interior. I went for the binoculars sitting on the passenger's seat anyway. I raised them to my eyes, but the sedan pulled onto the road again and continued on.

I was about to dismiss it, when the car made a U-turn about a quarter mile later. It proceeded to cruise past the gate again at the same speed, then pulled over near the gate on the opposite side of the road.

I trained the binoculars on the rear window of the car. I could only make out the silhouettes of three people. Men, from the shape of the hats they wore, and all had turned their heads in the direction of the gate.

A second sedan, a pristine two-door Bugatti, came up from the south, and that one pulled up to the gate. The two guards exited the kiosk. One of them leaned toward the driver's window. The gate lights illuminated the interior enough for me to see there were two men in the second sedan. The driver and guard seemed to be having a heated discussion.

While this was going on, I detected movement on my right. I swung the binoculars in the direction of the sedan on the side of the road. A guy had emerged from the back seat and stared intently at the gate. His face was mostly in the dark, but I recognized him as one of the three in the car that stopped next to me on the mountain road when the woman with red lipstick talked to me.

I dropped the binoculars and picked up my .45. I checked the magazine and loaded a bullet into the chamber.

Looking up again, I saw the sedan at the gate back out onto the road and drive south. It passed the parked sedan and continued. The man outside the first sedan on the road got back in, and that driver took off behind the other.

I started my engine, turned right, and followed.

27

This was the first time I was the one doing the hunting, and I didn't want to blow the opportunity by getting too close to the two sedans. The headlights might have attracted their attention, but I had to risk it. There was enough traffic on the road to minimize suspicion.

The two-lane road narrowed as it wound along the ridge of a Tuscan hill. Stone-and-concrete walls lined both sides. Because of the numerous twists in the road, I was forced to stay closer than I would have liked, but I didn't detect any difference in the driver's speed, no turning heads to look in my direction. We descended the hill and hit the denser suburbs of Florence. And because they were avoiding the main highway, I surmised their destination was somewhere in Florence.

Just before reaching the Florence city limits, the two cars turned onto a highway taking them southwest. They took a route across the Arno river and made several superfluous turns—probably to detect a tail, forcing me to keep more distance than I would have liked. When they were held up by a traffic light, I pulled over as if parking. Whether this trick was working, I didn't know, and I could have just as easily been falling into an ambush on a dark road.

We ended up south of the city, then made a big loop until I saw signs for the Porta Romana and the Boboli Gardens. A few moments later, we came to the big roundabout circling the ancient Porta Romana gate. The cars split up—the Horch with the three men turning to go back toward the Arno and Florence, while the two-door Bugatti went east on a road lined with ritzy villas.

It might have been a ruse to shake a tail, but I had to make a decision fast. I chose the battered Horch. I slowed to let a couple of cars enter the ring road to put them between me and the Horch, and I followed my quarry onto Via Romana heading for the Pitti Palace and Ponte Vecchio. Both the cars in front of me took the same road, helping me remain unde-tected on the narrow, one-way street.

Up ahead, the Horch turned on the first street on the left. I did the same a few seconds later. This street was just wide enough for a single car with parked cars to one side. One more hook to the left and the Horch pulled over and parked.

The driver doused the headlights, but everyone remained in the car. They were waiting to see if I was pulling over too. I turned my head away, passed them, and kept going. The road ended eighty feet later at a perpendicular street. I behaved like a sensible driver, stopping at the intersection, then calmly turned left onto another narrow street.

I went another fifty feet, parked, and hurried out of the car. I stuffed the .45 in my belt and rushed up to their street. I poked my head around the corner. One of men had gotten out of the car and was at a gate. He bent over as if to unlock it and opened it, letting the Horch enter the courtyard of a two-story house.

I waited until hearing the metal gate clang closed, then I quietly strode down the street, stopping at the gate. The house looked to have been built during the eighteenth century in Mediterranean style, with eight standard windows on both levels. A small stone balcony graced the middle two windows on the second floor. The only lights illuminated were in a couple of rooms on the ground floor.

I went a little further to a single gate for pedestrians. After fishing out my lock-picking tools, I knelt at the gate and worked the lock. It clicked back with little sound, but the hinges creaked when I opened it. I slipped inside, closed the gate, then ducked behind a tree. I was in a small courtyard of concrete and a small lawn. There were two cars parked on a strip of concrete, one of which was the Horch.

Fortunately, the house was closed up tight against the biting cold, which must have deadened the sound, as no one came to investigate. When all seemed clear, I stepped out from behind the tree and kept my eyes on the windows. Two lights came on in second-story windows on opposite sides of the house. I shifted to my right and looked up to the upstairs window. Someone passed through the light. As he pulled the curtains closed, I got a good look at his face—it was the guy I'd recognized from the mountain road. One of the men I didn't recognize stood in the living room as he switched off a floor lamp. They were packing it in for the evening.

It was time to move.

I sneaked up to the entrance and knelt at the lock. The old lock gave way easily. I stood, carefully turned the knob, and poked my head inside. All was quiet downstairs. I slipped in the door. A streetlight outside threw enough light through the curtains for me to see into the shadows. I was in a small foyer that connected to a hallway and marble staircase. Typical of the eighteenth-century architecture, there were flourishes in the ceiling and molding, with a tiled floor depicting a floral pattern. The living room was off to the right and a sitting room to the left, with presumably a dining room and kitchen to the rear of the house.

Thanks to the marble staircase, I moved up to the second floor in silence. At the top was a sitting area, then hallways serving bedrooms on both ends of the house. On each side of the staircase was a double door, which I figured were the main bedrooms. There were muffled voices in a room to my left, but the guy I'd recognized was in a corner bedroom to the right.

The door to the left bedroom opened, throwing light into the sitting area. I rushed over to a high cabinet and wedged myself between it and the corner of the room. Two men conversed at the doorway. One urged immediate action, that "they" were closing in, while the other said they lacked the resources, that their contacts insisted nothing could be done until they reached Rome. It was the end of a conversation, so the references were vague, but it sounded like they were in a bind. My guess was they had delayed getting to Rome in order to grab up Erika, and the delay had caused them to be even more desperate.

The door closed, and one of the men crossed the sitting area. I tucked in as deep as I could. He passed right by me.

In one stride, I was out of my corner and behind him. I put the barrel of my gun at the back of his head and pulled back the hammer. The man sucked in his breath and froze.

"Hands where I can see them," I said in German. "You make a sound, and I'll blow your head off."

He raised them. I grabbed his suit coat collar and guided him toward the staircase. He let out little puffs of air as if lifting something heavy. I eased the hammer back in place without a sound; I didn't want the gun to go off as we descended the stairs.

We got to the front door, and I said, "Open it."

He complied, and I pushed him outside. I whirled him around. "Now, close it quietly."

He did so, and we marched out of the gate and onto the sidewalk.

"Where are you taking me?" he asked with fear in his voice.

I shoved the barrel of the gun harder into his head. "Shut up, and you might live through this."

He let out a moan and let me urge him forward. As we turned the corner, I hoped no one was on the street. Otherwise, this little caper would go bad real fast. I got him to the car and forced him to his knees while I used my free hand to open the car door.

"Get in." I nudged him with the gun.

He was shaking and panting as he crawled in and slid across to the passenger's seat. I got in after him while keeping my gun pointed at his head.

Near tears, he asked, "Who are you? What do you want?"

"Shut up," I said and reached into his suit coat pocket and pulled out his wallet. He had an identity document issued by the Vatican Refugee Organization for a Dietrich Schiller claiming him as a displaced person, though I knew the papers were false and that the name was an alias. He had little else

228 | JOHN A. CONNELL

aside from about 10,000 AM-lira, or about a hundred U.S. dollars, and a small photograph of a woman and a baby.

"You see?" he said. "I have a wife and child. Please don't hurt me for their sake. Just take the money—"

I pushed the barrel of the .45 so hard it jammed his head against the passenger window. "I don't want your money. I want information. Where is Theodor Ziegler?"

The man stopped breathing. "I ... I don't know who—"

I pushed the gun even harder. "You try lying to me again, and I'll spread your brains on that window." I paused to let that sink in. "Where is ex-SS Obersturmführer Theodor Ziegler? Is he in the house?"

Schiller shook his head. "There are only three of us staying here. Me, Konrad Hoffmann, and Rudolf Lange."

"I know he's part of your group trying to get out of Italy."

"He's not a part of the—"

I pulled back the hammer. The noise made Schiller jump.

Schiller used his hands as if pushing against something. "Listen. Just listen, please!"

I said nothing and let off a little pressure of the gun barrel, prompting him to continue.

"He and some others latched onto us. They weren't welcome as far as I was concerned, but Kappler insisted. I knew they would be trouble."

"Why?"

"He and a fellow named Ludwig Klarsfeld promised to supply the group with a pile of money."

"The money from Klarsfeld's wife?"

Schiller tried to glance at me on instinct, as he seemed surprised that I knew of Erika and the fortune. He thought better of moving his head, stopped, and nodded. "I and my companions just want to get to Rome, but Kappler and some others insist on getting the money first. As far as I know, Ziegler has no intention of leaving without it. He's penniless and refuses to go to a foreign country to live in poverty."

That revelation surprised me. I'd assumed he was trying to flee the country as quickly as the others. I had worried that he would slip away before I'd ever track him down, but now I learned he'll continue to dog the convoy—if it ever got going again—which meant I still had a chance to corner him.

"If Ziegler is the one who's so hot on grabbing Klarsfeld's wife, then what were you guys doing there this evening?"

Schiller tried to look at me out of the corner of his eye. "Because there are some in our party who agree with Ziegler. So the quicker we get the money, the faster we can get out of here."

A police car cruised down the street. Schiller spotted the car when it was farther down the street. His eyes bounced in their sockets.

I pressed the barrel harder. "Not a good idea." I wanted to know more about the group, but the longer I lingered, the greater the chance of witnesses. It was better to stay on the main subject. "If Ziegler's not here, where is he staying?"

"Somewhere near the camp. That's all I know. I swear."

"How many others with him?"

"Maybe ten."

"Kappler?"

Schiller nodded.

"Who else?"

"I don't know them all."

"Try like your life depended on it."

"Franz Stangl and his mistress, Greta Schweiger. Dr. Ernst Fleischman."

"Who else?"

"I said I don't know them all. Gustav Wagner and Klarsfeld, but those are the only ones I'm sure of. There was an Anton Rudel, but someone put him in the hospital."

"That was me," I said.

Schiller choked down a sob. "Please, don't shoot me."

"Is that what you heard from the innocent Jews you shot?"

"I didn't shoot anyone."

"Gassed, then."

Schiller was near panic as he breathed rapidly with short breaths. "I was just a bureaucrat. I filled in numbers into columns. I made boring reports."

"They don't arrest bureaucrats, Dietrich—if that's your real name. You're trying to escape for something other than pushing papers." I dug the barrel of the gun into his forehead.

He screamed and said, "Sobibor. I was at Sobibor. But I didn't kill anyone. I just made sure the camp kept up its quota."

"Maybe you didn't kill anyone by your own hand, but you kept the killing machine humming, didn't you?"

The man was in tears. I wouldn't get much more out of him. A couple walked arm in arm for a late-night stroll and was heading my way. Two cars passed. I couldn't linger any longer.

I opened my door and put one foot onto the street. "You're going to get out the same way you came in."

"What are you going to do?"

"Follow my instructions without a sound, and you'll live through the night."

The man groaned but did as he was told. He slid across the bench seat while I kept the pistol at his head. I got both feet on the ground, then grabbed him by the collar and dragged him out. The couple was about eighty yards away and noticed us. I shoved Schiller to the back of the car, got out my car keys, and opened the trunk. "Get in."

"Please," he said. "I've told you what you wanted to know."

"That's why you're still breathing. We can't very well have you running back to your buddies. Get in and you'll live to see tomorrow." I couldn't promise him any more than that.

Schiller crawled into the trunk. He screamed, "Help!"

I slammed the trunk closed and went around to the driver's door. The couple had stopped. The woman clung to the man in fear, and they both stared at me. It was dark, so maybe they got a good look at my face, maybe they didn't.

I got in, started the engine, and sped away.

28

I managed to get some shut-eye before the sun rose above the mountains overlooking the camp. I felt revived after five hours of sleep, though my back and legs were stiff from sitting so long in a freezing car. Schiller was still in the trunk. He'd worn himself out long ago after hours of banging on the trunk lid.

Just before waking, I was dreaming of finding a long table full of food, and that memory triggered my stomach. I'd lost track of when I'd had something to eat, and those visions of food haunted me still.

I'd barely had time to rub the sleep from my eyes when a familiar black sedan came up the road and parked next to me in the opposite direction.

Barker rolled down the driver's window. I did the same.

"You got everything set up?" I asked.

"Get in," Barker said.

I pulled myself out of my car with my backpack and got into the back seat of theirs. "Well?"

Tilsit turned in his seat to face me. "You better hold up your end of the bargain."

"It'll be worth your time."

Tilsit grunted and turned away. Barker started up the car, did a U-turn, and drove up to the camp's gate. An MP guard came out from the kiosk and bent down to look into the car.

"CIC. Major Habersham is expecting us," Barker said.

The guard eyed the three of us, then straightened and signaled for his partner to open the barrier. Barker entered the camp's courtyard and parked in front of the administration building.

I grabbed my backpack, got out, and made my way to the hangar, while Barker and Tilsit entered the administration building to talk to the major. It wasn't a sure thing, this scheme I'd conjured up, but I was counting on the greed of these local CIC agents and Forester's ability to get things done.

I entered the hangar. Most of the people were stirring because the breakfast line was being set up at one end of the hangar. I was tempted to go over there and be first in line, but I had things that needed to get done before alleviating my hunger.

Erika sat on her cot next to a sleeping Kurt. She stared at something unseen and didn't notice me. She looked forlorn and lonely, and I wanted to go to her, but I had to talk to Feldman and Hazan.

They, along with Moishe, Aaron, Shimon, and Henri, were sitting on cots formed in a circle as if they hadn't budged since last night. Hazan saw me first. He bristled as he stood. Feldman said something to Hazan that I couldn't hear, but the words seemed to make him back off from attack mode. The others all turned to me but remained seated.

"We thought you had abandoned us," Feldman said as I got there.

"I had things to do," I said. "Like figuring out a way to get you all out of here."

The rest stood, and hope came to their eyes.

"Before you get excited," I said to the group, "I need to talk to Arie and David."

Feldman and Hazan followed me over to an empty area of the hangar.

"I worked out a deal with the two American CIC agents who got me out of here."

"I don't like it already," Hazan said.

"If you two want to get out of the charges of impersonating British soldiers and stealing their trucks, then you'll hear me out."

Neither of them said anything.

"Two cars with five Nazis swung by here last night looking for a way into the camp." I told them about following the cars to Florence and abducting Schiller. "The two others in the house were Konrad Hoffmann and Rudolf Lange."

"Lange?" Feldman said with surprise. "Standartenführer Lange?"

"Give us the address," Hazan said.

"What about the convoy?"

"What about it?" Hazan said.

"I got the CIC agents to arrange for everyone's release."

"Without trucks, the convoy isn't going anywhere," Feldman said.

"The CIC boys are working on that."

Hazan turned to Feldman and said, "If we're able to get out of here, then we can visit Lange before moving out."

"Now wait a minute," I said. "If we get the release, the Brits are not going to let all these people sit here while you guys hunt down Lange. Besides, Lange and Hoffmann have probably noticed Schiller is missing by now. They'll be gone but not too far. There are at least two groups of Nazis; each of them is separate but traveling in tandem. They'll follow the convoy. We get back out on the road, and they'll come to us."

"Mason?"

I turned to see Erika standing near.

"Get everyone ready to go," I said to Feldman.

Feldman and Hazan both looked like they wanted to hear more, but I gave them a look that said I was done for the moment. They marched off and started calling for everyone to pack up their things to restart the journey.

Erika stepped up to me. "What's going on?"

"You wouldn't come with me without the convoy, so I've arranged for everyone's release."

She said nothing, but her look told me what she was feeling. She smiled, and her eyes turned warm with a little sadness mixed in.

"You should wake Kurt and make sure you both get something to eat."

She nodded. "I'll get something for you, too. You look like a strong wind could blow you over." She turned and walked back to Kurt.

People began to collect their things, and an excited buzz of voices rose as the line grew for breakfast. Feldman and the others were going from person to person to get them moving.

Some appeared to ask questions, with Feldman or Hazan saying something while looking my way.

The main door opened, and Major Habersham came in flanked by two other British officers. One of them, a sergeant, was carrying a stepladder. Almost no one noticed the major until he climbed up on the ladder set up by the sergeant. That same subordinate blew a whistle to silence everyone.

When the room had quieted, Habersham said, "It seems the word has already gone out. I will make it official by saying that you are all free to go. Some private trucks have been requisitioned for your transport—"

The major was interrupted by sporadic cheers and excited conversations.

The sergeant blew the whistle and yelled for quiet like only a seasoned drill instructor could.

When order was restored, the major continued, "Once you leave this camp, you are on your own. You will be allowed to move through Italy, or any other legally sanctioned area, but you will not be welcomed in Mandatory Palestine. If you board any ship destined for that region it will be intercepted by the British Navy. All passengers on those ships attempting this crossing will be detained and sent to the refugee camp on Cyprus. We encourage you to remain at this camp. Here, you will be processed and sent to one of the Jewish DP camps in Italy. At those camps, the sick will be cared for, your children educated. Everyone will have warm clothes, shelter, and food. This journey you plan to undertake could face further perils. We urge you to remain, but it is not in my power to stop you. God bless you all."

Major Habersham descended the ladder. The sergeant folded it and tucked it under his arm. The major and two soldiers did a perfect about-face and marched out of the hangar.

The murmur of voices rose to a high pitch as everyone resumed getting their breakfast or packing their belongings. The energy of the adults seemed to rub off on the kids, and they started running around, playing games.

Hazan tried to give instructions over the cacophony, but without the aid of a drill sergeant or ladder, he went unheard. It was the roaring of three truck motors that got everyone's attention. Feldman opened one of the large doors meant for aircraft and revealed the three trucks pulling to a stop just outside the hangar. They were U.S. Army troop transport trucks with the star painted out. They were dirty, and the canvas coverings for the back were tattered, meaning they were probably surplus and had been left at a storage depot somewhere in Italy.

Erika came up with a cup of coffee and a tray of eggs, baked beans, and toast, and held them out to me. I took them, balancing the tray on one hand and holding the coffee in the other. I nodded my thanks and drank the warm coffee in one gulp. I nodded toward the trucks. "They're not pretty, but they'll do the job."

"I didn't know if you'd come back again," Erika said. "I don't know what to say."

I thought of a few things I wanted her to say having to do with the truth, but Kurt slamming into me made me change my mind. The tray of food teetered in my hand as Kurt wrestled with my leg.

"He's happy you came back, too," Erika said. She took Kurt's shoulders and pulled him off, saying, "Let Mason eat his food, okay?"

I stood there and ate as fast as I could. I never knew when or where the next meal would be coming from. "You'd better get your stuff together," I said with a mouthful of food.

Her smile faded, and she studied my eyes in what I figured was an attempt to discern why I was distant. Finally, she turned and escorted Kurt back to their cot despite Kurt's insistence to stay with me. My distance was partly from her refusal to tell me the truth and partly out of guilt that I was using her as bait.

Feldman and Hazan came up to me. "Are you still going to drive the third truck?" Feldman asked.

I nodded as I shoveled the last of the scrambled eggs into my mouth. I wiped my lips with my sleeve and fished out the car keys. "You can use my car to lead the way," I said and tossed them to Feldman. "There's a little present for you in the trunk. The guy I grabbed up in Florence."

"You want us to take out your trash?" Hazan said.

"He's still alive, if that's what you mean. His Vatican-issued ID card says he's Dietrich Schiller, but that's got to be an alias. He did admit he was a bureaucrat at Sobibor. Made the trains and gas chambers run on time."

Feldman and Hazan exchanged solemn looks.

I said, "This guy also said the Nazi I'm after, Ziegler, is traveling with Franz Stangl."

"We're going to have to find some way of getting at them," Hazan said to Feldman.

"Maybe you can get more out of Schiller than I had time for on a street in Florence."

"Let's get going," Feldman said, "and let the wolf pack come to us."

Feldman and Hazan turned back to the crowd gathering in

the center of the hangar. They moved with quick strides as if excited by the prospect of renewing the hunt. They began calling for everyone to gather in the courtyard. I walked over to Erika, who had their two bags mounted on her shoulder.

She gave me a fiery glance as I joined her. She put her hand on Kurt's shoulder and guided him toward the hangar door. All the boy's attention was on a slice of toast with jam, so Erika looked at me and said, "I noticed you spent a lot of time with those two. I suppose the only reason you came back was to continue using me as bait."

"You're getting to your destination, aren't you? And these people are getting to theirs."

"How long before you resort to dangling my son and me on the end of a fishing rod?"

"I don't work that way."

"I'm having a hard time believing you."

"That makes two of us."

She stopped abruptly outside the door. "What's that supposed to mean?" she said with enough force to get Kurt's attention. He looked frightened and confused.

I took a knee and faced Kurt. "You don't need to be scared. We're just figuring out the best way for you and your mom to go someplace safe and warm, where you'll have your bed and plenty of food and new friends."

"And Mommy, too?"

"Yes, of course."

"And a bed for you?"

"I have to help some other people, so when you and your mother get to that safe place, I'll have to go. But I'll visit when I can."

He looked crushed at the news and hid behind his mother's leg. I stood to face Erika's angry expression. She lifted Kurt to her hip. I went over to the last truck in the line and opened the passenger's door.

Erika helped Kurt crawl onto the seat, and said to me, "Something tells me we're not going to make it to that safe place." She didn't wait for an answer and climbed into the cab.

As I went around to get behind the steering wheel, I was glad she hadn't waited for an answer, because I didn't have one to give.

Like before, I took up the rear of the convoy, following Moishe's and Aaron's trucks out of the camp's gate. As I slowly turned left onto the road, I saw Feldman and Hazan standing at the rear of the car I'd left on the dirt road. Using my sideview mirror, I watched Hazan open the trunk. I figured they wanted to verify that Schiller was in there and let him know what fate awaited him. Seconds later, Hazan closed the trunk, and they hurried to get into the car.

They caught up to me, and I waved them forward when the opposite lane was clear. Their car raced past me to get to the head of the line. Kurt was kneeling on the floorboard and playing with his toy car on the seat. Erika glowered as she stared at the back of Moishe's truck.

The temperature had risen above freezing, and misty rain soaked the roads, and consequently the windshield. The roar of the engine and Kurt's car sound effects accompanied the clacking of the windshield wipers.

I was about to tell Erika what Schiller had said when I noticed a dark blue Opel parked perpendicular to the road. It looked very similar to the one that had hesitated on the mountain road. Because of the rain and reflections of the gray sky off the windshield, I couldn't get a good look inside, but I could make out the silhouette of a woman in the front passenger's seat, a man behind the wheel, and two rear passengers.

Erika sucked in her breath, prompting me to glance at her. Her eyes followed the parked car as we drove past.

"Greta Schweiger?"

"I think so," she said.

I watched the car in the sideview mirror, and it pulled out on the road a few seconds behind us. Erika had done the same, and she stiffened in her seat.

I said, "Like I stated before, they won't try anything against a moving truck in broad daylight."

Erika just nodded. She knew as well as I did that the problem would arise when we had to stop, for whatever reason. Having my .45 in my lap would have made me feel better, but the sight of the gun would surely upset Kurt. Erika must have read my mind, because she arranged my backpack so either of us had easy access to the two pistols nestled near the top of the pack.

"Do you know a Dietrich Schiller?" I asked.

Erika looked at me as if trying to see where that question was going. "Just from Tante Anna's in Meran. He talked with my husband, but we never spoke. Why do you ask?"

"Last night, when I left the camp, I followed him and his buddies to Florence."

Erika stopped breathing for a moment. "Did you kill him?"

"No. I abducted him from the villa where he was staying with a Konrad Hoffmann and Rudolf Lange." I glanced at her and noticed a tick of recognition of those names.

The word *kill* had gotten Kurt's attention. He looked at us. We both smiled at him. He crawled up on the seat and got in his mother's face. "Mommy, read me the book."

"Not now, *mein Schatz*," Erika said. "Go back to playing with your car. Mason and I have some things to discuss."

"Don't fight," he said to her firmly. He got down onto the floorboard again and began to play with his car, though I could tell he was listening.

"I only interrogated Schiller," I said, leaving out that I stuffed him in the trunk of the car Feldman and Hazan now drove. "You guessed correctly that I'm looking for a Nazi in the group." I expected her to admonish me, but she said nothing. "His name is Theodor Ziegler. He was with the Gestapo."

I told her the story of the incident on the farm in Czechoslovakia, how Ziegler had killed the girl I was trying to protect and then the family harboring us. I know Kurt was listening, so I avoided words like *kill* and *blood* and *murder*. The story affected Erika all the same; tears welled in her eyes as she listened to my story.

"You think by tracking down Ziegler you can relieve your guilt? It doesn't work that way."

"I know those aren't his only victims. I will not let him take another breath, walk another step on this earth. And don't lecture me about letting God be the judge, or that I would be stooping to his level. It's called justice in my book."

We drove in silence for a moment while we watched the Opel in the sideview mirrors.

"Schiller told me that Ziegler is traveling with the group trailing us. Apparently, he doesn't want to leave Italy without your money."

"He's with Ludwig?"

I nodded.

"They won't stop until they get it from me," she said.

"You're right, they won't. Schiller had an ID as a refugee issued by the Vatican Refugee Organization. I think they probably all do, which means they can travel in anonymity. At least within Italy. That can't last forever, but it could give them enough time to accomplish their mission."

"Why are you telling me this?"

"Because I want you to realize that they're not going to give up once you get to Naples or to Brindisi. Without the cover of this convoy, they'll move in for the—" I was going to say "kill" but stopped because of Kurt. "But being with the convoy also comes with a price: it gives them a perfect way to track you."

She studied me for a moment, and her face contorted with anger. "I suppose you want a share for getting me and Kurt to safety. Is that it?"

I wanted to yell at her but refrained. "I don't want your money."

"You expect me to believe that?"

"I don't care what you believe. I'm doing it because you saved my life, and I ... well, I think you and Kurt deserve saving."

"Despite my sins?"

"You've kept me in the dark. I wouldn't know what they are other than guilt by association."

"You saved my life more than once," Erika said. "I guess you deserve to know the whole truth."

"Let's start with where you learned those defensive moves," I said. "You didn't pick that up being a *hausfrau*."

Erika looked away as if weighing her response. "I was working as an asset for the Soviets."

I wasn't sure I heard her correctly. "You were a what?"

"I was recruited by a German agent spying for the Soviets. The agent had managed to get a low-level position in Hans Frank's office. He picked up on how miserable I was with Ludwig. How I hated the way things turned out under Hitler. He convinced me to gather whatever information I could on Ludwig's activities and that of his associates. Particularly, any information coming out of Frank's office. That was the reason for my frequent trips to be with Ludwig in Poland. He disgusted me, the whole thing disgusted me, but the agent convinced me how important it was."

"The Soviets trained you in spy craft and how to defend yourself?"

She nodded. "Over about ten days. He said I was an apt pupil."

Her revelation knocked me for a loop. I had operated under the assumption she was a closet Nazi sympathizer. Like so many Germans, she had regretted her decision to support the regime only after its devastating defeat. Then I learned she had been a Soviet asset?

I must have been in my head for a while, because she said, "You haven't said anything. I didn't tell you because I knew you'd find the idea of me working for the Soviets repugnant."

"I'm stunned, is all. I'm no fan of the Soviets, but they were on our side. It takes a lot of courage to do what you did."

"You thought I was lying to you about not being a Nazi."

"You're good at subterfuge. I can tell you that."

"I don't work for the Soviets anymore, if that's what you were wondering."

"I'm not."

"You can't tell anyone. Especially not your CIC agents. I'm still not sure I should have told you."

"Your secret's safe. You were actually helping to fight the regime that was trying to exterminate them. That's something to be proud of."

"It's hard for me to feel proud. I attended dinner parties with those pigs while I knew they were working on the extermination of all the Jews in Poland. I did nothing to stop them. I stood by and smiled and flattered and flirted and watched."

Kurt must have heard the anguish in Erika's voice, because he climbed up onto the seat again and hugged her. She cooed comforting words to him, and he seemed to relax.

My admiration of her grew, as did my guilt for using her as bait. The tangle of emotions left me speechless.

We fell into silence again. Even Kurt said little. I kept an eye on the car trailing us. It matched our speed and maintained a distance of fifty yards, even as the Italian drivers risked life and limb to speed past the slow-moving convoy. The vista had opened up, affording us views of the rolling Tuscan hills and leafless vineyards shrouded in misty rain.

Erika tilted her head to look at the sideview mirror. She stared at it for quite some time. "If I don't make it, I want you to find the money and ensure that my son is not left without anything."

It was so unexpected that I asked her, "What was that?"

"The family has a villa on the island of Capri—"

"Erika, you're going to—"

"Let me finish," she said and paused. "It's on the southeastern side off of Via Matteotti. At the end. The entrance has an arched wrought-iron gate with an opposing pair of rampant lions."

Up ahead, I saw that the highway would turn into two lanes, each way, and looked at the sideview mirror.

She leaned over to get in my face. "Are you listening carefully?"

"Yeah, I'm listening," I said and looked to her.

"They could torture me all they like, but they'll never find the money."

"Erika, everyone has a breaking point."

"It won't matter."

"What do you mean it won't matter?"

The highway opened up to two lanes. Cars that had been stuck behind our slow-moving convoy began to pass us. The Opel remained behind us, which gave other cars the opportunity to take the left lane.

Erika started to respond, but I yelled, "Get Kurt on the floor. Now!"

30

Kurt didn't have to be told twice. It saddened me to think that he now knew the routine of going for cover. Erika made sure he was secure. She grabbed the backpack and pulled out the .45 and Luger, while I kept the distance between our truck and Aaron's at a minimum.

As a small, open-bed truck came up beside us, the Opel accelerated and got into the left lane just behind it. The 1920s Fiat truck looked like it had been excavated from a dump somewhere and put into use. And because of this, it had a tough time getting up enough speed to pass us. The Opel was right up on its rear.

Erika loaded a round into the chamber of the .45 and placed it in my lap. I glanced at her as she did the same for the Luger. She had a fierce expression on her face; she was ready to go into action to keep her son safe.

I eased the truck over into the left lane in an attempt to force the old truck to slow down, effectively blocking the Opel. The driver of the old truck honked his horn and shook his fist at me.

The honking must have alerted Aaron, and he started to slow, forcing me to do the same. That gave the truck the room to surge ahead. The Opel was right on his tail and coming up alongside us.

I rolled down the window to have a clear shot. Just as I did so, the Opel's driver made his move. It swerved to the left, putting its left wheels into the gravel divider, then accelerated just enough to clip the back end of the old truck.

The old truck began to fishtail. As the driver tried to get it under control on the wet pavement, the truck started whipping from one side to the other. Finally, it was too much for the truck's suspension. It slammed sideways into my truck, then bounced off, tipped to one side and flipped. I tried braking, but everything unfolded too quickly. I slammed into the tumbling truck. The impact forced me to the right. I heard the screams of the people in the cargo area as I fought to keep the truck on the road. The old truck did one more spin and then came to a halt in the opposing lanes of traffic.

The Opel had tried and failed to stop my truck, but I'd lost speed and had to keep both hands on the steering wheel. The Opel came up beside me. I glanced down. Adrenaline slammed into my brain.

Ziegler was in the front passenger's seat, and he was staring straight at me with an MP 40 submachine gun aimed at my head. At the same moment, Erika leaned over me to point her pistol out the window.

"Get down!" I yelled and pushed her down. I hit the brakes just as Ziegler opened up with his submachine gun. I expected the windshield to shatter and rounds to penetrate the door, but he was aiming for the tires and engine hood. He was trying to disable the truck so they could abduct Erika.

Erika forced herself up and out of my grasp. She stuck her pistol out the window and fired. Her rounds hit the Opel's windows and both doors. The driver swerved and sped up to avoid more hits.

With the Luger's magazine emptied, she moved back to her seat to reload. The Opel's driver used the pause to slow enough to come alongside again.

Enraged, I aimed the .45 directly at Ziegler and opened up. My rounds hit the roof and rear door. The Opel veered to the left and onto the gravel divider. I continued to fire until the magazine emptied.

I must have hit someone or something vital, because the Opel braked hard. The tires dug up the gravel and mud as it came to a hard stop. Traffic had become a tangle on both sides near the shooting and because of the now-wrecked Italian truck.

As the image of the Opel grew smaller in my sideview mirror, I felt relieved that we got out of it safely and angry I'd missed a perfect opportunity to put several .45 rounds into Ziegler. I became aware of Kurt wailing with fear and Erika on the floorboard trying to calm him down. The poor kid was on the edge of hysteria.

Erika looked up at me. "Keep driving."

I nodded. She and I both knew the worst thing to do would be to stop. And I was glad Moishe and Aaron had continued to move forward. They must have known the convoy had to keep going and gain as much distance from the mayhem as possible. And no telling how many other Nazis would be still on our tail.

I just hoped the rounds from the submachine gun fire had

not damaged the engine too badly. Otherwise, our escape would be short-lived.

31

We were back on country roads and hadn't stopped since the attack. The convoy had left the main highway at Montevarchi and bypassed Siena, and we were on a two-lane road cutting through Tuscan farmland and vineyards. The rain had let up, making it easier to negotiate the twists and turns. It had just turned noon, and we'd have daylight for hours yet.

The images of Ziegler in that car with the submachine gun kept playing out in my mind. And not for the first time, I cursed myself for not shredding him with .45 slugs. I'd missed my opportunity, and now we were putting more and more distance between us and him.

Erika and Kurt were more important to me at the moment. As much as it burned my gut, I tried to resolve the idea that I might have to abandon meting out retribution for what he did to Hana and the family.

Kurt had curled up in a ball on his mother's lap and hadn't uttered a sound since the shooting. Erika sang softly to him and rocked him. I decided to pitch in and started to sing

"*Bache, Bache Kuchen,*" an old nursery rhyme my grandmother had sung to me when I was a child. Erika joined in, and we sang about a baker saying you had to have seven ingredients to bake a good cake.

We did our best to sound cheerful, and it seemed to have some effect on Kurt. He uncurled and alternated expressionless looks between his mother and me. Erika put her hand on my arm and smiled, which didn't go unnoticed by Kurt.

The convoy took another turn past fields of crops that had been harvested months ago. Moishe put on his blinker, and up ahead Feldman and Hazan's car and the lead truck had already pulled over onto a muddy road. I followed the rest into a patch of woods bordering two fields.

Everyone slowed and came to a stop.

"Finally," Erika said. "I really have to pee."

"Me too," Kurt said in a barely audible voice.

"You'd better find a private spot now. I think everyone needs to do the same thing."

We climbed down from the cab. People were already jumping off the truck and hurrying into the woods. I went around back to help Henri get everyone down to the ground.

"Is everyone okay?" I asked him.

"Some are pretty traumatized. The MP 40 has a distinctive sound, and it brought up terrible memories for many of us. Aside from that, just a few bruises."

After the last of the passengers got out of the truck, I went around to the engine hood. There were several bullet holes in the driver's door, but at least twenty rounds had pierced the hood on the side and front. Ziegler had obviously concentrated his fire at the front, because at least half the rounds had entered the area around the radiator. There were bullet hits on the front tire, but combat tires had thick rubber, and most of the bullets had bounced off.

A middle-aged man in tattered clothes came up to me with his hat in his hand. He pointed at his chest and said in accented German, "Mechanic." He then gestured toward the hood.

I nodded. He opened the hood and stood on the front bumper to examine the engine.

"How bad is it?" I asked him in German.

He shook his head while still looking at the engine block. "Not good."

"Will it still make it to Rome, at least?"

The man started rattling off words in what I assumed was Polish. Feldman and Hazan appeared, and Feldman said something to him in Yiddish. The man responded, and they had a little back-and-forth before Feldman turned to me.

"He said the engine block was hit several times and is leaking oil. The air filter is damaged, which will present a problem over time. The most concerning is a bullet lodged in the radiator. The bullet is keeping the water from leaking fully, but it could go at any time. One just missed the brake line. That was fortunate."

"Ask him if it can make it to the Rome camp," I said.

Feldman did. The man shrugged and said something to him.

"I don't need a translation," I said.

"We have to talk," Hazan said and tilted his head toward the front of the convoy.

I looked for Erika, but she was still somewhere in the woods with Kurt. I nodded and followed Feldman and Hazan to a spot near the lead car and away from the others.

"Having that woman with us has become too much of a liability," Hazan said.

"If you're talking about Erika, then I go too," I said.

Hazan stopped and spun to face me. "That's fine with me."

We were still close enough to passengers for them to overhear.

Feldman looked around and said in a hushed tone, "David, we're not going to abandon them. Are you forgetting that Mason is the one who got us out of that British camp, and Erika refused to go unless he did?"

"We can't risk the safety of the other passengers," Hazan said. "It's a miracle that no one got hurt. As long as she's with the convoy, we risk another attack, and it could be far more determined and deadly this time."

"We agreed to take her—"

Feldman stopped talking when Erika appeared in front of the lead car.

She wore a defiant expression, though she had tears in her eyes. "If I'm no longer useful as a piece of bait to you, perhaps you'll take my money," Erika said. "I'll give you half, if you get me to my family's villa."

"Erika," I said, "you don't give them anything. We can go faster and further without them." I said to Hazan, "If you want to get rid of us, then I'm taking the car."

"Fair enough—" Hazan started to say when Feldman interrupted.

"No. We're not mercenaries. We get everyone to Naples. No one is left behind."

Feldman and Hazan started arguing with each other about the morality of the commitments and the reality of the danger, and I took Erika's hand and started to lead her away. "Come on, we'll get our things and get out of here."

Erika pulled her hand away. "Don't lead me away like a child."

She faced all three of us. "Stop this, all of you." When she got Feldman's and Hazan's attention, she said, "I'm willing to give you close to a quarter million Swiss francs if you let us stay. Think of what you could do with that sum. Split it with these people, buy weapons for your fight for independence, bribe officials to get everyone to Palestine."

"Keep it and make a good life for Kurt," I said to her.

She ignored me and continued to stare at Feldman and Hazan.

"I don't want anyone to be injured because of me," she said, "but giving you that money for these people, for your cause, is worth taking the risk. Don't you think? We have maybe three hours to get to Rome, then another three or four to Naples, then Capri. That's it. Keep Kurt and me alive until then, and I'll hand over the money."

"Erika, that's way too much," I said.

She ignored me again as she glared at them. Hazan looked at Feldman, who, after a long pause, nodded his head.

"I've got to get Kurt," Erika said as she turned and marched away. "I'll meet you back at the truck."

Feldman and Hazan seemed indecisive as to what to do next. I wanted to throttle both of them.

"It looks like everyone has a price," I said to them. "Suddenly, risking the lives of the others doesn't seem so risky."

"How much is she giving to you?" Hazan said with a sneer.

I advanced on Hazan, determined to beat that sneer off his face.

Feldman got between us. "You two can settle this once the job is done. Not before. Right now, we have to figure out how to avoid another attack."

"The only thing we can do is remain vigilant," I said. "We're not going to find them on the road." A thought came to me. "Is your buddy in the trunk and still alive?"

"We were going to take care of him this evening," Hazan said.

"It's been pretty quiet back there," Feldman said.

"Let's see," I said.

The three of us walked up to the sedan. I pointed to a bend in the road. "We'll drive it up there, behind that stand of trees."

We all got in the car, and Hazan drove around the curve, about a hundred yards from the trucks, and stopped the car. At the back, I got my brass knuckles ready in case Schiller tried to cry for help. Feldman pulled out one of the deadliest-looking knives I'd ever seen. I knew it as an F-S fighting knife, a favored weapon of the British commandos. Hazan used the key to unlock the trunk lid and raised it.

The odors of a sewer hit us first. Schiller was lying motionless on his side with his back to us. He didn't move.

"Is he dead?" Feldman asked.

I turned him onto his back. His feet and wrists were bound, and he was gagged with a cloth. He must have defecated on himself, because the odor wafted up with the motion —certainly something that can happen at death. But then I noticed the veins in his neck still thumped with blood. He opened his eyes, but his gaze was unfocused.

"He must have passed out," I said.

"Exhausted himself, more like," Hazan said. "He was

screaming and banging up a storm when we were on the highway."

"Especially when we told him who we were."

I slapped his cheek a couple of times to bring him to consciousness. When his eyes focused on me, he recoiled and tried to get as deep into the trunk as he could. I put my index finger to my lips to remind him to not make a sound. He seemed to be teetering on the edge of delirium. I might have had pity for the guy, but all I had to do was remind myself what he and others did in the extermination camps to feel nothing for him but contempt.

I leaned into the trunk despite the odors. "You met my companions. They want to tear off your balls and make you eat them, but I said no. At least, not unless you answer a couple of questions."

He said nothing, though his eyes darted in their sockets from me to Feldman and Hazan.

"Dietrich, are you ready to talk, or do I let my friends get their wish?"

Schiller closed his eyes and nodded.

"You try to cry out, and they'll cut out your tongue."

When Schiller nodded again, I pulled down his gag. "What is your group's destination in Rome?"

He seemed to be confused by the question, and I worried his reason was too far gone for him to be of any use.

Using a quiet, friendly voice, I said, "I know you and your companions go someplace in Rome to get Red Cross passports and visas. And I know it has something to do with the Vatican. Where exactly?"

Schiller panted and continued shifting his gaze between the three of us.

I threw up my hands. "He's all yours," I said and backed away.

Feldman and Hazan started to move in, and Schiller cried out, "Wait, wait."

I stepped back up, dramatically pushing myself between them, and said, "The place in Rome, Dietrich."

"The Collegio Santa Maria dell'Anima. It's a papal college for Germanic priests."

"Rome is a big place. I need an address."

"It's close to the Piazza Navona on Via di Santa Maria dell'Anima."

"Are they going to be there?" Hazan asked.

Schiller looked confused by the question. "How would I know that? Please ..." He gestured at the lip of the trunk to indicate his present circumstances.

I glared at Hazan, warning him to let me do the interrogating. "Your group's destination is at the college. Is that where you planned to stay?"

"It's been proposed as a rendezvous point, but I heard we're often put up in apartments around the college."

"Where?" Hazan said.

"I have no idea," Schiller said. His fear and frustration had caused him to raise his voice in a shrill.

I glanced back toward the convoy to see if anyone had come around the curve in the road to investigate. No one appeared, but that wouldn't last much longer.

"We have what we need," I said. "And we're running out of time. Someone's bound to come looking for you two."

"Please," Schiller said, begging for his life.

I shoved the gag back over his mouth and turned away. Considering his complicity at Sobibor, I had no sympathy for him, but I found I didn't want to have anything to do with his execution. He wasn't worth it. He was too helpless, too pathetic, a low-level paper pusher who deserved to be tried.

I knew Feldman and Hazan couldn't continue to keep the man in the trunk, and he could alert his friends if we let him go. They would take care of him their way. As I walked away, I heard moans and the rustling of bodies, footsteps in the snow and dead leaves as the two carried Schiller deeper into the woods and toward a shallow grave.

Maybe I wore a sign on my forehead, maybe Erika was just good at reading my face, but whatever the case, her cold glare told me she had a decent idea of what had transpired with Feldman and Hazan. I kept my distance and chain-smoked cigarettes—something I hadn't done in months.

A good twenty minutes had passed since I left Feldman and Hazan to their grim task. The passengers had all answered their calls of nature and snacked on some meager provisions or talked among themselves. Moishe, Henri, Shimon, and Aaron knew not to ask about why we hadn't moved on. I stayed near the lead truck to run interference with anyone curious about the pair's whereabouts. When someone asked, I told them they'd gone to scout the road ahead. That and a stern look was enough to discourage further investigation.

The first few times, that had worked, but everyone was getting agitated by the mysterious delay. Fortunately, it was about that time that Feldman and Hazan made their appearance. I let them pass me without a word. They went directly to the drivers and Shimon and Henri and told them to get everyone ready to move.

Feldman and Hazan came up to me, and Hazan said, "We still haven't figured out a way to avoid another attack."

"We were talking about it on the way back," Feldman said. "Maybe we set up an ambush."

"Which road?" I asked. "They probably got off the main highway to avoid the cops, like we did. I say we hit them on their turf. And where they'd least expect it. We're going there, they're going there …"

"You're talking about Rome?" Hazan said.

I nodded. "The group is divided on whether to stay or get out of Italy while the going's good. Regardless, they'll need Red Cross displaced-person passports and then to hole up somewhere to wait for the visas. We know someone at the Vatican is helping them. And we know where."

"You're going on the word of a Nazi?"

"He was telling the truth."

"So we're supposed to break into a papal college in hopes of finding our targets?"

"I'll tell you what: You two stay in the camp in Rome, all cozy and warm. I'm perfectly happy to go in myself and do what I need to do."

Hazan and I glared at each other, while Feldman shifted his look between the two of us.

"Would you guys calm down?" Feldman said. He turned to Hazan. "Mason's right. The only way to stop these ambushes is to take the initiative. We recce the place, and if it looks promising, we go in. Think of who we might find there."

"That's your plan?" Hazan asked. "Do you know the layout

of the place? How many priests are we going to have to go through to get at our targets? Are we going to shoot them down in front of witnesses? Try to drag them away?"

"If you have a better plan, I'm all ears," Feldman said. "This way, not only do we take the fight to them, we each have an opportunity to get our men. We at least cripple them and get to our destination unmolested."

"I don't like it," Hazan said as he shook his head.

"And I think it's our best option," Feldman said. "Even if only one or two of the men from the group are at the college, they're important targets. Some of the worst of the worst. I say we recce the place and then decide from there."

Feldman looked over my shoulder to the trucks. I turned, as did Hazan, and saw a number of people standing around the back of the trucks and staring at us. Moishe stood outside the open door of his truck and made a hand gesture that we should wrap it up.

The three of us broke up. They headed for the sedan parked around the bend, and I went toward the convoy. The onlookers slowly climbed into the backs of their trucks. Moishe and Aaron started their engines. Erika stared at me from the passenger's seat of our truck.

I got into the cab, settled in behind the steering wheel, and started the engine.

"The men hunting us aren't the only monsters," Erika said in an icy-cold tone.

I said nothing, though the words made my temper flare, and I revved the engine a little too much. A loud bang came from under the hood. The engine began to rattle.

I stood out of the cab and whistled at Aaron's truck. It stopped. I leapt to the ground and lifted the engine hood.

Water was spewing from the radiator. The bullet had been dislodged by the force of the pressure.

I yelled for Erika to switch off the engine just as Aaron and Shimon joined me.

Moishe let out a sigh and walked to the back of the truck.

"Things are going to get pretty crowded," I said.

"At least it happened here and not on the road," Shimon said.

Aaron and Henri helped the passengers to the ground and began to split up the group.

I went over to the passenger's side and opened the door. "We're going to have to find accommodations in another truck."

"What were you and the other two plotting? How to steal my money and do God knows what to Kurt and me?"

I felt more relieved than angry; despite the insult, she didn't know the truth about Schiller's fate. "You might be surprised, but it had nothing to do with you. At least not directly. We were trying to figure out a way to avoid another ambush on the road."

"And did you?"

Kurt jumped into my arms and held on tight. "When we get out on the road, I'm supposed to open the door and push you out."

The venomous look faded from her face, and a faint smile replaced it. She picked up my backpack and tossed it, aiming for my head. I caught it, dropped it, and lowered Kurt to the road.

I offered my hand to help Erika, but she ignored it and jumped to the ground on her own. She got close to my face and said, "I believe you. But bear in mind, as a Soviet asset, I did learn a few ways to kill a man."

She gave me a mischievous smile, plucked Kurt out of my arms, and headed for the working trucks. As I watched her go, I prayed she would never have to use those skills.

Aaron had already managed to get three people from my disabled truck into the cab, and people were still trying to find space in back. I grabbed up my backpack and the two bags and joined Erika and Kurt at the tailgate of Aaron's truck.

Henri was about to climb in back, but I put my hand on his arm. "You ride up front with a couple of elderly folks. I'll keep Erika and Kurt company back here."

Henri nodded and guided a couple in their seventies toward the cab. I helped Erika and Kurt get in and then hoisted myself into the cargo area. The choice spots were obviously near the tailgate, as that portion was thick with people. The three of us stepped over legs and arms and found a corner at the front, behind the wall of the cab.

Once we got settled in, I understood why the tailgate area was so popular. There were more noxious fumes than fresh air where we were. We had to sit with our backs against our bags, our knees bent, and shoulder to shoulder, with Kurt tucked in Erika's lap.

"How long is this part of the trip?" Erika asked.

We were so close that when she looked at me to ask this, our noses almost touched. I could smell her, feel the weight of her body pressing against mine, and it gave me a warm flush. It made me self-conscious, and I looked away. "They'll stick to the back roads, so I figure four to five hours."

Aaron stood at the back of the truck. "We'll be at the camp

in Rome in a few hours. And I'll try to make the trip as comfortable as I can." He dropped the canvas back, plunging us into relative darkness.

She tilted her head toward my ear and whispered, "I hope I don't have to pee in the meantime."

"You're not the only one."

"Thank you for being back here with us," she said in an intimate tone.

Still self-conscious, I simply nodded. Out of the corner of my eye, I could see her smile, as she seemed touched by my uneasiness.

The truck started moving with an initial jolt, then rolled and bounced on the rough dirt road. The movements were exaggerated because of the darkness, and it illustrated to me what these people had put up with since beginning this journey. Especially during the attack on the highway.

Which brought me to the point that was nagging at me now: I had thought that being in the cargo area would reduce the risk of another attack. But being wedged in as we were, and in the dark, made me begin to doubt the wisdom of that decision. It made us more vulnerable. We would be unable to defend ourselves if the wolves moved in again for the kill.

33

Two and a half hours into the trip, the roads had flattened out, meaning we had to contend less with being jolted by changing elevation and were only bothered by the occasional sharp turn. The constant rumble and dim light had encouraged many of the other passengers to doze, including Kurt, who was curled up next to his mother's thigh. Erika had laid her head on my shoulder and dozed off thirty minutes ago.

The truck passed over a pothole, making it bounce and then bang against the tarmac.

She lifted her head and brushed her hand across my shoulder. "Sorry."

"Happy to accommodate."

She checked on Kurt, then turned back to me. "Does this woman love you?"

The question came out of the blue and left me silent.

"The one you've trekked across Italy to meet," Erika said.

I finally surmised where this might be going. At that

moment, I was happy to go along. "I don't know if she does or not," I said, answering honestly.

"From what you told me, she left you twice."

"When you put it that way …"

"What other way would you put it? She married another man only months after you two went your separate ways. Then, when you were still in jail in Vienna, she left you again."

I took a moment to search for a good response. "We came together like a bang, but we never seemed to find steady ground after that."

"Obviously by her getting married, she wanted something more stable."

"Gee, thanks."

She waited patiently for an answer with her soft eyes and an open expression. I didn't take offense.

After a pause, I said, "Probably."

"Someone more compliant to her wishes."

"More than likely."

"Yet you still chase after her like a heart-sick schoolboy."

"Her message made it sound like she's in trouble. We may not be lovers, but I will always go to her if she needs me."

She leaned in closer. "Something tells me she doesn't really know what she has in you."

The rumble of the truck, her body close to mine, her lips hovered near mine. I kissed her. It was soft, at first. Then we pressed into each other and our tongues explored. The world around me faded. We embraced with a passion that came from the release of tension and trauma, loneliness and need.

The truck hit another pothole, which made everyone stir. We broke our embrace and sat up. Kurt lifted his head just enough to lay it on Erika's lap. She stroked Kurt's hair and looked at her feet.

I hadn't expected the kiss or the passion. Maybe my feelings had been there for some time, and I hadn't been aware of them. Despite her background, despite the deceit and obfuscation, I felt close to her. There was no shame attached. I was still in love with Laura, and always would be, but now I felt confused. Erika had struck a nerve in me. By all appearances, Laura had cast me aside, and I had indeed often asked myself why I was chasing after her.

"I understand the burden you carry," Erika said while still regarding her feet. "Watching that man murder Hana and the Czech family must haunt you. I'm okay that you're using me as bait to get to him."

I found this touching, and it made me reflect on my motivations. "Using you as bait was an excuse for staying with you. Protecting you." Vocalizing it made me see something I'd hidden from myself.

She looked at me. "I just wonder if taking your revenge on Ziegler will really give you peace."

I smiled at her. "That was a very diplomatic way of persuading me to let him live. In truth, it *will* give me some peace. I won't have any if I let him go on with his life as if nothing happened. He has to pay for what he's done. And seeing he gets a fair trial is out of the question. He's already been arrested a couple of times and released."

The truck took a sharp turn and went over a bump before coming to a stop a moment later. The engine was shut off.

"We've made it to the camp?" Erika asked in surprise.

"I hope so. Otherwise, we have another problem."

Kurt had obviously had enough of emergency stops, and our coming to a halt drove him off the floor and into my arms for safety. With his arms wrapped around me and Erika smiling at the both of us, I felt part of my damaged soul begin to heal.

Shimon jumped down and pulled back the canvas flaps. I had to shield my eyes from the bright light of the setting sun. People struggled to stand on their cold legs. I, too, had a tough time, especially trying to hoist Kurt at the same time. And when I put weight on my feet, they screamed in pain. I resorted to using the frame for the canvas cover to steady myself.

Erika was already on her feet, and she took Kurt. Feldman waited for us as we made our way to the tailgate.

Erika must have spotted him at the same instant as me, because she said to me, "That's not a good sign."

I jumped down, and Shimon and I helped Erika and Kurt descend to the ground. What I saw in front of me left me confused: it appeared to be an ancient Roman forum. Though the facades looked real enough, the exposed backs of the temples and towering buildings revealed they were just hollow structures of wooden frames covered in plaster and paint. To the left was a long line of tall, warehouse-looking buildings with single-digit numbers painted on them. And beyond the buildings stood another row of similarly shaped structures. Some showed signs of bomb damage, with roofs gone and rubble piled in the narrow alleys between the buildings.

"Where are we?" I asked Feldman.

"Cinecitta. Italy's main movie studio complex. Or at least it was. The whole thing has been turned into a DP camp. Part for Italians left homeless by the war, and the rest for displaced Jews and a hodgepodge of international refugees."

While the sight of the place was impressive, I noticed the walls that surrounded the complex were easy to scale and left unguarded. Within the walls, a makeshift fence divided the immense complex into its two parts, but that was meant to be a demarcation and not a deterrent. People wandered on the grounds or hung laundry on lines strung along the fence line.

"We need to talk," Feldman said. He nodded toward a vacant spot near the perimeter wall. "Let's go over there."

Erika started to go with us, but Feldman said, "This might not be something for the boy to hear."

Erika told Kurt to stay with Shimon, who looked at a loss for what to do with the boy. Kurt kept calm, though he stared at his mother and refused to be led anywhere out of sight of her.

We followed Feldman to a space where other trucks and cars were parked.

"What's up?" I asked.

"Two Americans came across three of the Nazis in the group following us. They were trying to infiltrate the camp. Two men and a woman."

Erika sucked in her breath and put her hand to her mouth.

"You know this for sure?" I asked.

"I'm friends with one of the administrators, and one of the Americans told him to alert us as soon as we arrived."

"Do they have them in custody?" I asked.

"Only the woman, I'm afraid," Feldman said. "I don't know any more details."

"I want to talk to her," I said. "And find out who these Americans are." Though I had a feeling I knew who.

"I figured you would," Feldman said. "They're up at the administration building."

34

E rika and I followed Feldman toward the sound stages. On the way, Erika offered to relieve Shimon of Kurt, but he volunteered to take Kurt to a big playground set up for all the children. After some persuasion, Kurt went with Shimon. Erika waited until they had disappeared around the corner.

The three of us continued and turned down an alleyway between stages three and four. The complex was even bigger than I'd thought, and it took several minutes to weave through the labyrinth of stages to find the two-story administration building. I heard a dozen languages, including Arabic, and the mix of cultures and skin tones reminded me of my time in Tangier.

Two Italian policemen guarded the entrance to the building.

"Is this camp run by the Italians?"

"It's the main UNRRA administrative complex for all their DP camps in Italy. Italian police provide security. There's also an American presence here as well."

That explained what my two CIC shadows were doing there.

A man in a tailored suit stepped out of the building to greet Feldman. They spoke in Hebrew for a few moments, then Feldman introduced Erika and me to Elias Aronov.

"I'll leave you two," Feldman said.

"You don't want to see who they caught?" I asked.

"It's best if Hazan and I avoid much contact with those CIC agents. When you're done, we'll be in sound stage number two."

Feldman walked away, and Aronov ushered us inside. We followed him down several hallways until we were in the far reaches of the building. Another Italian policeman stood guard at a solid-looking door. Seeing the administrator, the guard came to attention. He knocked on the door and opened it.

Aronov left us, and we entered what appeared to have been a recording studio. We stepped into a small room with sound-dampening material on the walls and the remnants of a sound-mixing board. One wall was dominated by a thick window overlooking a larger room, where I figured the musicians played or actors spoke dialogue. The other portion of the room was clear of anything other than four wood chairs and a long table.

Sitting at the table was Greta Schweiger, Franz Stangl's mistress, the one who had stopped on the mountain road and was part of the party who tried to kidnap Erika at the Dolcé camp.

Erika stiffened, but not from fear. I thought I might have to restrain her from attacking the window. She took one stride toward it with balled fists.

I was so fixated on Schweiger that I didn't notice Barker and Tilsit sitting on lounge chairs in a corner of the room. They stood without saying anything and eyed Erika.

I said, "When I heard two Americans had nabbed some Nazi infiltrators, I figured it was you two."

Barker and Tilsit nodded greetings and moved up next to Erika. They had yet to say anything. Their expressions were neutral, but I could tell they were trying to intimidate Erika and send me a message.

"She stays," I said to them.

The agents continued their icy stares.

"You guys must be a real hoot back at headquarters," I said.

"We're not here to make jokes," Tilsit said.

"Good thing, too," I said. "How did you know we'd show up at this camp?"

"Most everyone comes through here," Barker said. "We got news of the incident on the highway and figured that had to be you. Heard there was a lot of shooting. We weren't even sure you guys had made it out in one piece."

"I hope you don't plan on staying in Italy," Tilsit said. "The local police aren't happy about all the shooting and bloodshed."

"They should worry more about all the Nazis hiding in plain sight."

"That's probably the only reason you're not in jail right now."

"It'll make them look bad," I said.

"That's about right."

I tilted my head at the window. "I heard you caught three of them."

"The two males got away," Barker said. "Stangl and

Wagner. They opened fire and pinned us down. The only reason we got the girl was because she tripped and twisted her ankle pretty badly." He held out his hand to stop me. "And before I hear any wisecracks about them escaping, the last thing we'd expected was to see their well-armed mugs nosing around here."

"I'm not the one you're going to have to explain that to."

"Does she have to be here?" Tilsit asked, glancing at Erika.

"She's the one they're after, and she knows Schweiger. So, yeah, she stays."

Erika walked up to the window and stared at Schweiger.

"Has she said anything?" Erika asked in German, still facing the window.

Tilsit looked at me, and I translated.

"Nope, not a thing," Tilsit said. "She even tried to bite me."

I told Erika what Tilsit said.

"It's our turn," I said.

"Knock yourself out," Barker said.

Erika and I went up to the door serving the two rooms.

Barker came over to us and said, "We'll be listening in, okay?"

I nodded. He unlocked the door and stepped aside. I let Erika enter first, with me right behind to watch for Schweiger's reaction. The woman looked up and blanched.

"Hello, Greta," Erika said in German.

Schweiger glared at Erika, which was a pretty effective look since she had steel-blue eyes and red hair tousled from her failed escape. It was the first time I'd seen her in the light. She had striking features: high, flared cheekbones, full lips, and a long, pinched nose. Her shoe on her right foot was missing, with a wrapped bandage in its place.

Schweiger put her hands on the table as if she would jump up and attack, but she was restrained by handcuffs bolted to the tabletop. "I will not talk to you or to him. Get out!"

"This time, we're the ones dictating terms," Erika said as she sat across from Schweiger.

I stood at the side of the table just out of bite range. "It must be terrible to realize that your boyfriend considers you expendable," I said in German and paused for effect.

She said nothing and looked away with her head high in a defiant posture.

"Franz isn't coming back for you," I said. "You're finished in his eyes. He'll do his best to get to some safe haven, while you go to prison for assaulting American intelligence agents. Then, once you get out, you'll be sent back to Germany. If he makes it out of Italy, he'll send for his wife and children and spend his days in some lush setting, while you'll have to scrounge for food and shelter."

Schweiger growled and slammed her fists on the table. Her head whipped around in my direction. "He won't do that. Once he cuts your throats, he'll come for me."

"You know that's not true, Greta," Erika said. "You were his plaything, and now he's happy to discard you like a child who's grown tired of a toy."

Schweiger spit at her. The spittle landed on Erika's coat, but Erika remained calm.

"I'm authorized to offer you a deal," I said.

I was pleased to see that Erika didn't react to my lie.

Schweiger blinked—a good sign. I continued. "You tell us what we want to know, and I'll see to it that those agents don't press assault charges. You'll stay out of jail, though you'll still be sent back." I stopped and looked at Erika. "Where is she from?"

"Berlin," Erika said.

"Berlin's just one big pile of rubble," I said to Schweiger and leaned in. "And in the Russian zone."

Schweiger's shoulders collapsed into her chest, and she slumped in her chair. "I'll never betray Franz. Never."

"You have to look out for yourself now," Erika said. "Berlin is a sad and dangerous place for attractive young women. Russian soldiers rove in bands and do what they want with helpless Germans."

"That's while you're starving and living in a hovel," I said. "But if you talk, I can see to it that you're sent wherever you want in the American or British zones in Germany. In fact, I can seal the deal right now."

I went over to the door and knocked. Barker opened it. I stepped into the recording room and closed the door.

"What do you mean seal a deal?" Barker said. "The worst she can be charged with is being caught with a firearm and leaving Germany without authorization. We'll hold her for a few days to see what we can get out of her, then hand her over to the Italians for deportation."

"She doesn't know that," I said. "How many interrogations have you guys done?"

Neither one claimed any experience.

"I came back in here to make her think I'm cutting a deal with you and to let her stew in the meantime. Work with me here. If I have to bring you in, I need for you guys to play along. If this works out, you may not need to go through the agony of trying to wrench something out of her."

Barker looked at Tilsit, who nodded once. I opened the

door and went into the studio. As I walked up to the table, I said, "The agents have agreed. You talk, and no jail time and the location in Germany of your choosing."

Schweiger said nothing as she stared at the wall. She tried to act indifferent, but she unconsciously picked at her nails that she'd already taken down to the quick.

"Is the group you're traveling with staying at the papal college Santa Maria dell'Anima?"

Her expression remained fixed, but her fingers had frozen in place.

"Greta, you have one minute to answer me," I said, raising my voice. "The jail they've picked out for you is one of the worst in Rome. And just imagine what the Italian prisoners will do to you in there when they find out you're a Nazi. And when they find out who your lover is, your life will turn from miserable to impossible."

"Yes," Schweiger said.

"Yes, what?"

She jerked her head in my direction and yelled, "Yes, they're at the papal college."

"How many are in your group?"

She started digging at her nails again, and she didn't seem to notice she'd drawn blood from several fingers. "Eight."

"Their names. We know Gustav Wagner and Franz Stangl, but who else?"

She said nothing.

"Greta, please," Erika said. "I know you weren't a fanatic. You were with Franz because you wanted a better life. I'm sure he told you he would leave his wife—"

"Shut up!" Schweiger said. "You're a whore and a traitor to your country."

I slammed my fist on the table next to Schweiger. She jumped in her seat and covered her face with shaking hands.

In a voice one notch below yelling, I said, "Tell me, now, Greta, or I'll call for the agents to take you away."

She put her hands down, exposing her tears. She jabbed her finger at Erika. "That whore's husband for one."

"Ludwig Klarsfeld?"

She nodded.

"Who else?"

"I don't know them all. Theodor Ziegler is one of them."

Even though I knew it was coming, hearing Ziegler's name made the hairs on the back of my neck stand up. I had to resist rushing out the door.

"Is everyone staying at the papal college?" I asked.

"How would I know that? I've been in custody for hours. Everyone's aware of that by now. Do you think they would simply go on like nothing happened?"

She had a point, and it was sobering to hear it. Greta Schweiger's capture would surely throw a wrench in the group's plan. They'd feel exposed and paranoid. That meant they'd be unpredictable.

"What about surrounding apartments? Was anyone in the group put up in one of those?"

"I wouldn't know."

"Were Vatican DP passports issued to everyone?"

"As far as I know."

"What about travel visas to South America?"

"That's why we were to pause in Rome. If someone has been issued a visa, I wouldn't know about it."

"There are others traveling in tandem with yours. Were they supposed to go to the papal college?"

"I'm just the mistress. Some of the people I've been traveling with don't trust me. They see me as a liability. They certainly aren't going to share everything with the likes of me."

"So it is possible."

Schweiger glared at me. "Do you want me to guess now?"

Erika stood, stepped up to me, and whispered in my ear.

I relayed Erika's question to Schweiger. "What are the names of the people planning to kill Frau Klarsfeld and steal her money?"

"It's not that whore's money. She stole it from her husband. It's his to do with what he wants."

"I'm not interested in arguing about where the money came from—"

I stopped when Erika charged Schweiger. She got in the woman's face. "That's a lie. That is my family's money. That bastard has no right to claim it."

I put my hands on Erika's shoulders and pulled her back before Schweiger was tempted to take a chunk out of her face.

Schweiger sneered at Erika. "Don't cry to me about who has the right. You're the idiot who married that bastard."

Erika pushed against me to get at Schweiger. She growled and fought to get free from my grasp. She had completely lost control. I had to get her out of there, and I gently urged her toward the door.

She only put up a little resistance as she shouted at Schweiger past my shoulder. "Whatever happens to me, I have the satisfaction of knowing you'll be living in poverty. You've been discarded like the trash that you are. You'll have to trade your body for a morsel of bread."

The door opened, and I guided her out of the room. Barker closed the door.

"You stay out here while I finish with her," I said to Erika.

She nodded. "I'm sorry. Just being the in same room with her finally got to me. I kept thinking back to when she bragged about dressing up in an SS uniform and making the rounds of Sobibor with Wagner, laughing at his cruelty and encouraging him to shoot the Jews."

"Then I'm not going to feel guilty when we renege on the deal."

Erika looked at Barker. "Put her in a deep, dark hole and let her rot."

Barker didn't know what to say. I didn't wait to find out if he came up with a response. I opened the door and went back into the studio. I marched up to her, planted both hands on the table, and leaned in.

"I want full names, Greta. Now. All of them."

Schweiger looked shaken, as if she had finally realized her coming fate. She swallowed hard and said, "Franz Stangl, Dr. Fleischman, Konrad Hoffmann, Rudolf Lange, Friedrich Kappler, Ludwig Klarsfeld, Gustav Wagner, and Theodor Ziegler. There might be others, but those are the only ones I know."

"And they plan to kill Erika and her son if they can get their hands on the money."

"That's seems obvious, doesn't it? And I hope it's a slow death."

My rage boiled up. I gripped the edge of the table with so much force that the wood planks groaned in protest. Schweiger saw the look in my eyes, and she reared back as far as the chair would allow. I turned around and walked out.

E rika, Barker, and Tilsit were standing at the window of the studio when I exited. I remained at the closed door and tried to calm myself. Barker and Tilsit said nothing, but Erika came over to me and took my arms.

"It's all right," she said in a soft tone. "It's not anything I haven't heard before."

Her touch and voice helped release most of the anger, and with it came clarity. I looked down at Erika and smiled, then I took her hands and placed them at her sides.

She saw something in my eyes change, because she said, "You're going after them, aren't you?"

I nodded.

"You plan to break into that college for priests and hunt them down."

"They have to be stopped."

"This is about exacting revenge on Ziegler. Nothing more."

Tilsit moved forward. "You're not serious about attacking those men on Vatican property."

"You don't want to land a bunch of mass murderers?" I asked Tilsit.

"We want them as much as anyone, but breaking into a papal college to round them up is out of the question. Not without authorization, anyway. You may have ruined your career with your reckless behavior, but we prefer to do this by the book."

"The Vatican will never agree to allow American intelligence agents to enter one of their properties. And while your superiors get tied up in diplomatic efforts, those men will slip away."

"We can't support what you're doing," Barker said. "If you go in there and get injured or arrested, we won't do anything to help you. Is that clear?"

"I say we warn the authorities," Tilsit said. "The CIC has been working with the Vatican—"

I said, interrupting, "Isn't enough that you guys are recruiting ex-Nazis, now you want to help some of them escape?"

"The reasons for the hands-off orders with the Vatican come from the top. It's way above our paygrade."

I was speechless. I had respect for the CIC, but there were some darker secrets among their policies. "Why are you guys even bothering to gather information on them if you're not going to use it to grab them up?"

"You were in the army," Barker said. "You don't question orders. You follow them."

"Don't try to reason with him," Tilsit said to Barker. "The army kicked him out for doing just that."

I wasn't about to get into the reasons the army and I had parted ways.

"What about if they're outside the confines of the Vatican's properties?" Erika asked.

Her question left the two agents silent for a moment. Barker glanced at Tilsit, then said, "We *are* authorized to pick up any of them for questioning in that case."

"I know I can't stop Mason from going, but I'd feel better if you two were there. You could wait outside while Mason flushes them out."

Barker looked at Tilsit again, who nodded his agreement.

I was impressed. She'd said it so logically, yet sweetly, that it had turned the two bull-headed agents to her way of thinking. Doubtless she had used the same combination of persuasion and subtle flattery to get others to do her biding while working as a Soviet asset.

Tilsit said, "We go in a separate vehicle. We can offer you support outside the confines of the college. If things go south while you're inside, don't expect us to come to the rescue."

I nodded my agreement, took Erika's hand, and led her out of the room. We were silent until exiting the building and walking across the paved courtyard.

"In there, I said I couldn't stop you," Erika said, "but I'm asking you now to stay."

"This may be the only opportunity I'll have to make Ziegler pay."

"Killing him won't change what happened. It won't bring back Hana."

"I'll sleep better knowing he's in hell. It will put some of my nightmares to rest."

"I have my own sins to atone for, but reliving them isn't going to make them go away. It's what I do right now, and in the future, that will heal me."

"I'm not you," I said. "If we pull this off, we won't have to worry about them hunting us. You can get your money and meet up with your sister without having to look over your shoulder all the time."

Erika got in front of me to stop my progress. "You'll be going in there without knowing the layout, where the men are, or if they'll be waiting for you with guns."

I looked around to see if there were any witnesses. I took her arm to pull her close and kissed her. She had her eyes closed and got lost in the moment. I broke the embrace and stepped around her.

She caught up with me just as we reached the entrance to sound stage two. "I want to go with you."

I stopped and turned to her. "I'm not about to risk taking you. I can't do what I need to do and worry about keeping you alive at the same time. You're capable. I'll give you that. But your job is to keep yourself and Kurt safe and make sure you get that money to give you both a better life."

She balled her fists and grimaced as if in pain. "I don't want to lose you."

"I'm pretty hard to get rid of," I said as we entered. I could tell Erika wanted to stop and continue our discussion, but I knew that if we did, I might decide to listen to her and stay.

The vast interior of the stage was filled with partitioned spaces no more than ten by twelve feet. The forty-foot-high catwalk bounced back the cacophony of voices and crying babies. A food line stood along one of the narrow sides, and an aid station was on the other. Feldman, Hazan, Moishe, Aaron, and Henri stood together supervising the food service.

We joined their circle. Shimon spotted us and said something to Kurt, who ran up to Erika and wrapped his arms around her thigh. He talked a mile a minute, and Erika had to calm him before returning her attention to us. Shimon hurried over to join us.

"Well?" Hazan asked.

"It's Greta Schweiger, Franz Stangl's mistress," Erika said.

"Those agents missed catching Stangl?"

"Stangl *and* Wagner," I said.

There were groans and accusations flung at the two CIC agents. I glanced around to see who might be eavesdropping. I turned back to the circle and told them what Erika and I had gotten out of Schweiger: the names of the Nazis holing up at the papal college; the group hunting Erika were still intent on stealing from her; and they all had their Red Cross DP passports and were waiting for their visas.

"Leaving Klarsfeld out of the equation, that's at least six mass murderers under one roof," I said. "I'm going in. And the two CIC agents will take a position outside the college. They won't come inside, but they will pick up anyone in the group going in or out. That way, our backs are covered."

Hazan looked at Feldman, and something unspoken passed between them. They turned back to me and said, "We're going, too."

"I was hoping you'd say that."

Moishe said, "If all of you go, that might leave Erika vulnerable. Three of them have already tried to infiltrate the camp. What if others attempt the same thing?"

Shimon turned to Erika. "The three of us—me, Henri, and Moishe—will be your protectors. We're trained soldiers. And this camp is certainly big enough to find a safe place while we wait for them to return."

"*If* they return," Erika said.

"I have no intention of dying in a Catholic enclave," Feldman said with a slight smile. "We'll make it back."

I said to Erika, "Do you feel okay with that arrangement?"

"I'd feel better if I could go with you."

I gave her a look of impatience.

She looked at Moishe, Henri, and Shimon, and said, "Thank you all for doing this. I'm sure you'd rather spend your time on something else other than guarding a mother and her son."

The three of them nodded. Henri blushed, and I got the idea that he had grown fond of Erika. Shimon grinned and seemed excited about the prospect of separating Erika and me. His look left me a little cold, but I knew Erika could handle herself if he got too aggressive.

"All right," I said. "It's all set. We leave at midnight. That'll give us enough time to get something to eat, get some rest, and sharpen our knives."

36

From the front passenger's seat of the car, I studied the exterior of the Priests' College of Santa Maria dell'Anima. Hazan was in the driver's seat, and Feldman sat behind. We were parked on the appropriately named Via di Santa Maria dell'Anima, which was just one block west of the Piazza Navona. At two in the morning, there were still quite a few people on the streets, and the bars were still open. Like most every old city in Europe, there was no divide between commercial and residential properties; a city block consisted of one solid mass of brick and stone.

From the south corner, there were several residential and commercial establishments, then the east wall of the college. It looked formidable, with solid, high walls, few accessible windows, and two sets of doors, which were sealed. There was only one usable door at the northeastern corner. On the other side of the cobblestoned street were several restaurants and a bar, with patrons coming and going.

Barker and Tilsit were parked somewhere a block west of us and across from the main entrance, which was situated in a small square formed by intersecting streets at the south-western corner. I glanced down at the handie-talkie they'd given me. They were to notify me if they saw anyone suspicious entering or exiting, or if the Italian police happened to be nearby.

We'd been observing the intersecting streets for a good hour without seeing anyone from the group. I was anxious to go in, but we'd agreed to watch for any of the men in the group to verify that at least some of them were staying in the college.

Before leaving the camp, I'd accompanied Erika and Kurt to the hiding place that Moishe had chosen, a film editing room on the second floor of a building adjacent to the administration building. Erika and I said little on the way, but Kurt had picked up on the tension we all felt, and he clung to his mother, saying little to me. Moishe and Henri tried to be cheery and assured all would be well. Shimon had disappeared to somewhere in the camp to scrounge up food and drinks. They'd even placed a couple of mattresses in a corner partitioned by sheets for their privacy. The three men knew how to secure the place, which made me feel better about leaving on my mission.

Feldman leaned forward, bringing me out of my reverie. He extended his head past my shoulder to peer out the windshield. "Hard to tell from here that the interior's a maze of interconnected buildings. And it's a lot bigger than it looked on the map."

"Having second thoughts?" I asked.

"No. I'm just repeating what Itzhak said about the place."

Fortunately, Feldman had found someone among the

refugees, a man named Itzhak Epper, who was familiar with the college.

I was having some misgivings about my two companions. It took a lot of determination and guts to track down and abduct so many Nazis, but they had done so with precise planning. They'd gone into hideouts knowing exactly what they were getting into, and in controlled environments. Now we were about to break into a sprawling location with a lot of unknowns. Hazan constantly fiddled with his revolver, while Feldman kept nervously peering out the windows and at the college.

Hazan glanced at the rough map that Itzhak had drawn for us. "According to this, the college's classrooms are in that larger building. The buildings of apartments must all be connected somehow. Then a small courtyard divides the church on the far side, with the residential quarters, dining halls, lecture rooms, and library on the other. That's a rough idea, anyway."

I pointed to a set of double doors on our side of the compound located at the far corner. "That's why I selected that door. I'm betting it serves the apartments and classrooms."

"Then let's get this over with," Feldman said.

His tone of reluctance concerned me, but I stayed quiet. I lifted the handie-talkie and said, "All clear?"

Barker's voice crackled over the handie-talkie. "The front looks like it's shut up tight. No one spotted, so far."

I checked my .45. Feldman and Hazan did the same with their Webley revolvers. I also made sure my hunting knife was secure in my boot. Feldman slipped his F-S knife into a sheath strapped to his thigh.

"Are you ready?" I asked them.

Hazan got out without responding.

"We're moving in," I said over the handie-talkie, and I got out with Feldman.

We concealed our pistols because of the people on the streets and moved out at a walking pace, trying to appear normal, but our grim expressions and hats pulled low on our foreheads would have given us away to an eagle-eyed observer.

I continued to scan the area around the door in case one of our quarry happened to appear. I hadn't counted on so many tipsy people on the streets, so it was better we hadn't encountered one of the Nazis and created a scene witnessed by dozens of onlookers.

We got to the double doors. I knelt in front of the large lock, while Feldman and Hazan stood in front of me, doing their best to conceal me. The old-fashioned lock gave way easily, though turning it took some muscle. The heavy bolt moved a bar, releasing two large pins, top and bottom. The whole mechanism clacked back with a sharp thwack.

I stood, tapped on my companions' shoulders and pushed the door open just enough for us to slip inside. Hazan closed the door, silencing the din of revelers outside. We were in a small foyer. To our left was an elegant staircase serving the two upper floors. Straight ahead was a short hallway and high double doors. Two wall sconces with dim bulbs barely illuminated the space. The air was heavy with the scent of wood polish.

Hazan pointed that we go up. I nodded, and we climbed the worn marble stairs to the second floor. We had two upper floors to search. I'd memorized the crude map Itzhak had drawn and figured we were in the main section of the college. A few wall sconces had been left on to give minimum lighting during the late evening hours. Tall windows in the second floor's foyer looked out onto the small courtyard. On either end were pairs of doors of solid oak.

I wasn't expecting to find any apartments in this section, but we snuck up to each door and looked inside. One appeared to be a lecture room and the other a library. Both were dark and empty. We checked for access to the other buildings and found one at the opposite end of the library.

Hazan started to head for the connecting hallway, but I put my hand on his arm to stop him.

I shook my head and whispered, "We clear the upper floor, first."

Hazan glanced at Feldman, then nodded. We backed out of the library and took the stairs to the second floor. The foyer on the third floor was the same, but behind the doors lay a series of smaller classrooms, one following another by connecting doorways, until we got to one that offered access to another building.

Before us was a narrow hallway with a handful of single doors on either side.

"Apartments," Feldman whispered.

A door opened in the hallway, and we ducked back behind the return. A man in a bathrobe and slippers stepped out, closed the door, and walked down the hallway in the opposite direction. He went to a door at the end of the hall, opened it, and turned on the light. It was a bathroom. He turned, so we could see his face as he closed the door.

The elderly man resembled no one that I knew from the

group. I looked back to Feldman and Hazan. They both shrugged.

"Probably a priest," Hazan said.

We waited several minutes before hearing the toilet flush. The priest emerged, shambled down the hall, and entered his room.

"Are we actually going to search every room?" Feldman asked.

"And how else are we going to find them?" Hazan said.

Feldman looked unconvinced but said nothing in response. Hazan moved out first, prompting Feldman and me to follow suit.

Now that we had reached our objective, the way to proceed was unclear. With Hazan chomping at the bit and Feldman overly cautious, I knew I'd have to do something drastic to get things done in a hurry. My usual answer was to go straight at the target.

The first door was to the room where the priest had exited to go to the bathroom. Without saying anything, I swiftly opened the door and strode in. The old man was in bed and was reaching for his bedside lamp when I burst into the room.

He sucked in his breath and opened his mouth to cry out, but I got my hand over his mouth before he could do so. I used all my weight to pin him down. He thrashed and fought against my hand as he uttered muffled screams.

I looked behind me and saw Hazan and Feldman had entered behind me but left the door open. "Close the damn door."

Feldman did so, then I turned back to our panicked priest. I put my finger to my mouth and shushed him. He had to be close to seventy, and I was afraid I might give him a heart attack.

"I'm not going to hurt you," I said in German. He seemed to understand, so I continued. "We're here for some other people, so everything will turn out fine for you if you tell us where they are. Are you with me so far?"

The man still breathed heavily through his nose, and his eyes were wide with fear, but he stopped fighting. He nodded.

"We know there are several Nazi war criminals here, fleeing justice." I flashed him my expired CIC pass with the U.S. Army seal at the top. "We're American agents here to arrest them. Our intelligence operatives have informed us that Franz Stangl, Rudolf Lange, Ludwig Klarsfeld, Gustav Wagner, Dr. Ernst Fleischman, Friedrich Kappler, and Theodor Ziegler are staying in apartments on the college's premises. All I need for you to do is tell us which apartments they're staying in. Do you understand?"

He shook his head violently and tried to speak through my hand.

I had no intention of using it but, with my free hand, I slipped my ten-inch knife out of my boot and showed it to him. The old priest stiffened and closed his eyes. I heard Feldman suck in his breath and Hazan take a step forward.

I looked at them and shook my head. I turned back to the priest. "I'm going to lift my hand so you can speak, but if you try to cry out, I will use this. Do you understand?"

The priest nodded, and I slowly lifted my hand. He took in deep breaths and put his hand to his chest as if experiencing some pain.

I spoke as calmly as I could, while still holding the knife in his field of view. "I know you're aware those men are staying here, so I don't want to hear any lies. You're going to tell me which apartments they're staying in. Nothing else."

"Threatening an old man with a knife," the priest said. "You are no better than the men you seek—"

I clamped my hand back on his mouth. "You open your mouth again without telling me exactly what I want to know, and it will be the last thing you ever do. I'll leave you drowning in your own blood, and we'll just go to the next room, to the next of your brethren, until we get an answer. Do you want that to be the last thing you do before you die? Sending us to the rooms of the other priests? You have one more chance. Where are they?"

I lifted my hand again. "Speak."

The old man took a moment, as if wrestling with his thoughts. Finally, he closed his eyes, and said, "There is only one of the men you speak of staying here. The others stayed two nights and left this morning."

Alarm and disappointment coursed through me. I wanted it to be a lie, but experience told me he was telling the truth. I glanced back at Feldman and Hazan.

"He's lying," Hazan said.

"We'll find out for ourselves," I said to him, then turned back to the priest. "Who's still here?"

"A fellow priest. Friedrich Kappler. But he had nothing to do with the mass murders—"

I grabbed his chin to stop him from speaking. I leaned in close and said, "Which apartment?"

"There are no numbers. He's in the middle of three buildings on the west side of the courtyard. It's where some of the refugees have stayed in the past. Second floor, second door, overlooking the courtyard."

I clamped back down on his mouth and used my other hand to signal Feldman and Hazan to come forward. The two men approaching caused the old man to panic, but I pinned him to the bed to keep him from thrashing, while Feldman and Hazan used a sheet from the bed to bind and gag him.

The priest tried to cry for help through the gag, but I felt sure the thick walls and heavy door would keep the noise to a minimum.

"We find out you're lying, we'll be back," I said to him.

"They must have left when your agents caught Schweiger," Feldman said.

"We'll worry about that after a little conversation with Kappler," I said.

37

I could hardly contain Hazan. He was rushing down hallways without concern of waking the other residents. I'd seen it in other men; his blood was up. I wanted answers as much as he did, but something had snapped in him.

Feldman had tried to slow him down by pulling on his arm, but Hazan shook him off and kept going. I was worried that Hazan might kill Kappler before we could get anything out of him, but tackling him or trying to reason with him would only create more noise. I kept pace with him and stayed a little behind in case someone came out wondering who had intruded on their peace and quiet.

We went down several hallways paralleling the southern side of the courtyard. We passed through connecting doorways of three small buildings housing what appeared to be more apartments, then classrooms, until finally turning right. We moved through another hallway that ran along the western side, and passed through another doorway into what I assumed was the middle building.

Just before Hazan crashed through the second door, I took

him by the shoulders, pulled him back, and got in his face. I whispered in a harsh tone, "The only way this works is if we get out of here without raising the dead."

"Let me go," Hazan said.

"Calm down."

"I know what I'm doing."

"Just make sure you get what we need before you kill him," I said to Hazan.

That seemed to give him focus. He nodded. I released his arms and let him go in first. Feldman and I rushed in after him. I closed the door just as Hazan pounced on Kappler, slamming his hand onto the man's mouth and putting the barrel of his pistol against his temple. He'd been sleeping, but now he was wide awake and frozen with fear.

Hazan had come on too hot; he should have slowly ratcheted up the threats to get Kappler to talk, but he'd compromised his chances by showing his intention to kill.

Kappler put his hands near the headboard as if surrendering. In a lightning move, he pulled a knife out from under the pillow and plunged the blade into Hazan's chest. Hazan grimaced, dropped off the bed and tumbled to the floor.

Kappler was up in a flash and went for Feldman, yelling as he did so. Feldman caught Kappler's hands, but the man's forward momentum pushed them both toward the door. As they passed me, I struck the back of Kappler's head with my sap. Stunned, Kappler fell to his knees. I hit him again, and he fell face-first to the floor.

Feldman and I rushed over to Hazan. He was up on his knees and writhing in pain as he tried to pull the knife out of his chest. The eight-inch blade had gone in about halfway, just below the collarbone. Blood stained his overcoat and dripped beneath the bottom of his sleeve to form a pool on the rug.

Feldman ripped the pillowcase from the pillow, then supported Hazan and yanked out the knife. Hazan moaned and wobbled on his knees. Feldman slipped the pillowcase underneath the overcoat.

Hazan's face was drained of blood, but his eyes were clear. He took Feldman's hand away and put his own over the wound.

"Can you walk?" Feldman asked.

Hazan, out of breath, nodded. "I'm fine." He pointed to a motionless Kappler. "We're taking him."

I pulled the top sheet off the bed and repeated what we did to bind the old man.

Feldman pointed at Kappler. "Taking him is a bad idea. Someone's going to see us carrying a bound priest through the college and out in the streets."

"What did you think we were going to do?" I said. "Leave him here so he can alert the others?"

I tore at the sheet and began to tie Kappler's hands behind his back.

"How are we going to get him *and* David out of here?" Feldman asked, raising his voice.

"Keep your voice down," I said.

Hazan stood, though he had to use the bed to steady himself.

"Are you sure you can make it?" I asked him.

"I'm sure," Hazan said to me, then to Feldman, "Help Mason. We're out of time."

"But what if the priest was lying, and there *are* some of the others in the group staying here?" Feldman said.

"We don't have much of a choice," Hazan said.

Feldman helped me finish binding and gagging Kappler. We lifted him to his feet. He was still out, with blood streaming from the two wounds on his skull. I hoped he didn't have a serious concussion. We wouldn't get anything out of him if that was the case. I hoisted him on my shoulder, pulled out my gun, and nodded that I was ready. Feldman went over to Hazan and used his shoulder to take some of his weight. I pulled open the door and went as fast as I could down the hallway. I tried to minimize the noise of my footsteps, but with around 170 pounds on my shoulder, each step resonated in the narrow space.

Fortunately, if anyone came out of their room to investigate, that happened only after we'd passed. We made it to the last classroom before the stairs and the exit without being seen, but then Kappler came out of his stupor. He cried out for help and fought against my grip.

Behind came the sound of doors opening and alarmed voices. We doubled our speed down the staircase, but Kappler's struggles nearly caused me to tumble. I had no choice. I stopped mid-flight, twisted my body, and swung his head into the marble wall. The struggling ceased.

We burst out the door and onto the street. Running for the car, we passed only two couples. Both dashed for cover. At the car, Feldman left Hazan leaning against the side door and came around to open the trunk. I dropped Kappler inside. I checked his breathing and pulse. He was still alive. I shut the trunk lid and helped Feldman get Hazan into the back seat.

By this time the two couples had come out of hiding. One pair ran in the opposite direction, while the other couple stared at us in disbelief. They could give a good description of us to the police, but there was nothing we could do except dive into the car. I got in the back with Hazan, while Feldman got behind the wheel. He started up the car and sped past the gawking spectators.

I got on the handie-talkie and said, "We're out. Only found one. The rest weren't there."

Barker came back and said, "We want to talk to him."

"I'm not sure he's in any shape to talk to anyone at the moment. We're going to make one stop then be back at the camp."

"He's to stay alive," Barker said. "You got that?"

"I'm not the one you have to convince. The guy knifed Hazan in the chest."

"Damnit, Mason—"

I switched off the handie-talkie and threw it on the floorboard before turning my attention to Hazan. He was sitting up in the seat and held tight to the cloth covering his wound.

"Turn up the heat," I said to Feldman. "I've got to take his coat off."

Hazan was aware enough to lean forward so I could remove his overcoat.

He grunted in pain. "Hurts like a son of a bitch," he said. "Hard to breathe."

I guided his hand off the wound and lifted the blood-soaked pillowcase. The bleeding had slowed to a trickle.

"It's high enough that I think it missed your lung."

"There's a first-aid kit," he said between grunts. "I put it under the driver's seat before we left."

I got it out and found what I needed. As I began to treat his wound, Hazan said, "I hope you know what you're doing."

"Don't worry. I had training in the field."

"Where are we going?" Feldman asked as he turned on the road running alongside the Tiber river.

"Just get us out of the city. We'll figure it out from there."

"I want first crack at him," Hazan said.

"You lost control of the situation back there."

He tried to say something, but I poured alcohol on his wound to cleanse it. He recoiled and growled at me instead. I threaded the suture needle and held it up for him to see.

"Don't move," I said, taunting him.

Feldman was lead-footing it through the tight curves in the road and jostling us in the back. "Arie, take it easy, would you? I'm about to stick a needle in your buddy's chest."

Feldman slowed the car, and I began to stitch up Hazan's wound. By the time we were outside Rome's city limits, I had finished stitching and dressing it. The painful ordeal left Hazan exhausted. I left him leaning back on the seat and sat forward to see where we were.

"Start making your way back to the camp," I said. "We'll look for a secure place to park. It's time we check on Kappler to see if he's still alive and ask him a few questions."

38

Hazan was slumped in the back seat and had fallen asleep. His vital signs appeared stable, so I had climbed in the front passenger's seat and consulted a map of Rome. We were on the eastern edge of Rome's city limits and heading south, back toward the Cinecitta camp. According to the map, we were crossing over the Aniene river and passing a natural reserve. The area had all the markings of a good place to stop. We no longer had to worry if Kappler had survived; he was pounding weakly on the inside of the trunk lid.

We were passing through the reserve when I spotted a primitive, single-lane road leading into a wooded field. I pointed it out to Feldman. "Turn there."

Feldman did as I asked, and we followed the road, passing scattered houses and corrugated-tin buildings, all dilapidated, with weeds and dumped trash on the properties.

I let Feldman continue in order to get as far from the main road as possible.

After a mile, the road narrowed to a dirt track. I hit

Feldman on the shoulder and pointed to a corrugated-tin shed that appeared to be abandoned. "That's looks good."

He nodded and turned off the road. The tires rolled over the trash and weeds until we were behind the structure. Feldman stopped the car. The jostling woke Hazan, and he sat up to see where we were. He looked like he might pass out again, but his eyes were focused and intense.

Feldman doused the headlights and shut off the engine. That encouraged Kappler to renew his pounding on the trunk lid. I removed my .45 from the glovebox and climbed out of the car. Feldman got out and went to the back door to help Hazan, but Hazan had already managed to get out on his own. He'd done it a little too quickly and had to use the car to steady himself. I whistled and held up my hand, prompting Feldman to toss me the car keys. Feldman helped his partner stand and gave him support. I unlocked the trunk and waited until Feldman and Hazan joined me.

I lifted the lid and flicked on the flashlight. Kappler shielded his eyes from the glare. His hair and face were caked in drying blood. One eye was sitting near the far edge of its socket.

He cried out through his gag and tried to wiggle his way out of the trunk. I shoved him back inside and held the pistol near his face.

I had to talk in a loud voice to be heard over his muffled cries. "Your only chance to live through this is to answer my questions. You do anything other than that, and I'll hand you over to my companions. And just so you know, we're in an isolated area. There's no one around to hear you scream. But just to save our ears, when I remove the gag, I don't want to hear anything other than your answers to our questions."

Kappler stopped struggling and fell quiet. He nodded, and I pulled down his gag. The man sucked in air, then spat out blood before sneering at us in defiance.

"The others in your group," I said. "Are they hiding somewhere in the papal college?"

When he didn't answer immediately, Hazan took an aggressive step forward. I put out my hand to stop him, which prompted Kappler to speak.

"You're such fools. They're gone," he said, then let out a fiendish chuckle that exposed blood on his teeth. "And you know where they went? To get that stinking bitch. Erika."

In a rage, I clamped onto his hair and crotch. He screamed in pain. I yanked him out of the trunk and dropped him to the ground. I walked away, leaving him to Hazan and Feldman.

Behind me, Kappler said, "I gladly sacrifice—"

A gunshot stopped him from going any further.

I opened the driver's door and said, "Let's get out of here." I got in and started the engine.

Feldman helped Hazan get in the back, and then he sat in the front passenger's seat. I backed out onto the road and hit the gas. I'd spent the last forty minutes studying the map of Rome, so I had a good idea of the fastest route back to the Cinecitta camp, and I did so with a lead foot, zooming down the two-lane highway at top speed.

Feldman instinctively grabbed onto the dashboard. "If you want to get back as fast as possible, getting stopped by the cops isn't the best way to do it."

I hit the steering wheel. "They knew exactly what we were going to do. And the only way that could have happened is if someone told them. It's how they could tail us in the mountains in the middle of a snowstorm. How they knew we'd stopped at that camp near Dolcé and where Erika was hiding. Someone in our group has been feeding them information."

Hazan grabbed the back of my seat to pull himself forward. "If you're implying that someone in our convoy is a traitor, then you're dead wrong. They could have guessed our moves. Guessed we'd come after them at the college and doubled back to take Erika."

"It could be those CIC agents," Feldman said. "Maybe they agreed to bail us out at the Florence camp to get us back on the road. They knew we'd go to the Cinecitta camp, and they knew exactly where and when we'd take the offensive. And you led those agents to us."

I said nothing and gripped the steering wheel so hard my knuckles turned white. On the surface, Barker and Tilsit seemed to be the most likely suspects, and it hit me in the gut the idea that they'd been playing me like a fool. The only hope I could grasp onto was that they didn't know where Erika and her bodyguards had hidden in the sprawling complex.

Hazan grabbed the back of my seat to pull himself forward and be next to my ear. "If it was those agents, and they helped the Nazi bastards take her, then you're on your own. Don't count on any help from us getting her back."

Feldman sat up in his seat as if hit by a jolt of electricity. "God, what if they found Moishe, Aaron, and Shimon with her? They'll kill them."

I hit the accelerator, heedless of the consequences. It was life and death now.

39

The Cinecitta camp was quiet when we returned. No police, no authorities of any kind, no panicked refugees. It gave me hope that Kappler had been wrong, or the Nazi assailants had failed to infiltrate the camp or find Erika and the others. I bypassed the parking lot and headed straight for the administration building, only stopping when I was within yards of the building housing the editing suites.

I got out fast and started running for the entrance. I stopped when I heard Hazan groan in pain and tumble to the pavement. I ran back to help Feldman get Hazan to his feet. Hazan had opened his wound in the fall, and I could see a fresh bloodstain spreading on his shirt through his open coat. With him in the middle, the three of us moved to the entrance. The main door should have been locked, but it sat slightly open.

My stomach dropped. Feldman muttered something in his alarm. We struggled with Hazan to the base of the staircase, when he made a signal for us to ease him onto the first step.

"Go, go," Hazan said. "I'll catch up."

314 | JOHN A. CONNELL

Feldman and I raced up the two flights of stairs and down a hallway to the editing room where Erika and the others were hiding. The door to the room was wide open, and it was dark inside.

I rushed in with Feldman right behind me. The two rolling bins holding strips of film lay on their sides. The film racks and chairs were tipped over. Feldman found the light switch. There were only two people in the room: Henri and Moishe, and they were both lying on the floor in pools of blood.

Feldman cried out in anguish and rushed over to Henri. I hurried over to Moishe and knelt at his side. I checked for a pulse. "Moishe's alive," I said.

Feldman was silent as he looked down in anguish at Henri's lifeless eyes. There were two areas of blood on Henri's chest, and a small entry wound at his forehead.

I slowly turned Moishe over, while supporting his head. He had two similar bullet wounds in his chest, though the shooter had not shot him in the head. He sputtered blood and opened his eyes.

Hazan arrived and stopped at the doorway. "Oh, God. I'll call for an ambulance." He stepped over to a phone and dialed.

Feldman joined me and checked on Moishe's wounds. He'd already lost a massive amount of blood and only had a faint heartbeat.

When Moishe saw Feldman, he raised his hand to put in on Feldman's cheek.

"Don't move, Moishe," Feldman said. "David is calling an ambulance. Okay? Hold on."

Moishe's breathing sounded wet and congested. His eyes fluttered as he looked at me. "I'm sorry."

"Don't talk," I said. "We can talk when you get better."

Hazan got off the phone and joined us.

"It was Shimon," Moishe said. "He shot us and took Erika. I tried to fight him—" He stopped and passed out.

We all were stunned into silence.

While my two companions did their best to care for Moishe's wounds, I stood and walked aimlessly to the windows. Rage and heartache battled for my attention. The blinds were askew—another sign of the struggle—and I looked out onto the plaza through a gap in the blades. The woman and boy who I had come to care for deeply were surely in the hands of the Nazi killers. Erika would be tortured, murdered, and dumped somewhere. I tried to block images of Erika in agony; I knew firsthand what that was like. I couldn't even contemplate what might happen to Kurt.

And they could be anywhere.

"No telling when the ambulance will get here," Feldman said as he paced the room.

I grunted an acknowledgment and went back to staring out the window. Hazan sat by Moishe, who was still bleeding out. Hazan wasn't doing very well either, though all his attention was on Moishe. He must have been in pain, but he took it stoically.

I desperately ran through the possible places the Nazis would have taken Erika. She had said that, even if they tortured her, she would never reveal the location of her fortune. I was sure she could put up a fight, especially for the sake of her child. But breaking was only a matter of time, even if she had received some training in resisting torture from the

Soviets. In the truck, before we were attacked south of Florence, I'd said that very thing to her. Then I remembered she had said something curious: that it wouldn't matter. I searched for a meaning to that phrase. It wouldn't matter if she broke under relentless pain? Unfortunately, she didn't have the chance to clarify. But one thing became clear.

I turned to the room and said to Feldman, "I have to get out of here before the police arrive."

"What are you talking about?"

"I can't be tied up in a police inquiry. It'll be too late by then."

I went over to Hazan and knelt next to him. He was pale but alert. "David, I think we can get these bastards."

He gave me a puzzled look, then his eyes brightened. "They'll be after Erika's money."

"Exactly. I have to get out of here before the police and ambulance medics get here."

"I'm coming with you." Hazan tried to stand but collapsed to the floor.

Feldman came over and knelt next to us. "You're not going anywhere, my friend. I should go, too, but I hate to leave you with this mess."

"Go," he said. "And if you see Shimon, cut off his balls for me." He held out his hand to me, and I shook it. "Make sure you bring my friend back. We still have to get those people to Naples."

"Will do," I said.

Feldman and Hazan embraced, then Hazan pushed him away. "Get out of here while you still have the chance."

Feldman and I stood. He glanced back at Hazan before we rushed out of the room. We ran down the stairs and out to the car. I got behind the wheel, while Feldman took the passenger's seat. I started up the car and backed into an alley between sound stages to make a three-point turn. Just as I was tucked in the alley, a police car and ambulance raced past, heading for the plaza.

When the vehicles were clear, I hit the accelerator and sped out of the alley. I headed for the rear gate, near the exterior ancient Rome set, to avoid any police or guards at the exit. I turned right off the main street and saw the rear gate was closed but unattended. I increased my speed.

A sedan shot out of an alley and stopped directly in my path. I hit the brakes and skidded to a halt. Furious, I jumped out of the car with my .45 tucked in my belt. Barker and Tilsit got out of their car, with their hands on their holstered guns.

"What the hell are you doing?" I said. "Get out of the way!"

"I can't count the ways you guys screwed up back there," Tilsit said. "You were supposed to go in and get your men without rousing the entire college, assaulting a priest, and being seen by several witnesses while carrying a bound man to the car."

"Where *is* that man, by the way?" Barker asked.

"We decided to drop him off on the way here," Feldman said as he came up beside me.

"After you tortured him," Tilsit said.

"We got what we wanted from him, so we left him," Feldman said, lying.

"Bullshit," Tilsit said. "We know your and Hazan's reputation—"

Tilsit stopped when I drew my weapon in an instant. I pointed it at both of them. "I'm sorry, boys, but I'm going to have to ask you for your weapons. We don't have time for this."

Out of the corner of my eye, I saw that Feldman had drawn his as well. Barker and Tilsit kept their hands on their pistols but made no move to draw them.

"Please, ease your hands from your weapons and raise them," Feldman said.

They complied, and I moved forward cautiously. I pulled out Barker's gun from its shoulder holster. He glared at me but said nothing. When I removed Tilsit's pistol, he said, "Once you've finished your business, you better keep going, because you'll be a wanted man as far as the CIC is concerned. Forester won't be able to bail you out of this one."

I said nothing as I leaned into the car and grabbed the keys to their sedan. I backed away and gave one of the pistols to Feldman. We continued to the car and got in a quick as we could. I hit the accelerator, the tires squealed, and I reversed the car out the far end of the alley.

We blew through the rear gate and raced away from the complex. Now I'd have the CIC after my hide, a bad prospect, indeed.

But first, we'd have to worry about going up against seven or eight desperate and well-armed men.

40

It was an hour before dawn when the taxi driver entered the Piazza Umberto, a small square with ritzy shops on the eastern side of the island of Capri. It had taken us almost four hours to get there. I hated open water, so it was much to my displeasure that the only way onto the island was by boat, and at that hour, the only option was to steal a motorboat at the Naples docks.

The taxi driver pulled his cab over to the curb and parked.

"Why is he stopping here?" I asked Feldman.

Feldman asked the driver something in Italian. The driver nodded, saying "*Si, si,*" while pointing at a narrow walkway of paving stones, flanked by jewelry stores and high-fashion shops.

"No vehicles allowed on that walkway," Feldman said. "We get out here."

Feldman and the driver exchanged a few more words, presumably the man giving directions, then Feldman paid him.

We exited the vehicle, each with a knapsack containing our pistols and spare magazines.

"It's about an eight-minute walk," Feldman said as we crossed the plaza.

We followed the walkway as it meandered through the village. The cobbled path narrowed, and the shops became houses and boutiques. It left the village behind and cut along a high point that jutted out into the Mediterranean. On the left, the land sloped downward gradually then finally became a sheer drop to the water. On the right, the rocky land rose steeply. The wind had picked up, announcing the coming dawn, and it brought up the scent of sea air.

Most of the houses sat high off the road and were served by staircases carved into the rock. A small sign indicated we were on Via Matteotti. We passed, ironically, a sign for the Villa Krupp, then a moment later we arrived at a wrought-iron gate with rampant lions.

"This is it," I said.

The gate was latched but not locked. We slid through the gap and stopped to assess the sprawling house and the property. From the walkway, the land rose sharply and had gardens and exotic trees that benefitted from the Mediterranean climate. Two formal fountains and a pair of statues of some mythical woodland nymphs stood in contrast with the house's mix of Mediterranean and modern architecture. Balconies and floor-to-ceiling plate-glass windows offered expansive views of the Mediterranean far below. It had two main levels, with a lower expansive terrace and pool attached to one side and below the main quarters. Even though that level was lower than the others, it stood on stilts and extended out over the cliff for unobstructed views of the sea.

We stood in the shadows and studied the house. The walls of the first level were floor-to-ceiling glass panels, and a balcony extended the whole length of the building. Most of the curtains were drawn but in a haphazard fashion that left gaps. With all the lights on, that made it easy to observe the interior. To the left was a grand living room with an immense stone fireplace and three walls of glass overlooking the sea. A narrow, long hallway ran along the front and led to a spacious dining room with an opulent antique dining table and armoire.

The second floor also had a full-length balcony serving what I figured was a series of bedrooms. The curtains on the arched windows and doors to the balcony were closed, though all the lights appeared to be on.

"Somebody's home," I said in a low voice.

"What if it's someone in Erika's family and not our targets?" Feldman asked.

His question was answered when we saw Dr. Fleischman walk past a gap in the curtains. He didn't look happy and was yelling something to someone unseen in the living room.

Then that other person walked to a spot where he was visible.

"Rudolf Lange," Feldman said. "The mass murderer of the Latvian Jews."

Silhouettes of at least two men moved in the curtains of the upper floor.

"How many do you think are here?" Feldman asked.

"Kappler's no longer in the picture, but then there's Shimon. Best guess is eight."

Feldman gave me a sideways glance, then checked his Webley and the Browning Hi-Power pistol he'd nabbed from

Tilsit. I did the same with my .45 and the other Browning courtesy of Barker.

We shifted to the left to get a better look at the lower terrace. From this new position, we were too far downhill to see more than the upper third of two rooms through the plate-glass windows. Shadows moved across the ceilings. They, too, appeared to be moving in a chaotic fashion, probably in a frantic search for Erika's money.

"They haven't found it yet," Feldman said.

That realization raised my hopes that Erika might still be alive. "No one's been posted as a lookout, and they've left the curtains partially open—they're not expecting company."

"And they won't be tearing up the house with guns in their hands," Feldman said.

"We go in quiet and fast." I looked at Feldman. "Are you ready?"

Feldman nodded. Despite the odds, he looked determined. He'd been a soldier and probably had fought in close quarters, so I felt confident he'd know what to do.

We moved across the property toward the front entrance. I kept my eyes on the windows, trying to estimate how many men might be on the first floor and where they might be when we broke in. Our only advantage was surprise. If we could subdue the men on the first floor without making a sound, we had a chance at overtaking the others.

We stopped at the front door and listened. There was a lot of banging in the living room and crashing of dishes on the floor, presumably in the kitchen. I could only speculate that the kitchen was off the dining room and toward the back of the house.

I tried the front doorknob. It was locked. I pulled out my

lock-picking tools and knelt in front of the door. In less than a minute, I turned the lock and the doorknob.

"We stay together and take them one at a time," I said in a low voice. I pointed to the left. "Living room first."

Feldman nodded and slipped out an F-S knife with his left and raised his revolver, ready to shoot. I slipped my brass knuckles onto my right hand, then pushed open the door. We snuck in and found ourselves in the center point of the hallway. At that position, there was a perpendicular hallway leading to a spacious foyer and a glass-and-steel staircase to the upper floor. We moved left, toward the living room. We could only see a sliver of the room, the back of a plush sofa and ornate antiques. We crept forward. The banging noise we'd heard earlier was actually the sound of books being tossed on the floor.

We got to the end of the hallway and peered inside. A man in his late thirties stood at the wall-to-wall bookshelves and was pulling off books, leafing through them, then tossing them to the floor. It was Rudolf Lange.

I signaled for Feldman to take him, and I would stay at the junction of the hallway to cover him. While Feldman stalked his prey, I alternately watched him and glanced down the hallway.

I didn't know whether Lange sensed Feldman's presence, or Feldman alerted him, but Lange whirled around. His eyes widened in surprise. He opened his mouth to cry out, but Feldman's lightning-fast swipe of his blade across Lange's neck put a stop to that. He made gurgling sounds as he tried to hold back the blood streaming from the wound.

"That's for the thousands of Jews you murdered," Feldman said.

Lange became limp, his knees buckled. As he went down, his head collided with a small table. He and the table crashed to the ground.

A man darted from a back room. He whined in panic as he ran.

It was Shimon, and he was going for a pistol on an end table by the sofa.

In two strides, I was on him. I grabbed him from behind and wrapped one arm around his neck with the other covering his mouth. He struggled against my grasp and tried to scream through my hand. I had him pinned, and I offered him up for Feldman.

Feldman advanced with his knife ready, but Shimon bit my hand. His teeth sank deep into my palm. I flinched from the pain, which gave Shimon enough wiggle room to break my hold.

Shimon cried out and tried to run for the back room. Feldman tackled him and pinned him with the knife at his throat.

"Please, Arie," Shimon said. "They offered me a lot of money. But I was going to get it, then kill them and bring it back. You've got to believe—"

He didn't get a chance to finish.

Feldman drove the knife into his chest. "That's for Henri and Moishe." He twisted the blade, but Shimon had already become still.

The clattering in the kitchen stopped. "Shimon? Rudolf?" the voice said.

I rushed down the hallway, toward the dining room, with as much stealth as I could muster. I reached the end and got two strides into the spacious room when Dr. Fleischman came out of the kitchen.

He stopped, puzzled for an instant, but then recognition spread across his face. "You!"

I didn't stop. He had a seven-inch kitchen knife in his hand, but my charge and grim expression must have terrified him. He screamed, turned, and ran. His terror gave him speed, and he got to the opposite side of the kitchen just as I entered. He grabbed his pistol off a kitchen countertop and swung around. He fired. The bullet impacted the wall beside me.

Before he could get off another shot, I fired my .45 three times, hitting him in the chest. He fell back against the counter and fell like a limp rag to the ground.

Now the others knew they had intruders, and they would be ready for us.

41

I raced back down the hallway and met Feldman halfway.

"Dining room and kitchen are clear," I said just above a whisper.

"I checked a billiard room and library," Feldman said. "Access to the terrace level is off the living room."

"I'll take the bedrooms, and you take the terrace level."

Feldman glanced at the staircase and then back to the living room, as if weighing my strategy.

"As far as we know, the only exits are on this level," I said. "They can't go anywhere, so take your time. See if they'll come to you."

He nodded and moved quickly for the living room. I moved silently over to the base of the staircase and paused to listen. All was quiet. Someone had turned off the hallway lights, though the soft glow of dawn coming through plate-glass windows gave me a pretty good idea of what I faced. At the top of the stairs there was a sizeable landing with hallways going to rooms to the right and left. They were waiting for me. Two, three? Or more?

I took the granite steps one careful step at a time with my gaze straight ahead, trying to watch for movement from either direction. My ears stood up as I listened intently. I reached the top. The landing accommodated a small sitting area with a sofa and two lounge chairs.

I chose the left hallway and snuck up to the return wall to peer into the darkness. No sounds and nothing moved. I crept down the hallway while staying against one wall. There were three doors toward the front of the house and two to the rear.

With rapid glances to check my rear, I made it to the first room on the right. The door was open, the room dark. I leaned in enough to see past the doorframe. The bedroom appeared vacant, though the armoire was open, and the dresser drawers lay on the floor. The mattress had been pulled off the bed and slashed open.

I stepped out into the hallway.

The booming of pistol shots echoed in the house. The exchange of fire stopped abruptly. In the sudden calm, I heard footsteps coming from a bedroom farther down the hallway. Either the person had been spooked by the gunfire or tried to use the noise to cover his movements.

Heedless of the possible danger behind me, I charged toward the sound. I kicked open the second door on the left and ducked. From somewhere in the darkness, two gunshots rang out. One impacted the wooden doorframe, and the other whizzed past the top of my head. I blindly fired twice in the hopes the man would respond, revealing his position.

Glass was smashed, and running footsteps sounded on the balcony. A silhouette of a man rushed past the curtains. I sprinted for the door to the balcony and rolled out onto the decking.

Konrad Hoffmann was running toward the opposite side of the house. He turned and fired, but I had a bead on him just as he pulled the trigger. Two .45 rounds hit him in the chest, and he tumbled to the decking.

I feared whoever else was upstairs would try running for the staircase. I raced through the bedroom and out into the hallway, ready to stop whoever might try to escape. The hallway was empty, and no sound of footsteps on the stairs.

Feldman and the men on the pool level traded occasional shots, but on this level all was quiet. I finished searching the rest of the rooms in the left hallway. I went from room to room, repeating the process of using the doorframe as cover and throwing open the door. Each room I checked was vacant though thoroughly ransacked. The last bedroom on the front of the house must have been Kurt's, because there were toys and children's books strewn on the floor. An oversized wooden castle lay in pieces on a short table.

Feldman and the men he had trapped continued lobbying shots at each other. Feldman was bound to run out of ammunition. I had to hurry.

I took long, silent strides across the landing and into the right-hand hallway. Like the left, the right hallway led to five doors, but then one door at the end. I figured that to be the master bedroom since it would have the best view of the sea. I kicked open the first door. It was empty, but a rustling noise came from the room at the end of the hallway. A high-pitched, muffled voice became distinct as I got closer.

I kicked open the door and ducked behind the doorway. Whoever was inside didn't take the bait and shoot at the door. A lamp from somewhere inside threw a dim glow in a room twice the size of the others. The muffled voice came from somewhere deeper in the room, near the glass door to the balcony. And it was clear to me who made those sounds.

Kurt!

I jumped to my feet and thrust my gun arm inside, aiming at the sound.

Klarsfeld held Kurt to his chest with one hand clamped on the boy's mouth. His Luger was pointed at the boy's head. The man's eyes were wide with a crazed panic. Kurt was in tears and his entire body shook.

"Put down your gun, or I kill him," Klarsfeld said.

My chest clenched in fear for the boy, but I knew that if I complied Klarsfeld would kill him after taking care of me. "Go ahead," I said to him. "The boy means nothing to me."

"You're lying!" Klarsfeld said, his voice shrill with desperation. "The boy told me. He said you were his father now and would come to rescue him." He pressed the barrel of his pistol harder against Kurt's head. "Now, put down the gun and back away."

Kurt started screaming and fought savagely against Klarsfeld's grasp. I was terrified that either Klarsfeld would pull the trigger in rage and panic, or Kurt's struggles would cause the gun to go off.

Kurt's violent struggles distracted Klarsfeld, and the man looked down. I had an opening, but the risk was extreme: in the involuntary contraction of his muscles, he could pull the trigger, even in death; and shooting Kurt's father in front of him might damage his mind forever.

I fired my pistol. The round entered Klarsfeld's forehead passing just three inches above Kurt's scalp.

Klarsfeld's eyes went blank. He dropped Kurt and the gun at the same time.

I leapt across the room as Klarsfeld wobbled on his feet for a split second before collapsing onto the floor.

The gun went off when it hit the ground.

"Kurt!"

I fell onto Kurt, who had gone still. I checked his entire body for any wounds. Nothing. I didn't know if he had fainted or gone into shock. I scooped him up and got him away from Klarsfeld's corpse before he could see his father's lifeless stare.

Kurt's eyes popped wide, and he took in a deep, desperate breath. Relief flooded over me when he sobbed in my arms. I carried him out of the bedroom took him into a bathroom farther down the hallway and set him in the tub. I looked into his eyes and wiped at his tears. His crying slowed.

In the calmest voice I could muster, I said, "Kurt, I want you to stay here. Okay? You'll be safe."

He lifted his arms to me and cried out of panic.

"I have to rescue your mother. And you can help by staying here. As soon as I get your mom, we'll come up to get you."

He became eerily quiet, as if the shock might return if I left him alone. But I had no other option. I stood and backed away, despite his protests. "I have to go get your mother. Okay? Don't move."

I got into the hallway and shut the door, then dashed down the stairs, across the hallway to the living room, and found the staircase leading down to the pool level.

Feldman was halfway down and sitting on a step as he reloaded his Webley. "I think I wounded one of them, but there are at least two more and in good covering positions. Did you find Erika?"

I shook my head and nodded toward the lower level. "That's why I've got to get down there."

"There's a bar and lounge area at the base of the stairs. One's behind the wooden bar to the right of the stairs. Then there's a billiard room to the right of the bar. One's in there, and then one near the door to the terrace and the pool."

I ran the scenarios in my head and turned to Feldman. "Go up to the living room balcony and fire down at the terrace."

"I won't be able to hit anything from there."

"You're going to create a distraction. They'll be looking in that direction, at least for a moment. That's when I'll go."

"We attack together."

"We can only go down one at a time. They'll pick us off before we can get one step into the room. As soon as you hear shooting inside, you come down to back me up."

Feldman hesitated and stared at me as if it might be the last time he'd see me alive. Finally, he gritted his teeth and climbed the stairs. I shot off a few rounds to keep the men below pinned to their positions, then loaded another magazine into the .45 and waited.

I didn't have to wait long. The distinctive reports of Feldman's Webley boomed in the house. I dived down the stairs and rolled to the left. I opened up with my .45 on the wooden bar, pinning one of them, while the other two shot at me.

I managed to take cover behind a lounge chair. Rounds punctured the chair and wall behind me. I emptied the magazine into the bar.

Someone cried out in pain and dashed for the billiard room. I pulled out the Browning pistol and fired at the doorway between the bar and the billiard room. The powerful weapon put several holes through the wall.

Two men, Franz Stangl and Gustav Wagner, ran from their

positions at the door toward a plate-glass window. I aimed for Wagner, but then I heard firing from the terrace and Feldman cry out in pain.

I peered around the chair and looked toward the terrace.

It was Ziegler.

42

Ziegler stood near the swimming pool and was aiming high, toward the living room balcony. He pulled the trigger. Nothing. The gun was empty.

I shot at him but was off the mark.

At the same moment, I heard the smashing of the plate-glass window in the billiard room and the two men scrambling out.

Out of danger from Wagner and Stangl, I jumped up and charged for the terrace. Ziegler pulled a revolver from his waistband and fired at me. I dropped behind the sofa, but the shooting stopped. I popped up just in time to see Ziegler leap off the balcony.

I ran out the broken glass door to the terrace and dashed around the pool to the terrace railing. It was a good twenty-foot drop to the rocky terrain. I heard the crashing of bushes and saw Ziegler racing down the hillside. He was limping badly but still making good time.

I calculated the jump and was about to go over when Feldman cried out, "Mason!"

I turned to see Feldman hanging by one arm from the upper terrace and dangling thirty feet to a rocky surface. The left sleeve of his coat was soaked in blood.

I glanced back at Ziegler. He was still in sight but almost to the walkway.

I groaned in frustration, raced back into the house and climbed the stairs to the living room. I got to Feldman and grabbed him by his overcoat.

Feldman kicked and got a foot on the terrace decking. I pulled. He cried out in pain as he fought for a foothold on the terrace railing. In one final effort, I got him over the railing and onto the decking.

Blood was streaming down his upper arm and onto his hand. I started to check his wound when he said, "Go, go," and waved in the direction of Ziegler's escape.

"Kurt's in a bathroom upstairs. I'll be back."

I sprinted through the house and out the front door. I made a beeline for the gate and reached the walkway. He could have gone in either direction. If I picked the wrong way, I'd lose him again, possibly forever. I looked up the walkway heading from the village shop. A man was walking his dog in a leisurely fashion—not the manner of someone witnessing a man running for his life. It was a gamble, but I chose the direction leading to the rocky point.

I went no farther than fifty yards before the walkway began descending the cliff face. I looked over the short wall. The walkway was a series of switchbacks clinging to the sheer cliff as it wound down to the sea. Then I spotted Ziegler. He was on the third switchback, fifty feet below me. His limp looked worse, but fear was pushing him to his limits.

I tore down the first leg, then the second, but the sharp

turns in direction slowed me down. I wouldn't make it in time.

At the third turn, I leapt over the wall and scrambled down the undergrowth to the level below. I repeated the move and nearly tumbled on the damp and icy ground. The next level down was steeper than the rest, with a fifteen-foot drop.

In a Hail Mary, I leapt over the wall. Somehow, I landed on my feet, and slid down the rocky face to the walkway. I froze.

Ziegler was at the next hairpin turn with his gun aimed at my chest.

I dived for cover just as he fired. He fired again, then I heard the click of an empty revolver. I stood.

"Who are you?" he yelled in fear and confusion. His chest heaved from running.

I was surprised he didn't recognize me. I aimed my pistol at him and took a step toward him. "You've murdered so many that you can't remember all of their faces."

"I was a lieutenant in the army. I only killed as my duty commanded."

"You were an SS Obersturmführer in the Gestapo. You murdered a little Polish girl and a Czech family in front of me."

I could see his eyes darting in their sockets as he struggled to recall. Then he must have remembered, because his facial muscles went limp, and he took a step backward.

"I was the American intelligence officer you captured at the Czech farm. I told you then that I would find you and kill you. And now here we are."

He threw down his pistol and raised his hands. He said in English, "I surrender. You can't shoot me if I surrender."

I took another step forward. "That's not how this works—"

Ziegler whipped out a derringer-style pistol and fired both rounds. The first ripped through my overcoat, but the second grazed my skull. The impact felt like I'd been stung by a hornet, and my head swam. It was only by sheer rage and determination that I ignored the pain and went after Ziegler.

He had already made the next turn and was nearing the next. I poured on the speed, though my steps were all over the place. He made it around the next turn, and I hit it a second later. I took aim and fired but was wide of the mark. I couldn't run and shoot at the same time in my condition.

I stopped midway on the fifth leg. We were still a good eighty feet to the bottom. I steadied myself and took aim for a spot at the halfway point of the seventh leg and waited.

He came into my field of view, limping and running. I pulled the trigger. His coat at the shoulder disintegrated. Flesh and blood erupted from the impact. He hit the outer wall at a dead run and flipped over it. He screamed as his body struck the stone wall the next level down and finally impacted on the rocky shoreline, sixty feet below.

I didn't go down to check if he was still alive. His neck and back were twisted at an odd angle. Blood pooled around his head.

The man was dead.

I turned and ran back up the walkway.

43

Feldman was in the dining room. His forearm was wrapped in a ragged piece of cloth, and he was improvising a sling from a piece of fabric torn from the tablecloth. He furrowed his brow when he saw me. "Did you get hit?"

In the frantic run up to the house, I'd forgotten about the bullet grazing my skull. I touched my temple. Blood had soaked my hair and the right side of my face. I went to the kitchen and washed away the blood as best I could; the last thing I wanted to do was to terrify an already traumatized Kurt.

"We should split up and look for Erika," Feldman said. "I've already searched this floor."

I nodded. "I'll take the bedrooms."

Feldman headed to the terrace level, while I climbed the stairs to the upper floor. I went from room to room, keeping one hand on the pistol in my belt in case someone else from the group was waiting in an ambush. I went about this task with a sense of urgency and held my breath each time I pulled back a curtain or opened a closet or checked the three remaining bathrooms.

I passed through the foyer dividing the two hallways to check on Kurt, when Feldman called me. "Mason," he said grimly from the bottom of the stairs.

I knew what he meant. My chest and throat constricted. My legs became rubbery. I glanced down the hallway toward the bathroom where I'd taken Kurt. I felt lost and empty as I descended the stairs. I followed Feldman to the terrace level.

We crossed through the bar and billiard room. I saw where Wagner and Stangl had broken the plate glass and jumped to a strip of lawn below. I concentrated on Feldman's back as we passed through another door and into a laundry room. Beyond the furnace and electrical distribution panel, we came to a storage room filled with unwanted furniture.

There she was. Erika. Tied to an antique high-backed chair. Her head hung low. Blood from her ears and eyes had begun to dry. She was almost unrecognizable with her face so bruised and swollen. There were burn marks on her arms.

I knelt in front of her and checked her pulse. Her skin was cool to the touch; she had been killed some time ago.

"I didn't find any bullet wounds," Feldman said. "They must have gone too far, and she died of internal hemorrhaging."

I kissed her forehead. "I'm sorry."

I was numb, like a steel casing had sealed off the emotional part of my brain. The sorrow, the guilt, and the rage would come later. But first I had to take care of Kurt.

"I'll see to her," Feldman said. "Go get Kurt."

I turned to Feldman. "If Kurt's going to be an orphan, I want him to have as much of an advantage as possible."

"What makes you think we can find the money when those eight bastards failed? After torturing Erika? And one of the neighbors must have heard the shooting. The police could show up any minute."

"You should get out of here. I have to try to find it, and I think Kurt might be able to help."

"I'm not leaving."

I didn't have time to argue. I left Feldman to do what he could for Erika, and I went up to the bedroom level and the bathroom. Before opening the door, I said softly, "Kurt, it's me. I'm coming in, okay?"

I heard nothing in response and opened the door. Kurt was in the bathtub, where I'd left him. He stared blankly at the tub's faucet. He didn't blink or move when I sat next to the tub.

"Those men won't hurt you anymore," I said.

"They hurt my mommy," he said in a hollow voice that cut into my heart. "My daddy showed me. He said he would hurt me if she didn't talk."

I felt I lacked the words to comfort this boy, though I had to try. I'd finally succeeded in avenging Hana's death by killing Ziegler, but where I had failed to save her, I now had the opportunity to help another of his young victims.

"Where is my mommy?" Kurt asked. When I couldn't find the words, he said, "She's dead, isn't she? Those men killed her."

I couldn't lie to him. With my eyes filled with tears for the boy, I nodded. "God and the angels have her now."

There was no change in his expression. It seemed he'd known before I affirmed it. Like me, the loss was too devas-

342 | JOHN A. CONNELL

tating to handle. He and I would grieve later. For his sake, for Erika's sake, I wanted to find the money for Kurt.

One thing that had bothered me all along was that, if the fortune consisted of stacks of money or gold coins, and if Erika had found some way to get something that large and heavy down here from Germany, then how could she have left Germany and brought such a burden to Italy? And aside from burying it under the foundation, eight men with hours to search would have surely found the stash somewhere. My hunch was that when Erika said her death by torture wouldn't matter, she meant it was Kurt who was the key to finding it.

"Your mom wanted you to have something. Something important. The same thing those men wanted, but now it belongs to you." When Kurt said nothing, I continued. "Was there something your mom told you was the most precious thing in this house? Maybe a favorite thing that she showed you the last time you were here?"

He remained silent.

"Your mom wanted you to be safe even if she wasn't here, and she told me that she could do that for you by making sure you have her gift."

I waited for him to process this. If he remained unresponsive for too long, I would give up and get him out of here.

Feldman knocked on the open door and stepped into the room.

Kurt looked up at him. "You're hurt."

"I'm fine, but thank you. I'm very happy to see you're okay."

Kurt looked at me. "Do you want to see my room?"

That came out of left field, and I didn't know what to make of him asking such a question after everything that had happened. Chances were, he was in some kind of shock, but I knew kids were resilient, and I hoped his abrupt change was a good sign he might make it through this intact.

"Mason, we should get out of here," Feldman said.

"Sure," I said to Kurt. "But it's kind of a mess."

Kurt lifted his arms, and I picked him up took him in mine. He held tightly to my neck.

As I walked past Feldman, he gave me a look of warning. I was worried about how Kurt might react to the things in his room being tossed or smashed, but when I brought him in, he seemed to have no reaction other than to signal that he wanted to get down.

He walked among the jumble as if it were an everyday occurrence—maybe leaving his bedroom in chaos was his usual MO. His back was to me as he took small steps and scanned the room. His eye caught something, and he walked up to the destroyed castle sitting on the table.

Feldman and I stood back and looked on as Kurt picked through the pieces. Feldman showed me his wristwatch to let me know we'd run out of time. It was 8:15 a.m., but with the heavy clouds, the rising sun threw only a dim light into the interior.

Kurt turned around and held up a three-inch tin knight in armor and sitting on an equally armored horse. "This isn't mine."

"Are you sure?" I asked. "You've got so much stuff in here, maybe you forgot."

"It's not stuff," Kurt said.

I joined him and noticed there were about twenty-five tin knights, some on horseback and some standing. They lay haphazardly on the table as if someone had swiped them away before crushing the castle.

I picked one up to examine it. "You've never seen any of these guys before?"

Kurt shook his head, and I looked closer at the mounted knight. Feldman came up to us. He rubbed Kurt's hair before picking up another of the tin figurines.

I noticed a spot on the horse's back that appeared to have been hastily painted over. I held it for Feldman to have a closer look and tapped on the spot. "That doesn't look like the original paint."

"So? The maker could have seen a flaw and fixed it."

I rubbed at the spot, and the paint flecked off easily, revealing putty over a quarter-inch hole. Kurt lost interest and went over to a stuffed rabbit in the center of the floor. He sat and picked it up. I looked at Feldman and put my index finger to my lips, then glanced at Kurt before snapping the horse in two.

Two small diamonds dropped into my hand. I tilted the open ends toward the floor, and two more fell onto the table. Feldman picked up the ones from the table. We looked at each other, then we glanced at Kurt. He was still enthralled with the rabbit, so each of us picked up another piece—both knights on foot—and did the same thing. Two diamonds fell out of each. It made sense: the family's royal fortune would be in property, art, and jewels, not cash or gold bars.

We quickly attacked the other pieces and snapped open each one, while Kurt turned his attention to a tin car. I had a flash of guilt breaking his toys behind his back, but this would be his future. We collected about two dozen two, three, and four-carat cut diamonds, then a dozen rubies and sapphires and, in the last of the horses, a diamond that seemed to be about seven or eight carats.

I found a piece of cloth and wrapped the stones with it and pocketed it. Then we hid the broken pieces so Kurt wouldn't spot them.

"We've got to get out of here," Feldman said. "We can't be caught with these stones in a house full of dead people."

"Erika?" I asked him in a whisper.

"I laid her out and covered her. That's the best either of us could do under the circumstances."

I nodded. The hardened shell around my emotions was already eroding, but I suppressed the grief; I had to remain strong for Kurt. "Hey, buddy, we have to leave," I said to the boy in a neutral voice.

Kurt held on to the stuffed rabbit and stood. I took him in my arms, and Feldman and I walked out of the house and into the morning light.

44

I was expecting trouble when we pulled up to the front gate of the Cinecitta camp, but the Italian guard only performed a cursory examination of my ID. He also ignored the bloodstained bandage above my ear, and Feldman's bandaged arm. Or the fact that we had a little kid asleep on Feldman's lap. He told us to have a good afternoon in accented English and waved for his companion to raise the barrier.

I drove straight to the administration building, figuring they would have an infirmary there.

"Will you look at that," Feldman said with a growing smile on his face.

Hazan rose from a chair on the front porch of the administration building and strode toward us. I stopped the car just as Hazan reached it and opened Feldman's door. Feldman clutched a sleeping Kurt in his arms while Hazan helped him climb out of the car. They embraced in joy and relief—at least as best they could with both of them with their arms in slings and Kurt clinging to Feldman's side.

I got out of the car and said, "You guys are a matching pair."

"Did Moishe make it?" Feldman asked Hazan.

Hazan's smile faded, and his expression turned sad. He shook his head.

"I made Shimon pay for what he did," Feldman said.

Hazan nodded, and a moment of silence passed between us.

I went around the car, took Kurt into my arms, and shook Hazan's hand. Hazan glanced inside the car, then looked at me, which I guessed meant he'd put it together that Erika hadn't survived.

"Thank you for bringing back Feldman in—mostly—one piece," Hazan said.

"What are you talking about? I brought *him* back," Feldman said, obviously trying to lighten the mood.

"There's someone waiting for you inside," Hazan said to me.

I expected it to be Barker and Tilsit waiting with a pair of handcuffs and a couple of MPs to arrest me, but when I stepped into the lobby, Mike Forester walked out of the side office. He glanced at Kurt sleeping in my arms and gave me a sly smile.

I shrugged. "What?"

"Daddy in training," he said.

"I've got to find a spot for him," I said, gesturing with Kurt.

"Sure, dad, come on in here." Forester motioned for the small office. "There's a sofa for him."

I followed Forester inside, and he shut the door. I laid Kurt on the sofa. He stirred, then curled up in a ball and fell back asleep. Forester and I took chairs and sat across from each other.

Forester nodded at Kurt. "His mother didn't make it?"

I shook my head and had to look away for a moment to rein in my emotions.

"Did you get Ziegler?" Forester asked.

I nodded, thinking it might feel better saying it, but there was too much other pain. "We got six, but two got away. Wagner and Stangl. I winged Stangl. Maybe your men can search the Isle of Capri or Naples hospitals. Speaking of your men, where are Barker and Tilsit? I was expecting them to throw me in the stockade when I got back."

"I sent them on their way. They were just going to get into trouble down here." He glanced at Kurt. "What are you going to do with the boy?"

"Get him to his aunt. She's been waiting for him and Erika in Brindisi."

He studied me a moment. "You got pretty attached to them."

I nodded.

He held up an envelope. "Then maybe you're not ready for this. Or maybe it came just at the right time."

My heart leapt into high gear. I had a very good idea of its origin, but I asked, "Who's that from?"

He answered by wagging the envelope in my face. I took it.

Inside the envelope was a hastily written note in Laura's hand:

My Wandering Cowboy, I waited for you in Naples until I couldn't. If you're reading this, you managed to stay alive, and thank God for that. Mike filled me in on what you've been up to, so I forgive you for not showing up. I'm doing one last piece for the

Associated Press *before returning home. I'm on a ship packed to the gills with Jewish refugees bound for Mandatory Palestine. I want you to join me, if you can, because ...*

You remember that night in Vienna? Well, I'm four months pregnant with our child.

I dropped the letter to my lap. I gulped in air as I tried to hold back my tears and stop my head from spinning.

"I thought that might be your reaction," Forester said. "Congratulations, Mason."

I said nothing in return. I couldn't process the news. I looked at him, then raised the note to read the rest.

If our ship makes it through the British blockade, I'll be staying at the Imperial Hotel in Jerusalem. Please come as soon as you can.

I shot to my feet and turned in place; I didn't know what to do next.

"Calm down," Forester said. "It's going to take that tub a while to get to Palestine. *If* they make it to Palestine. The chances are, the Brits will intercept the ship and take everyone to their main refugee camp on Cyprus."

"Of all the crazy things to do," I said to no one in particular. "Four months pregnant and she takes a slow boat across the Mediterranean in February."

"Hey, you're the one who fell in love with her."

I remained standing. I *had* fallen in love with her and was prepared to take the good with the bad. I was simultaneously mad at her for making me chase her once again and exhilarated at the same time.

"I have to take Kurt to his aunt and make sure he gets his mother's money."

"I'll make sure you have the right papers for safe passage to Brindisi. If you agree to report your assessment of the situation in Palestine, then I can also see that you get traveling papers for Jerusalem." He held up his index finger. "But not the funds. Are you willing to do that for us?"

I nodded. "And I know the perfect way to get there."

Forester studied me for a moment. "You're hopping on a ship with those Jewish refugees. And the Jewish Brigade boys."

I nodded.

"I suppose those boys are satisfied with their haul of Nazis."

"How did you know about that?"

"Mason, this is the CIC."

Forester smiled and stood. I did the same, and we shook hands.

He said, "I may not be here when you get back from Brindisi, but we'll be in touch."

I thanked Forester, scooped up Kurt, and headed out the door.

45

I pulled the car up to the curb on Piazza Cairoli in the old center of Brindisi. Kurt sat beside me and played with his stuffed rabbit. During the seven-hour trip, I'd managed to talk him down from his panic about me leaving him with his aunt, though I knew that could change once we got out of the car and he faced reality. As I looked at him, my chest ached.

"Okay, cowboy, here's where we get out," I said to him.

"I'm not a cowboy," he said with a look of confusion.

"No, you're right." I leaned in. "Not yet anyway."

"Will you take me to see cowboys?"

"Maybe one day," I said, and I meant it. I opened the car door. "Let's get out and look for your aunt."

I expected him to cry or put up a fight, but he simply muttered an "Okay" and opened his door.

I rushed over to help him out of the car and straightened his clothes so he'd make a good impression on his aunt. I got a suitcase out of the back that I'd bought for him in Rome. That was at a store across the street from the less than scrupulous jeweler where I sold one of Erika's diamonds. The man paid less than its full value—a discount I was willing to accept for his discretion. It was, however, more than enough for Kurt and his aunt to get passage to Mikonos and live off of it for a good while.

The jewels were hidden in the lining of Kurt's suitcase. When I'd contacted his aunt, I told her where to look for them. I also assured her that I'd be checking up on him—and her—to make sure everything was all right. She understood what that meant, and I could tell after a couple of phone conversations that she'd loved Erika and Kurt. I felt assured, but I swore to myself that I would keep my promise.

A woman dressed in an emerald-blue overcoat and hat stood about fifty yards away. She looked to be a couple of years younger than Erika and as lovely as her sister. A big smile formed on her face, and she started running toward us with her arms wide.

She reached us and knelt next to Kurt and hugged him. She cooed and gave him pecks on the cheeks. His arms stayed by his sides, and he remained silent. Maybe it was her voice or her smells, but whatever it was, he suddenly wrapped his arms around her.

She picked him up and turned to me and thanked me. I handed her the suitcase. It struck me as we spoke that her eyes were completely different than Erika's: they weren't haunted and alert for danger; they didn't reflect a depth of loss, or a life of upheaval and heartache, or the trauma of being hunted by evil men.

I knew then that Kurt would be safe and loved.

Kurt and I said our good-byes—the lump in my throat made it hard to speak.

As I watched him walk away with his aunt, I felt I'd closed

a dark chapter in my life and was about to open another that had the promise of a brighter future.

But I knew how I always found trouble, or it found me.

Not to mention I was going to accompany Feldman and Hazan and the refugees on a rust bucket of a ship to the hotbed of Jerusalem.

The End

AUTHOR'S NOTES

As with all my Mason Collins adventures, I tried to anchor Where the Wicked Tread in historical facts. The Brenner Pass in northern Italy was, indeed, the main escape route—or ratline—for Nazi war criminals fleeing justice. It is also well documented that certain factions within the Vatican aided the Nazis escape Europe for countries offering safe harbor, principally several countries in South America and the Middle East.

South Tyrol retains much of its Austrian heritage to this day, and the towns of Sterzing (Vipiteno in Italian) and Meran (Merano in Italian) were known havens for the fleeing Nazis on their way to Rome. As was the inn located in Meran, named Tante Anna's, or Aunt Anna's, though the location of the inn in the book is my own. The Collegio Santa Maria dell'Anima in Rome is also a real place, and it had a history during the post-war years of harboring Nazis awaiting visas acquired by the Vatican to board ships bound for friendly ports. On the island of Capri, Erika's family's villa is fictitious, though the Villa Krupp and via Krupp, both built by steel magnate Friedrich Alfred Krupp in the late 1800s, are real. The surrounding area and path from the Piazza Umberto to via Krupp is mostly as described.

The history of the Jewish Brigade is well documented. Arie Feldman and David Hazan are fictitious, but they represent that faction of Jewish soldiers from Israel fighting in the British Army during the war, who decided to stay on after Germany's surrender to seek out and assassinate Nazis directly involved in the Holocaust. They called their loose organization, *Tilhas Tizig Gesheften, or "kiss my ass business."* They were also the principal players in smuggling Jewish Holocaust survivors to Mandatory Palestine. As in Mason's story, by 1946/47, those who had stayed on to assassinate Nazis joined the effort to smuggle Jews to Mandatory Palestine and augment the ranks of the nascent Israeli Defense Force.

The history of the ratlines (the escape routes for Nazi war criminals), is far more complex than I could possibly portray in one story. It spans several years, and the people involved are many. Some of the most notorious Nazis escaped this way: Klaus Barbie, Adolf Eichmann, and Josef Mengele to name just a few. However, these Nazis made their escape at a later date, and I didn't want to stretch reality too far.

The escaping Nazis in this story are a mix of real and imagined. Franz Stangl—the commander of the Sobibor extermination camp—and Gustav Wagner—the deputy commander of Sobibor and known as "the Beast" by inmates—did actually escape together through Italy and received Vatican aid to board ships. Stangl went to Syria and Wagner to Brazil. Some is known of their actual route, though I took some liberties with the process of their escape. I also took liberties with the real Rudolf Lange, an SS commander who was largely responsible for the Holocaust in Latvia. He disappeared without a trace at the end of the war, so why not have him escaping to Italy? Finally, the one who got away from Feldman and Hazan, Eduard Roschmann, was the SS commandant of the Riga ghetto. He did escape the Dachau prison camp in 1947 and made it to Argentina via the Italian ratline by 1948 with assistance from the Vatican.

If you are interested in learning more about the ratlines and the vast array of people and institutions involved, there are two principal resources I used in my research for this story:

Nazis On The Run: How Hitler's Henchmen Fled Justice by Gerard Steinacher

Unholy Trinity: The Vatican, The Nazis, and the Swiss Banks by Mark Aarons and John Loftus

While I referred to many sources about the exploits of the Jewish Brigade and *Tilhas Tizig Gesheften*, my principal source was:

The Brigade: An Epic Story of Vengeance, Salvation, and World War Two by Howard Blum

I found this slice of post-WW2 history intriguing, and maybe I'll revisit this time and place for another story in the future. And as you may have been able to tell from the ending, I do intend to have Mason wrapped up in the *Aliyah Bet*, the effort to take Jewish survivors to Mandatory Palestine and the tumultuous birth of Israel.

In the meantime, I hope you enjoyed Mason's latest adventure.

GET A FREE MASON COLLINS NOVELLA

GET A FREE MASON COLLINS NOVELLA!

*In **Malevolent Hands**: Three mysterious deaths, one terrible secret, and a host of suspects.*

While recuperating in an army hospital from multiple diseases picked up during his time in Nazi POW camps, Mason Collins begins to suspect that the deaths of three patients were not just a coincidence.

With nurses, doctors, and orderlies coming in at all hours, with access to drugs and syringes, the ward makes a perfect hunting ground.

The mystery deepens when Mason finds out the three victims were from the same outfit and wounded on the same day. Something happened on that day and three men died because of it, and anyone getting close to uncovering the secret is in mortal danger, including Mason.

If you are interested in going beyond what you read here and wish to receive occasional newsletters from me with details on my writing life, new releases, special offers, and other news, you can sign up to my mailing list, and I'll send you a free Mason Collins series prequel novella not available anywhere else.

You can get the novella *In Malevolent Hands* by signing up at: https://johnaconnell.com/subscribe/

ABOUT THE AUTHOR

John A. Connell is a 2016 Barry Award nominee and the author of the Mason Collins series: **Madness in the Ruins**, **Haven of Vipers**, **Bones of the innocent**, **To Kill a Devil**, and **Where the Wicked Tread**, and the standalone historical crime thriller **Good Night, Sweet Daddy-O**. John has worked as a cameraman on films such as *Jurassic* Park and *Thelma and Louis* and on TV shows including *NYPD Blue* and *The Practice*. Atlanta-born, John spends his time between the U.S. and France.

You can visit John online at:

http://johnaconnell.com

Or on Facebook at:

https://www.facebook.com/johnconnellauthor1/

And Twitter at:

https://twitter.com/johnaconnell

ALSO BY JOHN A. CONNELL

<u>The Mason Collins Series</u>

Madness in the Ruins (Book #1)

A mutilated body. No witnesses. The only clue, a message, "Those who I have made suffer will become saints and they shall lift me up from hell."

Winter, 1945. Munich is in ruins, and a savage killer is stalking the city.

U.S. Army investigator Mason Collins enforces the law in the American Zone of Occupation. This post is his last chance to do what he loves most—being a homicide detective.

But he gets more than he's bargained for when the bodies start piling up, the city devolves into panic, and the army brass start breathing down his neck.

Then the murderer makes him a target. Now it's a high-stakes duel, and to win it Mason must bring into deadly play all that he values: his partner, his career—even his life.

Haven of Vipers (Book #2)

A fairytale town with gingerbread houses has become the Dodge City of post-WW2 Germany. And the gang running things are ex-Nazis and crooked U.S. Army officers.

Not the best place for U.S. Army detective Mason Collins to keep his head down, serve out his time, so he can go home.

While investigating a rash of murders, Mason discovers a web of coconspirators more dangerous than anything he's ever encountered.

Witnesses and evidence disappear, someone on high is stifling the investigation, and Mason must feel his way in the darkness if he is going to find out who in town has the most to gain—and the most to lose…

Bones of the Innocent (Book #3)

Summer, 1946. Just as assassins from a shadowy organization close in for the kill, a flamboyant stranger offers Mason a way out: He must accompany the stranger to Morocco to investigate the abductions of teenage girls. Girls that vanished without a trace.

Once Mason lands in Tangier, he discovers that nothing—or no one —is what it seems. This playground for the super rich is called the wickedest city in the world, and he realizes those who could help him the most harbor a terrible secret.

But just as Mason begins to unravel the mystery, the assassins have once again picked up his trail. Now, Mason must put his life on the line to find the girls before it's too late. If he lives that long…

To Kill A Devil (Book #4)

1946, Vienna. When a shadowy organization fails to assassinate Mason Collins, they go after his colleagues, his friends, and the love of his life. Mason knows the only way to stop the killings is to cut off the head of the snake.

Armed only with the alias, Valerius, Mason treks across Franco's

Spain to war-torn Vienna to eliminate the man ordering the hits. But tracking him down seems to be an unsurmountable task; everyone speaks his name with awe and fear, but no one knows if he's real or a gangland myth.

Mason, desperate for answers, abandons his strict moral code, leading him down a very dark path, and to succeed in hunting one devil, he makes a pact with another.

But what Mason doesn't know is that, even if he does find his way in the darkness, the man they call Valerius has something special in store for him.

~

A standalone historical crime thriller

Good Night, Sweet Daddy-O

1958 San Francisco

Struggling jazz musician, Frank Valentine, suffers a midnight beating, leaving his left hand paralyzed. Jobless, penniless, and desperate, Frank agrees to join his best friend, George, and three other buddies to distribute a gangster's heroin for quick money.

What he doesn't know is that George has far more dangerous plans...

Inexperienced in the ways of crime, Frank quickly slips deeper and deeper into the dark vortex of San Francisco gangsters, junkies, and murderers for hire. To make things worse, Frank's newfound love, a mysterious, dark-haired beauty, is somehow connected to it all.

And when it becomes clear that a crime syndicate is bent on his destruction, Frank realizes that the easy road out of purgatory often leads to hell.